Rave Reviews for CRUSH

"*Crush* is my absolute favorite book that Lacey has written to date. She has weaved into the pages betrayal, deception, obsession, love, secrets, suspense, drama, twist and turns around every corner. This is not your typical high school crush book—it is a coming of age book that mixes jealousy, drug use, conformity, and love. I highly recommend purchasing this book!" *~Lisa Markson, Mommy Reads Too Much*

"*Crush* is an unforgettable, stimulating romance that will have you reeling in astonishment when the unthinkable strikes in Cami's world! Which of these characters will come out of this deceitful web carefully designed by this wonderfully talented author, Lacey Weatherford! I give this book my thumbs up!" *~Jessica Johnson, Book End 2 Book End*

"Once again, Lacey Weatherford has delivered a romance so exhilarating, you'll be left in a puddle of swoony sighs. *Crush* has it all – romance, suspense, angst, humor . . . not to mention amazing one liners from a guy so deliciously sexy, it'll leave you breathless and blushing for hours to come! I don't just have a crush . . . I have an addiction!" *~Belinda Boring, The Bookish Snob*

"I absolutely loved, loved, loved, this book! Lacey takes us on an electrifying ride—there were so many times I could feel my heart beat faster in anticipation wondering what was going to happen next! *Crush* is a 5 star page turner full of passion, secrets and intrigue...A MUST read!!!" *~Holly Malgieri, I Love Indie Books*

"I love the cover for *Crush* by Lacey Weatherford and I went into reading it with the idea that it was going to be a hot, contemporary romance. I'm happy to tell you that whilst this is indeed the case, the book is about so much more. The romance was present but there was also something else going on and this made for one of the best books I've seen from Lacey. It's a great story and one that needs to be read. I dare you to fall in love with *Crush.*" *~Lynsey Newton, Narratively Speaking*

"I love a good romantic novel laced with suspense and danger and *Crush* is all that and more. Perfectly paced and plotted, there was no lull in the action. Weatherford has crafted what I consider to be the perfect book and I am looking forward to many re-reads in the future." *~Melissa Simmons, Girls Heart Books*

"*Crush* is AH-MAY-ZING. Sparks were flying off the pages throughout the entire book. The romance isn't the only thing going on, it has many different levels to it. I absolutely loved the plot—I was amazed once all the pieces started coming together. I soooo did not want this book to end!" ~*Tishia Mackey, Paranormal Opinion*

"Jenny: What a delicious and engrossing read this was! I really did enjoy it! The anticipation kept me eagerly flicking the pages and it kept me riveted until the end! Gitte: Lacey absolutely has a knack for creating storylines with depth and her characters are real, credible and relevant. I got sucked in right away again and couldn't put it down. *Crush* was a FAB YA story!" ~*Jenny & Gitte, Totally Booked*

"Weatherford has a distinctive writing style with the ability to create storylines with depth and realism; her characters are real, believable and relatable. If her name is on a book I immediately want to read it, regardless! *Crush* is yet another success for the amazing author!" ~*Tammy Middleton, Tam's Two Cents*

"So far I've loved everything Lacey's ever written, but I generally prefer fantasy to contemporary. So, I expected to love it, just not quite as much. Hah. I was wrong. This is probably Lacey's best novel yet. Whether or not you like contemporary YA, you'll like *Crush*. It was fun, serious and adventurous all at once." ~*Natalie Richards, Songs and Stories*

"I loved, loved, loved this book! I was so captivated by the characters and story line. I felt like I was back in high school living out the tale with Hunter, Cami, and Clay. You want to know SO bad what Hunter is hiding from Cami. Should she even be trusting this guy that she barely knows, yet feels so drawn to? There are some seriously steamy kisses too. Make sure you add it to your pile!" ~*Stephanie Shaw, Steph's Book Club*

"Lacey has a way of creating stories that speak to your heart. She really knows how to capture her readers with every story she writes. It's real, it flows perfectly and flawlessly and I really feel like I'm there experiencing the journey along with the characters. If I could give *Crush* more than FIVE stars, I would no questions asked, but alas I can only give it FIVE so that would have to suffice!" ~ *Anne Brewer, YA Romance Author*

"Wow, what an amazing story. Once again Lacey Weatherford has done it. I would rate this as a must read book." ~*Becky Warnick, Avid Reader*

OTHER BOOKS BY
LACEY WEATHERFORD

Of Witches and Warlocks series:
The Trouble with Spells
The Demon Kiss
Blood of the White Witch
The Dark Rising
Possession of Souls

Chasing Nikki series:
Chasing Nikki
Finding Chase
(Available December 2012)

Anthology:
A Midsummer Night's Fling

CRUSH

BY
LACEY WEATHERFORD

YA F WEA
1691 4502 04/10/13 ESB
Weatherford, Lacey.

Crush
      sch

Copyright © 2012 Moonstruck Media
and Lacey Weatherford
Edited by Irene Hunt, Third Eye Tight Editing Services
ALL RIGHTS RESERVED

ISBN-13: 978-1479398775
ISBN-10: 1479398772

Published by

Moonstruck Media

Arizona

ACKNOWLEDGMENTS

Crush was a story that popped into my head suddenly and took over. After continuously struggling to put it on the back burner so that I could finish the projects scheduled ahead of it, I finally gave in and listened to the advice of my business partners, Bels, and Kam. They said if the story was eating at me that badly, then I should just write it.

I'm glad I listened to them! This tale literally poured out of me in a matter of days and was sent off to my editor a whole month ahead of schedule. So thanks to them, thanks to my family for not growling at me while I wrote on our vacation, thanks to my editor, Irene, for all her help and amazing suggestions, and thanks to all the amazing reviewers who read the ARC and spread so much love for the story!

Another one bites the dust! ;)

Love,

Lacey

DEDICATION

my "besties" from high school:
Barbara, Kim, and Deanna.
ere's to the memories of all the awesome
crushes we had!

***

For my cousin, Chris Napier.
You are missed!

CAMI

PROLOGUE

Cami-

It was magical. We danced and swayed to the music as fake snow fell from above, catching the glitter of the giant silver disco ball as it spread the flickering mood lighting around the gym. Despite the Winter Formal's snowflake theme, the room was hot from the crush of bodies, but no one, including me, seemed to care. It was beautiful, and I was thoroughly enjoying this night out with Clay, my best friend in the whole world.

There was a small commotion off to my right, and I saw Jordan Henley stagger toward me. My first thought was to wonder who spiked his punch. He abruptly lurched forward, falling against me.

"Cami, help me. Please," he said in a desperate sounding whisper, spitting on me as he spoke.

"Get off her!" Clay yelled in disgust, shoving him.

Jordan fell—his head hit the floor with a resounding crack that vibrated under my feet. My loud, horrified scream pierced the air. The dancing teens stopped and scattered outward in cries of disbelief, forming a wide circle around the twitching boy in the center. I was frozen to the spot until Clay grabbed me, yanking me backward as well.

Teachers rushed forward, pushing through the packed crowd trying to discover what was wrong with the school's champion running back. He was foaming from the mouth, his eyes rolled back into his head.

"Somebody help him!" I screeched out.

"Call an ambulance!" one of the teachers yelled, and several students produced their cell phones all at once.

Jordan suddenly gurgled and gagged then quit moving. The teacher, Mr. Russo, laid his head near Jordan's mouth before quickly straightening and checking for a pulse.

"Get these kids out of here!" he ordered the rest of the faculty as he ripped open the buttons of Jordan's shirt.

Several girls started crying as he placed his hands on Jordan's chest and started doing compressions . . . but I could tell it was too late. Jordan Henley was already dead.

CAMI

CHAPTER ONE
Cami- Three months later

"Can someone please tell me the ruling for comma placements in this particular sentence?" Mrs. Stuart tapped the board with her old-fashioned, stick pointer as she peered over the top of her small, gold wire-rimmed glasses. Her gaze floated around the classroom, looking for a volunteer as she absently reached up to pat her French twisted gray hair.

I raised my hand from the back of the classroom and she stopped on me, smiling.

"Anyone besides Miss Wimberley?" she amended.

I lowered my arm quickly, accidentally hitting the edge of my binder, which was hanging off my desk. The action caused it to pop up and fall to the floor. The three rings burst open, and papers scattered everywhere.

Laughter twittered through the previously silent classroom, and my face flushed in embarrassment as I slid to my knees, hurriedly trying to gather the mess.

"Attention! Please!" Mrs. Stuart's voice snapped, directing everyone to look back at her. "Mr. Wilder, please help Cami pick up her things."

I groaned internally. *Not Hunter*, I thought.

My humiliation was complete. It was bad enough almost all my classes were seated alphabetically, bad enough the computer had somehow managed to put him in four of my seven periods when he'd moved in a few weeks ago, bad enough he'd risen to immediate 'in' status and was now considered the hottest, coolest—and maybe the worst—partier in school. Despite the two of us being from entirely different social classes, him the king of stoners, me the queen of nerdy chic, I still managed to have a crush on him—a crush I did my absolute best to hide from everyone . . . especially him.

"That was a sleek move you did there, Cami," Hunter whispered as he knelt down next to me and began to gather papers. "I didn't think notebooks could fly like that. Did you have to get special training?" He glanced up at the board where Mrs. Stuart was continuing with the lesson. "Too bad it didn't work."

"What?" I sighed in exasperation, trying to figure out what he was talking about. He flashed a bright smile, and my gaze settled first on his perfect, white teeth, then on those deliciously plump lips of his.

I bet he's fun to kiss. I blinked. *Whoa! Where did that come from?*

"Are you saying this whole knocking of the binder was truly an accident?" he spoke.

I jerked my attention from his mouth back to the floor and the task in front of me.

"And here I thought you were trying to save the rest of the class from answering the question," he continued.

I paused to stare at him. "Really? You did?"

He leaned past me, reaching to grab some papers under a vacant desk, and I caught a whiff of his cool scented aftershave, mixed with the faint smell of cigarettes.

"No." He chuckled quietly, and a lock of his black hair tumbled over his tanned forehead. He straightened and handed me the papers. "I was trying to give you an out so you didn't feel quite so humiliated." He winked, and I couldn't help but notice his chocolate colored eyes looked like they had little drops of caramel scattered through them. I'd never been this close to his face before.

"Oh." I suddenly felt uncomfortable under his scrutiny. "Thanks . . . I think."

His smile widened. "Anytime. I may have only been here a short while, but I'm sure I've been in enough of your classes to have you pegged."

"Is that so?" I began arranging things in my binder so I wouldn't have to look at him or his tight, black t-shirt stretched across his perfectly muscled physique. It should be a sin for a guy in high school to have a body that good. Besides, I was pretty sure he was messing with me.

"I do. It didn't take me long to figure out

you're sweet, probably the smartest girl in school, maybe the most talented as well, and you're definitely every teacher's pet. You always pay attention and do your work like a good student should." He shook his head, as he stared. "Little-Miss-Goody-Two-Shoes. Do you have a life outside of class? I haven't seen you around. I bet you've never even been to a party before, have you? I just can't picture you kickin' back with the homies."

He was baiting me—and it was working. "Of course I have," I snapped under my breath, not knowing why I cared whether or not he thought I was cool. "My mom throws the most amazing parties, and I hang out with my best friend, Clay, all the time."

"I don't think birthday parties count. And Clay? Now there's a nerd for you—pocket protector and everything. Someone told me he has a girlfriend." He snorted a little too loudly. "I find that hard to believe."

"Hurry up you two," Mrs. Stuart called out before turning to her desk.

I snapped my binder back together. "Thanks for your help, even if it was required of you." I got into my seat feeling irritated.

He slid into his beside me, slouching and stretching his long frame into the aisle. I could tell he was still looking at me, so I stared straight ahead, determined to ignore him. He was such a punk.

"You need a partner for the next part of this lesson, so buddy up please," Mrs. Stuart said as she started passing out a worksheet.

There was a bunch of noise as everyone hurried to find whom they wanted to work with. Hunter promptly slid his desk over next to mine before I had a chance to move.

"Hey buddy." He smiled.

My eyes widened. "Back to degrade me some more?" I grumbled.

He looked surprised. "What do you mean?"

"Isn't that what you were doing a minute ago? Telling me what a nerd I am and how I have no social life?"

"Is that what you thought?" He leaned forward, placing his arms on his desk and turned to stare at me.

I didn't answer. He was so close he seemed intimidating, like he noticed everything about me with just one glance. It made me feel self-conscious.

Mrs. Stuart paused at our desks and handed us a piece of paper before she returned to the front of the room. "As you can see, there are several paragraphs on this. All but one are punctuated incorrectly. You're to take turns reading aloud to each other. In the space below each paragraph, rewrite it the way you think it should be. When you find the correct one, circle it. Put both your names in the top corner, and turn it in before the bell please. You may begin."

Hunter grabbed the paper and penciled his name in before sliding it over. "I'm glad I picked you as a partner. Maybe I'll get a good grade on this now."

"Why? Because I'll do all the work?" I hissed. I knew guys like him. They sucked up to you until they got what they wanted and then acted like you were no one the next time you were around. There was no way I'd let him do that.

He looked at me funny. "Did I do something to piss you off? You seem mad."

"Never mind." I picked up the paper to begin reading, but he placed his hand on it, flattening it against the desk.

"What's wrong?"

"Nothing." I wouldn't look at him. I wasn't sure why I was getting so upset. It shouldn't matter if some party boy thought I was a nerd. It's not like I would ever go out with him even if he didn't. I was positive he was into the whole drug and alcohol scene, just from the friends he'd made already. I'd seen him smoking in the parking lot a couple of times, trying to hide his cigarette in the curl of his hand so no one would notice. I always wondered why the kids in this school were still stupid enough to party after Jordan Henley's overdose on meth three months ago. You think they'd learn, but no, everyone seemed content to keep on using. "Can we do this please?" I gestured to the assignment.

He removed his hand and leaned in closer, following along as I read the first paragraph.

"Okay, where do you think the punctuation goes?" I asked, not wanting to share my knowledge all of a sudden.

He pointed to a spot. "Comma here, I think."

Dang. He was right. I begrudgingly penciled it in.

"I can tell you're a singer. You have a musical quality to your voice. That's so cool, by the way. I hear you're pretty good. Do you think you'd ever want to do it professionally?"

"Whaa . . . ?" I couldn't finish the comment, his remark caught me so off guard. I fumbled, trying to find words. "Where did you hear that?" I narrowed my eyes. "Have you been talking to people about me?"

He laughed. "Of course. Guys always talk to each other about the pretty girls at school." He bumped his shoulder into mine in a friendly gesture.

My mouth popped open, and I was reduced to the facial movements of a fish. I was stunned, unable to believe what he'd just said.

"I needed to be brought into the loop about who's hot and who's not, when I moved here. You know how it is," he added. "Social status and all that."

And then I was deflated, because I understood what he meant.

"Yes, I'm sure they were happy to fill you in that I'm part of the 'who's not' category. In fact, I'd imagine I'm probably on the top of that list."

He lifted an eyebrow in question, and I noticed the color of his eyes again for the second time today. "You're kidding, right? I don't think any guy has you on his 'who's not' list."

"Then please, enlighten me as to which lucky category I've fallen into. It's always nice to be sorted like inanimate objects."

He appeared unfazed by my objection. "I think you're more on the unattainable list. Guys figure you're too good for them, so they don't bother asking."

I laughed in spite of myself. "I can't imagine why anyone would think that. I've never acted that way."

He shrugged. "Must be that Goody-Two-Shoes attitude then."

"Stop calling me that."

"Why? I kind of like it. I think it's going to be my nickname for you from now on." He grinned.

"Are you this irritating with everyone you know?" I glared at him.

He laughed loud enough that Mrs. Stuart sent a disgruntled look in our direction.

"Pretty much, yeah." He grabbed the paper, read the next paragraph, and we took turns marking the punctuation together. He got a couple wrong, and I had to explain the rules to him.

I chewed lightly on the tip of my pencil eraser as I quickly skimmed through the next paragraph. "I think this is the correct one. Do you want to read it before I circle it?"

"No. I trust you," he said, waving it off. "So what are you doing this weekend?"

I stiffened, suddenly worried about where this conversation might be headed. "My dad has a fundraiser concert and dinner on Saturday for his Jazz band. I may attend that, but I haven't really decided yet. Why?"

"Your dad plays in a band?" he questioned.

"Yeah, my mom is the choir director at New Mexico West University, and my dad is the band director. They're always putting on concerts together. It was their dream jobs to find two positions together like they did here. I've participated in all their concerts and musicals since we moved here when I was little."

"Really? That's interesting. Where'd you live before?" He seemed genuinely interested.

"Tucson, Arizona."

He looked shocked for a second before he laughed. "What a small world. That's where I'm from. So you know how painful it is to move from there to a middle-of-nowhere place like Copper City then."

I nodded. "I do. Of course, I don't really remember Tucson that much. We moved when I was five. It's not so bad, once you get used to it. There's lots of fun things to do here, like visiting the museums, checking out the local artistry, or driving out to see some of the Indian ruins and mines in the . . ." I let my sentence dwindle off at his horrified look. "Yeah, Copper City is definitely not your kind of thing."

He slouched back into his chair with a sigh. "I know. My life is over."

"I believe your life can be whatever you want to make of it." I lifted my chin defiantly, daring him to challenge me.

"Is that how it works? Well then, I want my life to be a big, giant, keg party."

I pursed my lips together and glanced over him.

"What?" He squinted his gorgeous eyes. "You think I'm a loser now, Goody-Two-Shoes? Just some worthless partier?"

"Actually, I was trying to imagine what you might look like with a beer belly."

He grinned and sat up, grabbing the paper on the desk in front of me. "I like you, Goody. No one mentioned you were so snarky."

He started reading the next paragraph out loud before I could respond. I wasn't sure what to think of him. He'd hardly spoken to me before, except to ask for a pencil once. Now he was suddenly Mr. Talkative? It didn't matter really. He would probably forget all about me by tomorrow.

HUNTER

CHAPTER TWO
Hunter-

Dude, the girl is freakin' hot, I thought to myself for the thousandth time as I stared at her during chemistry lab. Initially, I'd been disappointed this class didn't have alphabetized seating like the others, but I'd grown quite happy with admiring the view from behind without her knowing.

I cast another glance over her form— slender, yet round in all the right places. Her curly, red hair bounced with every shake of her head as she talked animatedly to her best friend, Clay.

He was almost the classic nerd stereotype. Slick hair combed with a rigid part, plaid shirts, with pens in his pocket protector. He wore glasses, but they were decent looking ones—not the typical thick coke bottle glasses that were taped in the middle that most people associated with the type. My attention returned to the beautiful girl at his side.

What a pair. I wondered if she knew he was the real reason guys didn't ask her out much. She was considered nerdy by association, which was a shame seeing how she was drop-dead gorgeous. Even though Clay claimed to have a girlfriend in another town, there was still some speculation on whether or not these two might actually be an item.

I released a frustrated sigh. I wished I hadn't talked to her yesterday. I liked her instantly. It was fun to push her buttons and mess with her for a bit. But I wasn't looking for a girlfriend, nerd or otherwise—no way, no how. There was enough on my plate right now, and having a relationship with anyone, especially her, would complicate things so badly I didn't want to consider the repercussions.

I dragged my stare away and looked at the lab sheet in front of me, as I tried to forget the conversation we'd had. She was unsure of me. I could tell from the way her honey eyes rounded in surprise and how she chewed on her apricot colored bottom lip, her perfect skin blushing softly like an overripe peach.

Growling, I shifted slightly in my seat. I made her sound like she was a fruit salad just waiting for me to take a bite. *There will be no biting of anyone,* I reminded myself, frowning at my internal dialogue. *Strictly off limits.*

"You okay, man?"

I glanced over to find my lab partner and new friend, Russ, staring at me strangely.

"Fine, why?"

He shrugged. "No reason. You were just making some funny noises."

"What's the next step in this lab?" I asked. If he wondered why I was taking a sudden interest in the project I'd basically been letting him do alone, he made no comment about it.

He chuckled. "We're done."

"Oh, sorry." I wasn't really. I could think of a million other things I would rather be doing right now. I hated being stuck in this dumb science lab, or any class for that matter. I was so over high school.

"It's okay. You seemed . . . preoccupied." He cast a glance in Cami's direction before looking back.

I gave a soft grunt and ran a hand over my face. I needed to pay better attention to what I was doing and who was watching.

"I get it," Russ continued on as if we'd actually been having a conversation. "I've always thought she's pretty."

"Who?" I asked, trying to bluff my way out of this situation.

He grinned. "That's really the way you're gonna play it?"

"Play what? I have no idea what you're talking about, bro."

He shook his head looking perplexed. "Okay, I get it. You don't want to talk about the girl you obviously think is hot. I don't understand it, but whatever. It's your deal."

"Going to any good parties tonight?" I asked, desperate to change the subject.

"I'm planning on heading to the one at Billy

Barker's. His parents are out of town. You going?"

"If that's where the good stuff is, then that's where I'll be." I needed to see if I could score something.

"Then look me up while you're there," he said. "We can chill together."

"Will do."

The house was easy enough to find, thanks in part to the massive amount of cars parked up and down the long driveway. I climbed out of my black Camaro and glanced around, noticing there didn't seem to be any neighboring residences close by. This was probably a good thing since the music was pounding so loud I was sure they would've called the cops by now. I grinned slightly at the idea of the house being surrounded and watching people scream and scatter while they tried to avoid arrest.

The gravel crunched under my boots as I made my way toward the two-story adobe, Santa Fe styled home. It seemed like the party was in full swing. The tree outside had already been toilet papered, and I could hear some poor person puking their guts out in the bushes.

I walked up the steps to the covered porch, choosing to avoid any eye contact with the couple heavily making out on the swing, and went inside.

Weaving my way through the crush of bodies that danced to the heavy bass, I moved toward where the kitchen appeared to be located. I found the giant keg I was looking for and grabbed a plastic cup off the counter.

"Fill me up!" I yelled over the loud music to the guy manning the alcohol, Johnny, if I remembered his name from school.

He grinned. "Will do!" He opened the tap until the amber liquid was close to foaming over. I nodded at him before lifting it and downing a healthy swig, draining the glass to nearly halfway.

Careful to keep from spilling, I moved through the gyrating crowd toward the open glass doors that led out to a pool area.

"Hunter!" A voice caught my attention, and I saw Russ give me a wave, motioning me over.

I turned in his direction, handing him my cup before I jumped up to sit on the short wall next to him.

"Wassup, dude?" I asked, as he handed my drink back. I sat it carefully beside me while I fished my cigarettes and lighter from my pocket. I lit up and took a long drag before blowing the smoke out the side of my mouth.

"Nothin' much. Just scoping out the girls."

"Finding anyone good?" I surveyed the ladies both in the pool and out and shook my head. I didn't think large crowds, beer, and water were probably the best mix. Plus, there was no way I'd be getting in any pool in March, unless of course it was heated. The weather this week had been quite a bit warmer though, so maybe it wasn't too bad.

"There's a couple I might try hookin' up with later." He grinned, ruffling a hand through his light-brown hair. "See anyone you like?"

I gave a slight shrug and shook my head. "Not really."

"Well, Gabrielle Martinez has been asking everyone if you're coming tonight. I think she has her eye on you."

I looked over to where the striking brunette was standing beside the pool in a skimpy turquoise bikini talking to her friends and groaned. The lights under the water were sending glowing ripples across her smooth, caramel-colored skin, highlighting her near-perfect body. She laughed at something—her smile lighting her face—and cast a glance in my direction.

"She's pretty, but not my type," I replied to Russ, reiterating my complete lack of interest in having any of these girls as a girlfriend.

"Oh, I already knew that. I just didn't have the heart to tell her that your tastes tend to run toward the nerdy, redheaded variety." He chuckled.

I stiffened at his reference to Cami and the disturbing fact I immediately knew who he was talking about. Images of the stunning redhead filtered through my mind, causing my pulse to jump up a notch. This wasn't good. If I were being totally honest, she was the first person I looked for when I walked through the door tonight, although I knew she wouldn't be here. I was glad she wasn't.

"Cami's gorgeous, but she's not my type either." I reached for my beer and took a sip before taking another drag on my cigarette.

"Could've fooled me with the way you've

been staring at her in school. If she's not your type, who is? I'm sure we can find you someone good to hook up with."

"No one's my type, I don't want a girlfriend. They're too complicated."

Russ arched his brow, looking at me as if I was crazy.

I decided to get chatty. "The last girl I was with did a real number on me. She was super possessive, always wanted me to meet her and do whatever she wanted. It seemed as if nothing I did was ever good enough. Then I found out she was cheating on me the whole time with some college guy. I broke up with her and she threatened to tell my parents and the cops I was doing drugs. She wanted me to stay with her while she was with this other guy."

"Wow, that's crazy. What did you do?"

"I told her to go ahead and tell them—she couldn't prove anything. Besides, she was the person I was always getting stoned with. I could've gotten her in just as much trouble."

"Sounds like she was a real winner."

I chuckled. Dang, I was a friggin' good liar. He totally bought it. "She was something. Who can I hit up here to score a little blunt?" I asked, successfully redirecting the subject as I glanced around the large group. "The last party I went to provided all the goods for us, but it was smaller. I guess that's not the case this time."

"Talk to Derek Johnson." He pointed to a guy standing by a girl in the far corner over by the house. "He can hook you up. I'm not sure where he gets his stuff, but he always seems to have something on him."

I saw the girl give Derek some money, and he slipped a small bag into her hand.

"Thanks. I couldn't find anyone at the party last weekend to spot me something for my personal stash, so I had to make do with alcohol. Thank goodness my uncle left his liquor cabinet open when he went out of town. That helped me pass the week a little easier."

"I heard you live with your uncle. Sorry about your parents." He looked at me sympathetically. "We've known each other for a couple of weeks now, but you've never really brought stuff up when it comes to your past. I didn't want to pry—figured you'd talk when you were ready."

I took another swallow of my drink and shrugged. "Accidents happen. I try not to think about it."

He looked uncomfortable. "So your uncle is gone a lot?"

I nodded. "Yeah, he seems to enjoy that jet-setter lifestyle of his—always flying around to his big corporate meetings around the country. I'm sure he wasn't thrilled to be saddled with me, even though we get along. I don't mind, though. I'd rather be alone."

"Well, if you ever need someone to just hang with, you know where to find me."

"Thanks, dude." I crushed out my cigarette, clapped him on the shoulder, and hopped off the wall. I headed toward Derek, feeling pretty good with myself—until the very curvy brunette, who'd been eyeing me since I arrived, waylaid me.

"Hey Hunter," Gabrielle said sliding up close and blocking my path.

"Hey," I replied, trying to keep my eyes on her face and not the rest of what she was so generously flashing.

"I'm glad you came tonight." She boldly traced a finger over my chest.

"Really? Why's that?" I tried to gauge if she was drunk, but I couldn't smell anything.

"Haven't you noticed I've been watching you at school?" She smiled flirtatiously, tossing some of her long hair over her shoulder.

"No." That was a lie. I'd noticed and was doing my best to avoid her. I knew her reputation and exactly what she was hoping to get from me.

"Well, I have been." She pressed in closer. "Wanna come sit by me at the pool? We can put our feet in together."

"No thanks. The chlorine bothers me." Another lie. I noticed Derek slipping into the house, and I felt irritated. I didn't want to lose him. The whole reason I came to this party was to get some sort of illegal refreshment.

Gabrielle gave me a pouty look. "Okay. How about taking me for a ride in that sweet car of yours then? I know a place with a great view of the city where we can go park."

Wow, this chick didn't take a hint very well, and she certainly didn't waste any time.

I pulled my cell phone from my pocket and glanced at it. "Sorry, Gabby, but my uncle will be home soon," I fibbed again. "I was just dropping into the party for a quick beer and to say hi to Russ. I gotta get going."

"Oh. All right." She looked truly put out. "See you at school then."

"Sure thing." I ducked around her, making a mental note to do my best to avoid her completely from now on.

I hurried into the house, looking around for Derek, but couldn't find him anywhere. "Hey, did Derek just come through here?" I shouted at the guy standing by the door so he could hear me over the music.

"I think he went upstairs," he yelled back and pointed.

"Thanks." I weaved through the throng in that direction, quickly ascending the staircase, but only saw a couple making out in the hallway. I walked around them, pausing by a door that was ajar. I knocked, opening it enough to stick my head in and was rewarded with a shriek.

"Lock the friggin' door people," I grumbled, wishing I didn't have that image stuck in my head. I paused, staring at all the other doors, afraid to open them now. "Derek Johnson! Are you up here?" I shouted.

The couple who'd been kissing stopped and stared at me like I was crazy. There was no answer from any of the rooms, and no one emerged.

"We haven't seen him up here," the guy said.

I gave a frustrated sigh and headed back down the stairs. After searching the whole ground floor unsuccessfully, I finally left the house and headed toward my car.

Damn. What a wasted night.

CAMI

CHAPTER THREE
Cami-

I stretched out in the poolside lounge chair, trying to catch some of the warm, spring rays, and get a jumpstart on my tan for the year. Once again, I thanked the genetics of my parents. Even though they'd given me the curly, red hair of my mother, I had at least been blessed with the warm skin tones of my father—skin that loved the sun.

Clay, who was not so blessed, sat beside me and continued to slather sunscreen over every inch of his white, glowing body.

"I think you've got half the bottle on you now," I joked as I watched him rub it in vigorously.

"Not all of us are gifted with the complexion of a supermodel, like you are."

I laughed. "Actually, most models avoid the sun. They're probably as pale as you."

He considered this for a moment before

flexing his mid section. "But do they have my great abs of steel?"

I snorted as I stared at him. He wasn't flabby by any means, but I certainly wouldn't call his stomach abs of steel. When I pictured a body like that, I saw someone like . . . Hunter Wilder. I groaned and hid my eyes behind my arm.

"That bad, huh?" Clay sounded defeated.

"No, no, no!" I hurried to reassure him. "Your comment just made me think of something that happened."

"Oh, well fill me in then." He finished rubbing his sunscreen in and settled into the seat.

"It's nothing really. Are those new swimming trunks?" I tried to change the subject. "I don't remember seeing them before." I gestured to the plaid shorts he was wearing. He'd had a serious obsession with plaid for as long as I could remember. Sometimes a little was okay, but when it came to Clay, he always managed to overdo it.

"Don't you *even* try to dodge me. We've been best friends since kindergarten, and I know when you're hiding stuff. You've been quiet and reflective all day. Tell me what's going on."

I laughed again. "Are you this bossy with your girlfriend?"

"No. It's hard to tell Marcy what to do when she lives three hours away."

"Well, at least you're close enough to see each other once in a while. That's nice."

He made some sort of noncommittal sound in the back of his throat. "Back to the original subject. What's going on?"

"Nothing. I just had a weird moment with Hunter Wilder. I'm not sure if he was trying to discretely be insulting or if he was flirting with me."

Clay's eyebrows furrowed. "If I were you, I wouldn't have anything to do with him. He's not your kind of guy. In fact, I advise you to stay far, far away." His tone had taken on a decidedly agitated quality.

I narrowed my eyes and observed him closely. "You sound upset. Do you know him?"

"Not really, but I know enough. Rumor has it he's hardcore into the drug scene. He also has "womanizer" written all over him." He scratched his head as he scowled. "He's one of those guys that girls just lay down in front of. He can have his pick of anyone."

"Oh, I get it. You're saying you don't think he was flirting with me. Thanks a lot." I made a screwed up face.

He shook his head. "No, I'm saying I *know* he was flirting. I've seen him look at you. Trust me, Cami. He wants you to be another notch on his headboard."

My breath caught, surprised at his remark. Clay had never spoken to me this way about other guys. He seemed truly upset.

"I'm not the notch-making kind of girl, in case you've forgotten," I snapped, suddenly irritated by his remark.

"Of course I haven't." Clay reached over and slid his hand down my arm. He grasped my hand, squeezing it. "And I want to help you stay that way. Who knows how this guy would try to take advantage of you?"

"He can't take advantage of me if I'm not interested."

"You're interested. You know you are. I've seen the way you look at him too." He sighed and released me.

I grabbed him back and laced my fingers with his. "I don't need any guy in my life besides you. Things are perfect just the way they are."

He visibly relaxed and smiled, looking at me sweetly. "I agree. Stick with me, baby," he added in an exaggerated attempt at a suave voice, and I laughed hard.

It always amazed me that no one noticed how cute Clay was. Well, I mean I guess Marcy did, but she wasn't around to show it. Clay met her when he was staying at his aunt's house during winter break, and he was constantly talking about and texting her.

True, Clay had no sense of fashion whatsoever, but when he was laying here like this—mostly undressed, no glasses, his blond hair spiked from being in the water—he actually looked kind of adorable. I would've probably been impressed with his attempt at abs even if I hadn't been in such recent proximity to Hunter. Clay had obviously been working out; he was getting some definition to his physique. I didn't know why, but the mental image of him lifting weights made me snicker.

"What?" Clay asked, lifting his head a little to squint with one eye. "What's so funny?"

"Nothing." I grinned and bit my lip.

"Don't make me come tickle it out of you."

"You'd have to be able to actually see me for that to happen. I know you're nearly blind as a bat without your glasses," I teased.

"I'm not that bad." He looked upset by my remark.

I nudged his arm. "I'm just kidding."

"Whatever."

"That's it." I moved and tickled him first.

He jerked away in surprise over my attack and laughed before coming back after me.

I squealed and curled up in a ball to protect myself. He rolled over from his chair onto me, tickling me all over as I wriggled. I tried to get away, but he grabbed my hands and pinned them up over my head.

"I surrender!" I shouted, unable to stop my fit of giggles.

"Good choice," he replied as he stared down. His smile slowly slid from his face and he was suddenly serious.

I squirmed underneath him trying to get free, and he shifted, looking uncomfortable. "Time for a dip, I think." He stood up and scooped me off the chair while I kicked and screamed. Then he jumped into the ice cold water, drowning us both.

"You haven't been around as much, Clay. How are you liking your classes this semester?" my mom asked as she cut some more of her famous chicken salad sandwiches into fourths and slid the heaping plate toward us.

Clay shrugged, fidgeting a little with the hem

on his shorts. "It's more of the same, I guess. They're all right. I wish I had more classes with Cami, though."

"Aw, that's sweet!" I leaned against him, and he wrapped his arm around me, giving my shoulders a squeeze.

He smiled radiantly. "Classes are always more enjoyable with you."

"I feel the same way. I'm glad we have band and chemistry together at least. We've had lots of good times in those."

"And lunch! Don't forget that," he added, making a gagging motion.

"Of course not. I need someone to make fun of the cafeteria food with me. We've made some great sculptures with that stuff."

"Things worthy of a science project on occasion."

"The food there *is* a science project."

"Hopefully the school board will decide to let us have open lunches again."

A solemn wave washed through the room, and I thought about the crack down by the school after Jordan Henley had died. They were worried about the kids doing drugs and had closed the school campus in an attempt to make things safer.

"I'm assuming you've decided not to attend the fundraiser. What plans do you two have for this evening?" Mom asked, deftly changing the subject.

"I thought maybe we could go see the newest, latest, and greatest action movie that's out," Clay said and turned to me. "What do you think? Are you up for that?"

"Sure. It'll be fun to get out and hang with you for a little while again. We haven't been able to do that much. You've been really busy lately."

"Just trying to keep up on all my assignments, like you."

"And talking to Marcy," I teased, winking.

His face colored. "And working at the theater, like you. I wish Jen would arrange the schedule again. I liked our shifts on the same nights."

I shrugged. "So talk to her. Maybe she can put in a word for us with Jon and get it switched back."

"Maybe," he mumbled. "I better go home and get ready. Do you want to grab a burger or something before?"

I nodded. "That sounds good. Is that okay with you, Mom?"

"As long as you two are home by curfew."

"Alright," Clay said with a grin. "I'll pick you up at six."

"See you then." I wrapped my arms around him and gave him a bear hug. "Thanks for coming over today."

"It's been my favorite thing to do since I was five." He hugged me back tightly. "See you tonight."

I resumed eating my sandwich, swinging my dangling legs from the barstool like a child.

My mom glanced up from the food she was preparing for herself with a puzzled expression.

"What?" I asked.

She gestured toward the door. "I wonder if you've noticed that the dynamics between you and Clay have changed. He likes you."

"He better like me. He's my best friend." I took another bite.

She shook her head. "No, I think you're missing the point. I think he *likes you*, likes you—more than a friend."

I choked on my last bite and started coughing. "No way." I kept coughing as she hurried and got me a glass of water. I took a heavy drink before placing the cup on the counter and staring at her. "You aren't serious, are you?"

My mom sighed as she continued chopping a tomato for her salad. "I'm just calling it as I see it. You haven't noticed the changes? Working out more, wearing nicer labels of clothing—even if they are still plaid. He finds reasons to touch you a lot more often too."

I couldn't help my gaping mouth; my world was turning upside down. Suddenly I was afraid. "I hope you're wrong about this, Mom. It will ruin everything."

"So, I'm guessing that means you don't reciprocate?"

I groaned. "Not. In. The. Slightest." I replied, emphasizing each word. "What should I do? Should I call him and cancel our plans? I think of him like a brother, and I don't want to lead him on."

"I don't think so. I may be seeing something that isn't there. I'd go and see what happens with him tonight." She stared at me pointedly.

"Just be careful. He seems different to me for some reason."

"Okay." I pushed my plate away, my appetite suddenly gone. "I'm going to go get showered now. Thanks for lunch, Mom."

She gave me a sorrowful smile, and I left. I closed the door to my room behind me and flopped onto my bed with a groan, burying my face into the pillow. This was so not what I needed to hear right now. I hoped she was wrong, but she seemed to possess an uncanny sense of intuition about things.

If she was right, I was going to have to find some way to put the brakes on, but I didn't want to come right out and crush him. Images of our tickle fight and holding hands by the pool popped into my head. Suddenly, actions that had seemed so intimately friendly took on another quality all together.

I got up and wandered over to my closet, trying to decide what to wear. Normally, I'd have thrown any old thing on to hang out with Clay, totally happy to be my comfortable self. However, tonight I was torn. Did I dress down to discourage him? Or should I dress up with the hope of flirting with some other guy there. That would show him I wasn't into him romantically. Actually, that might not be a bad idea. Maybe I needed to try and do some things with other people so he wouldn't think we were having some kind of exclusive arrangement.

I reached into the closet to get my newest outfit I'd been saving for something special.

"Oh, Clay. Why'd you have to go and

change? It ruins everything," I said aloud. I hugged the clothes to me before laying them on my bed and heading into the bathroom.

I was going to hate doing this to him.

CAMI ♥

CHAPTER FOUR
Cami-

My hand trembled as I reached for the doorknob after the knock sounded. I took a steadying breath and tried to appear normal as I swung it open.

"Hey, Clay," I said casually. That was as far as I got. My jaw fell open, and I quickly snapped it shut.

He was completely transformed. His blond hair was no longer slicked back, instead styled to perfection in the latest messy trend. He wasn't wearing his glasses, and due to the extreme, startling, blue shade of his eyes, I quickly gathered he'd gotten contacts. There wasn't an ounce of plaid anywhere on his body— instead he was wearing a blue t-shirt in a shade that only further complimented his eyes and his newly-trimmed physique. His jeans were a dark indigo, slung low on his hips, and a pair of black checkerboard vans completed the ensemble.

He chuckled. "You look amazing," he said as his eyes drifted over the short, green, halter summer dress I was wearing, along with a pair of matching sandals.

"Um, so do you. What happened?" I shook my head. "That didn't come out like I meant. I mean . . . I never knew you cared about being fashionable."

He shrugged. "I decided it was time for a change, so I've been saving up some money for it. I've been trying to slowly switch things up, just to see if you would notice but then after today I was tired of waiting."

I wasn't sure what to say. He looked great, but not like *my* Clay either. "Well, you look . . . good."

He shifted a little and glanced away for a second as if he were uncomfortable. "So, you ready to go?"

"Yeah, just let me grab my sweater really quick in case it gets chilly later." I went to get it off the couch. "Mom, I'm heading out with Clay now," I called.

She appeared and came to give me a kiss. "Have a good time. Be home by midnight. Love you."

"I will. Love you too."

I left the house, and Clay walked me to his old, white VW Rabbit, pausing to open the door. I slid in. "Thank you," I mumbled under my breath.

I couldn't remember him ever doing this for me before. Something had definitely changed. I thought back to our tickle fight beside the pool today and felt a little sick. I didn't want things to be different between us. I was happy with the way they were. I was beginning to think my mom was right. Clay liked me.

"Oh, shoot!" I exclaimed as I glanced down, realizing I'd forgotten my purse.

"What is it?" he asked.

"I left my bag on the couch. I need my money for dinner and the movie." I moved, intending to get out.

"No worries. This is my treat." He smiled.

"Wait!" I heard my mom. She came running from the house with my handbag. "You forgot this, Cami! Hi, Clay. You look nice tonight," she added, giving him the once over.

He blushed a little and glanced away. "Thanks," he mumbled.

"Here you go, sweetie," Mom said, handing me my purse.

My relief was palpable. "Thank you. I just realized. I didn't want to make Clay pay for everything. It defeats the whole point of going Dutch, right?" I laughed nervously hoping I didn't sound stupid while I tried to make him understand we were *not* on a date.

My mom looked at me curiously. "Okay. Have fun!" She stepped back to the curb and Clay shut my door.

I clutched my bag tightly as I watched him walk around the car. I felt like I'd been cast in a role for a horror spot in *Invasion of the Body Snatchers*. My BFF had suddenly disappeared, replaced with someone who sort of looked like him, but this person had designs on me. I was having a hard time coming to terms with it. It was impossible to just wake up one morning and decide you weren't a science nerd anymore, but a jock instead. The social ladder didn't work that way—did it?

Clay slid into his seat and started the car. "I think I'll replace this beater-mobile next. What do you think about that? Maybe get a sports car . . . like a Mustang or something."

"Who are you?" I asked, unable to keep it to myself anymore. "Why are you doing all this? And I like your car! We have good memories in it. Where would you get that kind of money anyway? Buying a car is a lot different than saving up for contacts."

"It doesn't have to be brand new. There are nice, used cars out there, Cami." He sounded frustrated. "Besides, I thought you'd like all of this. You were the one who inspired it."

"How?" His remark surprised me.

"Don't you remember the day those guys were picking on me in class? You told me not to listen to them because they couldn't see how wonderful I really was. You said it was up to me to be what I wanted. Well, this is what I want to be—someone girls will notice, and people will want to hang out with. Sure, I'm good at school—really good. I can get a blue ribbon at any science fair, but I don't want to just be smart. I want to look good doing it. I want to have more friends—not that you won't always be my best friend—but I'm tired of sitting on the sidelines and watching life happen to everyone else. So I made some changes. I thought you'd be pleased." He glanced over, a hurt expression on his face.

"Clay, I think you look amazing, but I did before too," I said softly.

"You did?" He glanced at me with a hopeful expression.

I nodded. "I've known you since we were five. You're like my favorite brother who I adore."

His jaw clenched. He put the car into gear and headed off down the road without speaking.

I felt my hands trembling, wishing he would say something, but hoping he wouldn't either.

"I never wanted to be your brother, Cami."

Biting my bottom lip, I turned away to look out the window and blinked back the tears, which threatened. I hated hurting him. I wasn't sure what else to say, so I didn't say anything as we drove the rest of the way to the restaurant.

Dinner was brutal. We ate mostly in silence. It didn't matter that we were at our favorite mom and pop diner, Francesca's, eating our favorite burgers and crispy French fries. Everything tasted like sawdust in my mouth, so I just sat and stirred my thick, strawberry shake while I watched Clay texting madly on his phone to someone.

"Who you talking to?" I finally asked.

"Marcy," he replied shortly.

I felt a sudden burst of relief. Maybe he didn't like me in that way after all.

"Let me see your phone." I gestured for him

to hand it to me, but he pulled back. "Give it to me. I want to take a picture of you so you can send it to her. She needs to see how hot you look tonight."

A slow grin crossed his face, and he slumped back into his chair. "You think I look hot?"

I nodded. "Yes, and don't move. The slouch you're sitting in is perfect."

He pushed a button and slid the phone across the table. "Here you go." He'd already pulled up the camera.

"Okay, give me some sexy smolder."

He laughed and pursed his lips together. "Not duck face!" I groaned. "Sexy smolder. You know, you're looking at that gorgeous girl who you always wanted and you're thinking, "Come to me, baby."

His look changed immediately and instantly there it was, smolder. Wow, he could actually do it. I snapped the picture and handed the phone back.

"Here you go. Marcy's gonna love that!"

His expression fell a little, but he glanced at the picture anyway. A small grin crossed his face. "Thanks, Cami. I like it. You're a good photographer even when you don't have your big camera."

"Thanks. I love photography. It's always fun in the dark room, watching the pictures develop."

"Maybe you can show me sometime," he said, staring at the image on his phone. "I'm gonna message this to you so you can put it as my contact photo."

"Sweet. Sounds good." I pulled my cell out and waited for the text to pop in.

"Aren't you hungry tonight?" he asked, motioning to my barely-touched food.

I shook my head. "Not really. I've just had a nervous stomach for some reason. Don't worry, I'll get some snacks at the movie theater if I need to."

He shrugged. "Suit yourself." He tossed several bills onto the table. "I've got dinner tonight."

"No really, Clay. Let me get my own. You said yourself you wanted to save for a new car."

"I'm paying for dinner," he said in a no-nonsense voice.

"All right. I'll leave the tip then." I put a few dollars next to his. "Thanks."

He nodded abruptly and quickly stood and headed for the door. I sighed, not happy that we seemed to be back at awkward again. I'd been hopeful there for a few minutes.

I watched him walk to his car, but I headed toward the restrooms instead to check my lip-gloss, teeth, and pop a breath mint. Thankfully the movie was next. We wouldn't have to do a lot of talking there.

Smoothing my hands over my dress, I gave a sigh and turned to go.

HUNTER♥

CHAPTER FIVE
Hunter-

She was here, and I was so mesmerized with staring at her it took me a second to realize who the guy was standing next to her. I did a double take as I took in Clay's new look, amazed with the transformation. I couldn't believe this was the same nerdy kid I saw every day.

I glanced around the lobby of the theater, noticing he was getting much of the same reaction from the school kids who knew him. Some were pointing and laughing, though there were a few girls who looked at him appreciatively.

Returning my gaze to the two of them, I also noticed there seemed to be some sort of friction. Clay was looking at Cami as if she was the axis his world was spinning on. Cami was biting her plump bottom lip and doing her best not to pay any attention to him, studying everything around her instead.

I chuckled slightly and leaned back against the wall. Well, this was interesting. It seemed as if the guy was carrying a serious torch for his gorgeous BFF, and she was not willing to reciprocate. For some reason, I found a great deal of pleasure in this.

She looked amazing in her green dress, her soft, red hair falling in waves down to brush her bare-skinned shoulders. She was showing a fair amount of leg—something I hadn't really seen her do before—and I didn't mind one bit. She reminded me of some sort of green apple just ripe for the picking.

I grunted internally, realizing I was comparing her to fruit again. What was up with that? *You know exactly what's up with that*, my mind countered, but I couldn't force myself to look away. I knew she wasn't for me, though somehow, it didn't seem to matter much at the moment.

"Enjoying the eye candy again, I see," Russ said, joining me after getting his snack.

"Who? Clayton Bradley? I don't think so."

Russ snorted. "Yeah, we're both aware that's not who you were looking at. Dude, if you like her that much just go get her. You know you want her."

I shook my head and turned in the direction of the theaters. "Can't."

"Why not?" Russ pressured, trying to understand. "You got a girlfriend back home? Or are you saying you play for the other team?"

I snorted. "I just can't, okay? No girlfriend for me, period."

"So you're going to lust after her from afar?" He elbowed me as he took a bite of his giant popcorn.

"Something like that."

We found ourselves a seat at the back of the theater. I liked sitting here so I could watch what everyone around me was doing while I was waiting for the movie to start.

"This is just a crying shame," Russ said.

"What is?"

"Sitting on the back row and not having any honeys to make out with in the dark. I need a date soon."

"Good luck with that," I replied. "Maybe you should try actually talking to a girl. That might help."

"Oh, look who's Mr. Advice all of a sudden— he who stares and drools from afar."

"At least I have an actual babe to drool over instead of just wishful thinking."

"Ah ha! You just admitted it. You do like her!" His face was lit up like he'd just discovered electricity or something.

And dang it, he was right. "Eat your popcorn like a good boy and leave me alone." I grinned.

He laughed. "There's not a good bone in this body."

"That sucks for you," I countered with a sly smile. "Good bones are all I have lately."

Russ choked, spewing popcorn out into the aisle.

"That's just sick, man," I chuckled with a shake of my head, observing the chewed popcorn on the back of the chair in front of him.

"It's your fault. Don't blame me." He took a napkin, wiping his mouth and then the chair.

"You're never gonna get a girl like this. Maybe I should show you how it's done."

"Well, master, here's your chance." Russ gestured into the theater, and I saw Cami and Clay enter together.

I stiffened immediately as I watched them. They chose some seats a few aisles down from where we were. Clay put his drink in the cup holder and leaned in close to her. Cami clearly shifted away from him.

This caused an alarm to go off in my head. She was obviously uncomfortable with his close proximity. I wondered if he'd tried to hit on her, and she didn't like it. It was as if they weren't the same people I'd watched in class together. Clay had changed his appearance, and it seemed to have the opposite effect of what he was going for—changing the dynamic between them completely.

He bent closer and whispered something in her ear and she leaned even farther. There was definitely something bad going on between them.

I reached over, grabbed Russ's popcorn, and got up.

"Hey, where you going?" he asked, looking confused.

I ignored him and walked down to the row Cami was on. I had to find something out.

"Hey, Goody," I said as I sat down in the chair right next to her. "I guess I don't know you so well after all. I never pegged you as an action adventure kind of girl."

Her face was a mask of complete surprise as she turned to look at me.

"Popcorn?" I asked her innocently, tipping Russ's bag toward her.

She shook her head. "No thanks." I saw what I was looking for after the shock wore away. Relief. It was plain—there was no way I was leaving.

"Can we help you with something?" Clay said leaning forward, annoyance written all over him.

"I don't think so. Just settling in to watch the movie here with my good buddy, Cami." I turned and glanced up behind me to where Russ was sitting with his mouth hanging open. "Come on, dude. These seats are *way* better than those up there. I told you they would be." I shoved a handful of his popcorn into my mouth, chomping happily.

Russ got up, moving in our direction. He ripped his popcorn out of my hand when he sat down and gave me a glare followed by a questioning look.

Cami was still staring expectantly, as if she were waiting for me to say something else.

I flashed her my most winning smile, hoping there was nothing stuck in my teeth. I was going to lay on all the charm I could and do some messing with Clay boy. "So how's your weekend been going, Cami?" I cast a glance over her rockin' body. "Looks like you got a little sun since the last time I saw you. That dress shows it off *very* nicely."

Her eyes widened in surprise, and I thought

I actually saw Clay bare his teeth at me. I had to work hard not to laugh out loud.

"Um, thank you." A smile faltered on her lips as if she weren't really sure if I was messing with her or not.

I needed to make things a little more clear. I was trying to send a message here. "I'm sorry I didn't get another chance to talk to you at school on Friday. I wondered if you'd like to go on a date with me sometime? Maybe get a burger or something—go to one of those art galleries you told me about?"

Russ choked on his popcorn again for the second time tonight as the previews for the movie started.

Cami was staring at me like I was someone who had just crawled out of a foreign film and she had no idea what I was saying.

"Cami," Clay growled, nudging her a bit. That brought her back to life.

What the hell was I doing? What part of 'no girls' was my brain not understanding? I hurried to amend. "No rush or anything. I shouldn't have put you on the spot like that. You can think about it during the movie and tell me afterward."

"Oh, okay," she spoke in almost a whisper and reclined back into her seat.

Clay hissed something in her ear I couldn't understand. He was not happy by any means, and I was irritated when Cami visibly became rigid.

She tapped me on the shoulder, and I leaned over so I could hear her better. "I don't need to wait," she whispered. "I would enjoy going out with you. Thank you for asking."

I smiled softly, wondering briefly why my heart sped up so much at her simple words. "I'm glad. I promise we can do something fun together. Nothing that will make you uncomfortable."

She nodded and returned my smile. "That sounds good."

I pulled out my cell phone. "Can I get your number so I can set things up with you later? You can have mine too."

"Sure." She pulled hers from her bag and handed it to me, taking mine, and we typed our numbers into them and switched back.

"Thanks," I said again. "Do you mind if we sit here with you for the show?"

She shook her head. "Not at all."

Clay huffed, sitting back into his chair, crossing his arms as he obviously pouted. Cami glanced at him, but he wouldn't acknowledge her, so she turned and watched the movie.

I leaned back into my chair feeling satisfied. She'd definitely needed some help. I looked at Russ who was watching me in shock.

"You're one crazy S.O.B. You stole her right from under the guy she was with," he whispered in awe. "I can't believe you got her to go out with you. How'd you do that?"

"I paid attention to what was going on around me, which is what you need to do. Then you'll start seeing the things you're missing."

"I have no idea what you mean, but feel free to teach me, Master Obi-Wan."

I snorted and Cami looked at me. I smiled and she gave me a shy one back before turning toward the screen again.

"You already have her wrapped around your finger." Russ said in a low voice with a laugh.

I elbowed him in the ribs. "Shut up and watch the movie."

"Yes, Master," he groaned, and I couldn't help the chuckle that burst from my lips. I faked a cough, lifting my hand to cover my mouth.

My humor didn't last long, though. As the movie started I couldn't help the guilty feelings, which coursed through me, and I found I had a hard time concentrating. Yes, this girl was beautiful, and it was obvious I liked her . . . a lot. The truth was I really had no business messing with her. Red warning flags were dropping all over, and suddenly I felt like I was standing right in the middle of a potential mine field. One wrong step and everything would explode in the worst way possible, and it would be a bloody, friggin' disaster.

I glanced at Cami again, watching her stunning eyes flash in the lights coming from the screen. I wasn't sure what was going on between her and her friend right now, but I promised myself I was going to find out. For some reason, I needed to make sure she was all right. One thing I'd learned was always listen to my intuition, and right now it was speaking loud and clear, telling me there was a big a problem.

I hope she's worth it, spoke that nagging internal voice again.

"She is," I whispered, answering myself

back.

CAMI ♥

CHAPTER SIX
Cami-

I wasn't sure what had just happened. Had I just agreed to go on a date with Hunter Wilder? The guy I swore I'd never go out with—even if we *were* both from the same social class? Not only that, but I was clearly excited about it, much to the dismay of Clay who felt it was his moral obligation to remind me Hunter was only after one thing. His plan backfired, though. As soon as he said it, I made up my mind I'd do it, just to tick him off.

I sighed heavily. This day had started out okay and gone to utterly confusing. Nothing and no one was where they should be. It was like living in the middle of the Twilight Zone. I kept expecting the creepy music to start playing any minute.

When the movie ended, Clay got up and stalked from the theater, pausing only to cast an angry glare, first at me and then at Hunter, before he continued on his way.

"What's his problem?" Hunter asked softly as his friend Russ left the aisle and headed down the steps, leaving the two of us alone.

"It's a long story. Maybe I should tell you another day and go catch up with Clay."

"He likes you a lot. You know that, right?"

"No. I didn't. I mean I do now, but I didn't. He just showed up at the house with no warning all . . . different. It's like he's not the same person anymore. I can tell he expects something from me, but I'm not sure what."

"I think he wanted you to be amazed—to finally see him in a new light. People at school told me they thought you two might be an item because of the way he acts about you. He's very possessive."

I was shocked. "Really? I had no idea. Honestly, I never got that vibe from him until today. Then something changed when we were swimming. Even then, I wouldn't have put the pieces together until my mom pointed it out. I didn't want to believe it." I stared at him for a moment. "If you thought we were a couple, then why did you come and ask me on a date?

He shrugged. "I could tell something was going on, and you looked extremely uncomfortable. I wanted to make sure you were okay."

This revelation didn't fit into the previously judged category I'd placed Hunter in. It was . . . nice. Did popular bad boy partiers *do* nice?

"Well, I appreciate your help, Hunter. But let's get some things straight right now. I don't party, I don't use illicit drugs, and I won't be a notch in anyone's headboard."

He choked and sputtered before smiling widely. "Wow. You've been reading the daily rumor mill, haven't you? You've already decided what kind of guy I am."

He looked disappointed, and suddenly I felt horrible.

"I'm sorry if that sounds harsh. It had to do with something Clay said earlier."

"Something about me, I gather?"

"Yeah, he told me to stay away from you."

"Really?" Hunter grinned. "So you were talking about me then?"

I blushed hard. "Um, I better go before Clay leaves me."

"Let him leave you. I'll take you home."

I shook my head, wishing I could do exactly that. "No, it would be even more unfair. I feel bad about screwing up whatever dreams or plans he had for this moment. I love him. He's like my brother. I don't want to hurt him—I just don't want to date him either."

"I thought he had a girlfriend."

"He does, but she doesn't live here."

"Ah, long distance relationships, huh? Those never work out."

I smiled. "I couldn't say. I've never had one." I stood and reached for my sweater.

"Here, let me help you with that," Hunter offered. He took it and held it up, allowing me to slip my arms inside, then he adjusted it on my shoulders before letting his hands smooth over it and down my arms.

"Perfect," he muttered, almost like he'd forgotten I could hear him.

"Thanks," I replied and his head popped up in surprise. "That was sweet of you."

"Just calling it like I see it." He grinned.

We were standing so close together now I could see some of those caramel highlights in his eyes.

"Hello, Cami! Are you coming or what?" Clay's voice interrupted us.

"Be right there," I called back before addressing Hunter again. "Sorry. I gotta go now."

"No worries, but do me a favor real quick. Can I see your phone again?"

"Sure," I replied digging in my purse before handing it to him.

He pushed a few buttons and gave it back. "Number 7. Just remember Lucky Sevens. That's my number on speed dial. If you ever need any help just call me, and I'll come get you."

I blushed. *Wow. This guy was beyond nice.* "Thanks, I will."

"Good. Text me and let me know you got home okay."

I laughed. "Clay would never hurt me."

"That might be true, but you see . . . I don't know Clay that well, so just humor me, okay? I'll rest better."

"All right. Thanks again for asking me out." I gave a little wave and walked away.

"I'm looking forward to it," he said softly, not moving as I made my way down to my very angry, best friend. At least I hoped he was still my best friend.

It was bound to be an interesting drive home.

Clay turned and huffed out in front of me. I followed him quietly to the parking lot, and he opened the door for me.

We didn't speak as he drove and soon pulled up in front of my house.

"Thanks for the ride," I said as I fumbled for the handle.

"Why'd you do it?" he asked.

"Do what?"

"Agree to a date with him." His hands were gripping the steering wheel tightly.

"Because you were scaring me and trying to tell me what to do. It made me irritated, and then he showed up and offered a way out." I was being brutally honest.

"So you just did it to make me mad?"

"Yes, partly. I like him too, I think. At least I like what I've seen so far, and I'd like to know more."

"I know everything there is to know about you, Cami, and I'd like to learn more about you still. I've wanted to for a long time." He looked and sounded so sorrowful.

"I'm sorry. I didn't realize you felt that way."

"Well, now you do. Will you give me a chance at least? Can I show you how good I think we'd be together?" He stroked the side of my cheek.

My shoulders tightened, and I felt the panic coming on. I shook my head. "I'm sorry—so incredibly sorry, but I don't think I'm on the same page. You already have a girlfriend, and I don't want her to get hurt. Plus, it would be so awkward for me. You're my best friend. You've seen and heard all my flaws and secrets. I think of you like my brother. I want things to stay as they always have been."

He sighed heavily. "And if I can't do that anymore?"

I felt the tears welling. "Then I'll be really sad not to have you in my life." I opened the door and got out. "Goodnight, Clay."

He didn't look at me again before he drove off. I watched until his car was out of sight before turning to go up the sidewalk to my house.

Safely home. Thanks, I texted to Hunter.

The reply was almost immediate. Glad 2 hear it. Text U 2morrow. Night.

I stared at the words in front of me. Hunter Wilder was going to text me tomorrow. Despite all that happened tonight with Clay, I couldn't help the little thrill that shot through me.

I sighed. What a crazy day.

CAMI

CHAPTER SEVEN
Cami-

It was late when I rolled over and checked the time. Wow. Ten o'clock and my mom hadn't been in to wake me. I reached for my phone on the charger and looked to see if Clay had messaged. There was nothing. I didn't know what to say so I didn't text him either.

Grabbing some shorts and a t-shirt, I made my way into the bathroom for a quick shower and then headed downstairs for some breakfast.

"Well, look who finally decided to grace us with her presence this fine Sunday morning." My dad smiled from his recliner where he was reading the Arts & Style section of the paper.

I bent and kissed him on the cheek. "Morning, Dad. How are you today? Did you enjoy your band fundraiser last night?"

"I'm good and we had a great time. The people in the hotel really loved the jazz performance, and we raised a lot of money. I'm pleased we live in a town that appreciates good culture."

Copper City certainly did cater to the arts. I felt like he and Mom were really happy here. It was definitely their dream place to live.

"I'm so glad. That's awesome. I'm going to grab some breakfast. Where's Mom?"

"She stayed up late helping with clean up after the banquet so I let her sleep in."

That explained why she hadn't been in this morning. I went to the cupboard and pulled out a bowl before getting a box of cereal off the counter and taking it to the island bar.

I was munching away when I felt my phone vibrate. I stiffened. Chances were this was either Clay or Hunter, and I was afraid to look, feeling nervous about hearing from either of them. I glanced at the text.

Nice day 2day. Wanna grab some lunch & eat @ the park around noon?

I smiled, letting out a sigh of relief. It was Hunter.

Sure. Sounds fun.

Gr8. Can I get UR address?

I texted it back to him with a little smiley face.

Awesome. C U in a bit.

Nervous butterflies danced in my stomach. I quickly finished my last few bites of cereal and hurried to my room.

"Where are you going in such a rush?" Dad called.

"I have a lunch date!"

"With Clay?"

"No. His name is Hunter Wilder. He's new. I'll tell you more about him after I'm ready."

"Okay. I want to meet this kid before you leave with him."

I rolled my eyes. "Yes, Dad." My dad was totally the overprotective father type. I knew he trusted me, but I was a little worried about what he might think of Hunter.

Yes, I'd been out a few times with guys other than Clay, but they tended to be more of the studious variety, or they were music and drama students—people who my dad would instantly approve of. He'd even let me go with one of his students from the college. I'd never dated anybody in the hot guy category of Hunter, though. It would be interesting to see if he said anything.

I raided my closet and drawers, finally deciding on a pair of tiny jean shorts and a cute square-cut tee with cap sleeves in a bright, cheery yellow. I carefully applied my makeup and then got my hot iron and painstakingly worked on my hair until my curls were bone straight. I pulled it back into a trendy-styled ponytail, and added some gold hoop earrings before slipping my feet into some matching yellow sandals that laced up my calves.

It was only eleven-thirty when I finished, so I went back down to the living room to visit with my dad, finding my mom had joined him as well.

"You look nice." She smiled, glancing up from a romance novel she was reading. "Dad told me you have a lunch date with a new guy.

Who is he?"

"His name is Hunter Wilder. He recently moved here from Tucson with his uncle. I guess both his parents were killed in a car accident. At least that's what the rumor mill says. I haven't really had an opportunity to talk to him about it yet, other than for him to tell me he's from Tucson."

"So is he in your music and drama classes with you then?" Dad asked.

"No, he's in my Chemistry, English, Government, and Photography classes."

"Oh, so does he hope to be a photographer?"

I laughed. "I have no idea. I don't know him that well. He's only been here a short while. We've never really spoken to each other before this week."

"Does Clay like him?" Dad smiled and I instantly sobered.

"No, I'm afraid not." I cringed. I knew my dad put a lot of stock in Clay's opinion about who I dated.

"Why doesn't he like him?" he pressed.

I shrugged. "Jealous, I think."

"Jealous?"

My mom chuckled. "You're a little out of the loop, Brandt. Clay seems to have developed a bit of a crush on our girl."

"Has he now? How do you feel about that?"

"Actually, it's quite awkward, and I wish he hadn't. I don't feel that way about him. It would be like dating my brother or something. He's making things difficult."

"So last night didn't go well?" Mom asked,

looking concerned.

"Not at all. In fact, I think Hunter asked me out as a way to try and help rescue me from a very uncomfortable situation." I twisted my hands together in my lap.

"That was nice of him, though I'm sad you and Clay are having problems. You've been friends far too long to let something like this come between you. I hope you can fix it."

"Me too. I love Clay, just not like *that*." I looked back and forth between them. "There's something else I should tell you about Hunter."

"What's that?" Dad asked.

"He won't be the kind of guy you're used to me dating. I mean he's maybe one of the most popular guys in school right now. He rose to fame around here pretty fast—drives a shiny new black Camaro—and may actually be the best looking guy I've ever seen in my life—I'm talking model worthy. I honestly have no idea why he would want to go out with me."

"Maybe because you're beautiful and sweet and he can see that." My mom smiled.

"You have to say that. You're my mom."

"She wouldn't lie to you either, honey," my dad added.

The doorbell rang, interrupting our conversation, and I felt nervous. He was a few minutes early. I answered it, surprised to find Clay, not Hunter, standing there.

He glanced over me before moving back up, locking eyes with me—almost a desperate plea in them. "Hey, Cami. Can we please go somewhere and talk?"

Right then a loud thumping bass sound filled the air. I looked down the street, and watched as Hunter pulled up in his Camaro with the windows rolled down.

I glanced back to Clay. "Um, I have a date right now. Maybe later when I get done?"

Clay's lips turned in an obvious frown. "He didn't waste any time, did he? Call me when you get home." He turned and headed down the sidewalk.

"Hey, man," Hunter said as they passed. Clay ignored him and kept on walking. He got into his car and drove away without a backward glance.

"Did I interrupt something important?" Hunter asked as he approached. He was holding a couple of roses loosely in his hand and I smiled.

"No, not at all. Come in and meet my parents. They've been expecting you." I stepped aside so he could enter.

He followed me into the living room, and my parents stood to greet him. I noticed my mom's eyes going wide in surprise, but my dad's narrowed as if he sensed a predator. His gaze traveled over the red t-shirt and down to the amazing, deep-blue hipster jeans and dark shoes, all designer of course. It was obvious he had money.

"This is my mom, Cecily, and my dad, Brandt. Mom and Dad, this is Hunter Wilder."

"Pleased to meet you," Hunter said with impeccable manners, shaking my dad's hand firmly. He handed my mom a rose. "This is for you," he added before turning to extend the other one to me. "And this one is yours."

I couldn't help the smile as I took a sniff. "It smells wonderful. Thank you."

He looked pleased. "You're welcome. I saw them, and they made me think of your pretty, red hair. Looks like it worked for your mom too." He laughed and gestured to her hair color.

"Well, aren't you just the charmer?" My mom giggled like a schoolgirl, and I knew he'd won over at least one parent. "Would you like a drink or something?"

"Oh, no thanks. I figured I'd pick up something with Cami, and we could go to the park and hang out together."

"What else do you plan on doing while you're there?" My dad asked sternly.

"Uh, well, I brought a Frisbee I thought we could toss around, if Cami's up for it." He glanced at me.

"Sound fun," I said, thinking how I couldn't imagine Hunter doing anything as lame as throwing a Frisbee.

"When will you have her home?"

Hunter shrugged. "I hadn't really planned on a certain time. I figured I'd take her to do whatever she wanted until she got sick of me. She said there's some good museums and stuff around. I thought I'd let her decide since she knows better than I do."

"I'm sure you'll have a wonderful time," my mom gushed. "Cami's curfew is midnight. As long as she's home by then, we are good."

I think my dad may have actually shot fire

out of his eyes toward my mom, and I bit my lip to suppress a giggle of my own.

"Very well. Please remember she's the most precious thing in her parent's lives and treat her accordingly."

I almost choked. Boy, he was laying it on thick.

"I'll be fine, Dad," I said, standing on my tiptoes to give him a quick kiss on the cheek. I could tell he was very apprehensive. "I'll see you both later."

"Have fun!" My mom was glowing as she gave us a little wave, and I grabbed Hunter by the arm and dragged him from the room before things could get any weirder.

He walked me to the car and opened the door before jogging around and getting in the other side.

"Sorry for the craziness in there."

He smiled widely. "Nah, it was fine."

"I think my mom liked you."

"But not your dad?"

"I'd say the jury is still out. He'll form a better opinion of you after you've returned me safely home in the same condition you found me." I blushed.

"Well, I don't want to deliver you home in exactly the same condition I found you." His eyes flitted over my figure and my heart raced.

Suddenly I felt underdressed. "You don't?" I managed to squeak out.

He shook his head. "Nope. I want to bring you back exhausted from having an amazing day with me."

"Oh." I didn't know what else to say.

He started the car, and I jumped as the stereo roared to life with a loud thump. I covered my ears in reflex.

Hunter quickly turned it down significantly. "Sorry! I get a little carried away with the tunes while I'm driving."

"It's okay. It just caught me by surprise, is all."

"So, where do you want to go get food?" he asked.

"Well, if you like burgers and stuff, I like that little diner called Francesca's."

"Oh, I ate there with Russ one night. They had great food. Let's do that then." He turned in that direction.

Everything still felt so surreal—being here with him like this—but he was making me feel comfortable and at ease.

I sighed. I already liked him, and I didn't even know him.

HUNTER♥

CHAPTER EIGHT
Hunter-

Her eyes widened when I opened my trunk and pulled out the thick, heavy blanket I'd brought. I could almost see her imagining what sort of nefarious things I might be planning.

"I thought it would be nice to sit on while we ate." I smiled.

"That would be good," she replied, visibly relaxing.

I couldn't resist teasing her some more, though. "Yeah, it will be great for later when it's darker. I don't think I should ravish you right here in the middle of the park in full daylight."

She actually gulped, and I laughed loudly. "I'm just messing with you, Goody. You're safe. Here hand me the food, and I'll carry it."

She blushed and gave me a faltering grin. "It's okay. I've got it."

"You sure? I'm tough, I can take it all."

She lifted her chin slightly. "I'm tough too."

She was full of surprises. "Very well, tough gal. I was thinking we could set up over there under that big, leafy tree so we can have a little shade. Does that look good to you?"

"Yep, let's do it."

I cocked my eyebrow. "Did you just proposition me? I think you should know I'm not that kind of guy, Miss Wimberley."

"Uh . . . " She laughed nervously.

"Relax, Cami. It's all right." I was having entirely too much fun with her already. *Be careful,* my inner voice warned me again, and I wanted to shove it back down. This was just a friendly date between new friends—following through on something I'd done to help her get out of an awkward situation. I didn't ever have to ask her out again after this. Everything would be okay and back where it should be. I was safe as long as I kept things light and chill.

I spread the blanket on the ground and gestured for her to take a seat. She did and reached into the bag, dishing our food: two juicy-looking bacon cheeseburgers, crispy fries with ketchup and ranch for dipping, and two shakes—one chocolate for me, one strawberry for her—along with two pieces of thick, homemade apple pie.

"This looks fabulous," I said as I settled down next to her, stretching out and propping up on one of my elbows.

"Thanks again for inviting me. I know you didn't have to, but I appreciate you trying to help me last night."

I took a sip of my shake and stared at her.

"You are aware this isn't a mercy date, aren't you? I've been talking myself out of asking you to do something since I moved here."

Her eyes widened. "You have? Why?"

I shrugged. "I have some things going on in my life right now that make dating a little on the difficult side. I don't really want to get into it, but things are complicated. I figured it was easier to stay away rather than risk messing things up."

I breathed a sigh of relief when she didn't ask me any more questions. There was no way for me to explain. It was a secret I needed to keep to myself for now.

"Why me?" she finally asked.

Sighing, I touched the end of her hair, fingering it slightly. It felt so silky. "You were the first person I saw at this school. I'd parked in the lot and was walking past the auditorium and saw this gorgeous girl come out of the music room. The sun hit your stunning red hair, and it shone so brightly it almost looked like you had a halo. You were staring down at some music you were holding, and started humming something. I froze. I just stood there and watched you walk by. You were so engrossed you didn't notice me." I twisted the loop of her hair around my finger. "You straightened it today. I've never seen you wear it this way before."

She lifted her shake and took a swallow, licking her lips afterward. "I like to change it up every now and then. It's so thick it takes a long time to straighten."

I released it and picked up my drink again. "Well, I like it both ways, but when you wear it curly, it bounces like it has a life of its own."

She laughed. "Just wait until it gets humid in the summer. It frizzes out until I look like I have a crazy red Afro. You won't think it's so pretty then."

I shook my head. "Nah, I bet I'll think it's gorgeous no matter what."

"I'm glad you're so sure. There are times I'm tempted to chop it all off." She absently ran her fingers through the length of it.

"Now that would just be a crime. Don't ever cut it. It perfectly complements the rest of the package."

"I'm beginning to think you're a schmoozer, Hunter. I bet you really do have girls falling at your feet, if you talk this way to all of them." She gave me a soft smile.

"Just telling it like it is. And you need to quit listening to the rumor mill. They don't have the slightest clue about me and who I am."

"So you're saying you're not some crazy party boy?"

"Depends on who you're asking, I guess," I answered vaguely.

"I'm asking you." She unwrapped her burger and took a bite.

"Okay, tell you what. I'll give you permission to ask me whatever you want. I'll answer as honestly as I can, but I get to do the same with you." I opened my burger and took a bite too.

She looked surprised and appeared to think it over while she finished chewing and swallowed. "Okay. That seems fair. Let me think."

I dipped some of my fries in ketchup while I waited.

"Do you use drugs?"

I laughed. "Gonna go straight for the heavy questions first, are you?"

"Might as well." She was waiting for my answer as if she were looking for any kind of lie in what I said.

"Yes, I use."

She seemed shocked by my completely honest reply.

"A lot?"

A chuckled again. "It depends. Sometimes more, sometimes less—mostly a little weed that I score at some parties."

"Have you used harder stuff?"

"Yep."

"Why?"

"It was available once in a while when I was partying with peeps. Just one of those things." I wondered what she was thinking about me now.

"I don't mean to judge, but I've never been able to understand why anyone would want to try something they know could hurt them."

"Sometimes people just want to escape, Cami. They like the way it feels when they get high."

"And you like feeling that way?"

"I guess so, or I wouldn't be doing it, would I?"

She stared off toward the playground where kids were on the swings, cheering happily with each other. "I went to a dance with Clay a few months before you moved here. It was probably halfway over when one of the most popular guys in school came staggering up. He grabbed me, begged me to help him, and then he fell to the floor and started convulsing. He died a few moments later. He'd had a heart attack from a drug overdose. I keep replaying the scene over and over again in my head, wondering if there was something I could've done. I didn't know what was happening. I wasn't sure what to do. I thought he was drunk." She looked at me seriously. "I didn't know Jordan well, but I couldn't figure out why he was involved with all that. He was this amazing football player. He had several scholarship offers too. His whole life was ahead of him. I can't help but think what a waste of a promising future." She paused before she continued. "It scared me—scarred me. I know you and I aren't that well acquainted, but I can say you seem like a nice guy, and I'd feel horrible if something like that happened to you. I'm not gonna lie . . . I wish you'd stop."

What was I supposed to say to that? She'd bared her heart to me, and for one moment I couldn't imagine a plea that was as sweet as this one. How could anyone say no to something like this?

I shook my head. "The only reassurance I can give you is that I'll be careful. Lots of things you've heard about me are greatly exaggerated and aren't as bad as they seem. People see what they want."

She nodded. "I recognize how that can be

true. It happens in every social group, unfortunately."

I nodded; content to watch her for a moment. "So here's my question for you." This was probably going to come back and bite me later.

"What?"

"Will you go out with me again, even though you know I do drugs, or is this it for me?"

She looked down at her burger and played with the wrapper. "My parents wouldn't like it if they knew, and Clay would be furious."

"That's not what I asked. I want to know what you think about it."

She looked solemn. "I think I don't like the idea of you doing drugs at all, but I also think there's more to you than that. It wouldn't be fair for me *not* to be your friend because I didn't like something about you. So, yeah, I'd go out with you again."

Relief overwhelmed me and also made me nervous in the same heartbeat. She was attracted to me, but that could be so incredibly bad. I wished for one moment I was free to sweep her off her feet.

"My turn for a question now." She smiled. "Are you the womanizer people say you are?"

I grinned widely. "Maybe, once upon a time—a long time ago—but not recently. I really haven't had the time for girls in my life lately. That's the honest truth."

She scrunched up her nose. "Then why are you here with me?"

"I can't answer that. You already used your

question, so it's my turn now," I teased her and she laughed, breaking off a piece of her burger and throwing it at me.

"You're not seriously trying to start a food fight, are you?" I couldn't believe how she kept catching me by surprise.

"I never start something I can't finish. Now answer my question."

"No. I need to ask mine first."

"You just did. You asked me about starting a food fight." She laughed hard and threw another piece.

"That doesn't count!" I lunged, trying to grab her burger.

"Yes, it does!" She yanked it out of my reach, holding it high over her head.

I flopped back onto the blanket. "Fine, you win. Ask me something."

"I want you to answer my original question. If you don't have time for girls, why are you here with me?"

I groaned, running a hand over my forehead. "Because I'm stupid and a glutton for punishment apparently, and I mean that in the nicest way possible."

She looked at me skeptically, as if she didn't understand.

"There's just something about you that I like. I'm suffering from 'moth to flame' syndrome, I guess. Russ teases me about it. He calls you my eye candy." I paused, stumbling for what I should say. "There's something I like about you," I repeated lamely as I pushed forward. "You're beautiful, and you're real. I love that I can talk to you and get straight answers like this. You don't play games." I sighed in frustration. "Sorry, I'm rambling."

She shook her head and smiled. "You're very nice."

"Okay. I have one more serious question, and then we can move on to lighter stuff."

"All right." She looked like she was preparing herself.

"It has to do with what you told me about your experience. Why did Jordan come to you for help at the dance? Was there something going on between you two? Were you dating or something? Sorry, I'm just trying to get a better picture."

If she noticed I'd just listed three questions she didn't say anything. "I think I was just the unlucky person he happened to be by. I don't think he was asking me for help in particular though, just saying he needed help. And I do believe it was self-inflicted. He'd been known to party before, much in the same context you've shared with me. That's why I'm worried about what you told me. He partied like you."

"I get it," I answered with a nod.

"But you won't change."

"I can't promise that, no. I wish I could, but I don't want to disappoint you."

Silence hung in the air between us, and I wished I could tell her the whole truth.

That wasn't possible, though. I couldn't trust anyone.

CHAPTER NINE
Cami-

Hunter annihilated me at Frisbee. It didn't matter how badly I threw it—trying to make him miss it—he always seemed able to catch it somehow. It was quite impressive, actually.

"Are you like some kind of super secret athlete?" I asked, bending over, my hands on my knees as I gasped for breath.

"Hardly." He laughed.

"Seriously, you've had to play sports at some time."

"I used to play varsity football and basketball," he confessed.

"I believe you. You're amazing." I went to the blanket and collapsed. "You said you used to. Does that mean you don't do any sports now?"

"I weight lift still, but not so much of the other stuff. It just isn't my thing anymore." He dropped down next to me.

"Well, I've already figured out you weight lift."

He chuckled. "You did? How? Are you spying on my class schedule?"

"No, I'm paying attention to how your t-shirts fit." I laughed, hoping I wasn't crossing any weird lines.

"Oh! Nice." He grinned, looking very pleased. "Glad I could give you something to look at." He gently tossed the Frisbee in between his hands.

I tried to snag it, but he was too quick, snapping it out of my reach with a chuckle. "You thought you were being sneaky. I can see how you are."

"Whatever," I replied, shoving his arm slightly. "You're just trying to rub in all your physical prowess."

He laughed loud, turning to look at me. "I like you, Goody. I think you like me too. Come on, admit it."

"Never." I smiled.

"It's not that difficult, really—all you have to say is, Hunter, I like you. Now you try it."

"Nope. Not gonna say it."

"I bet I could make you say it." He quirked his eyebrow, and I saw it as a clear challenge.

"You could try," I countered.

"What do I get when I win?" he asked grinning.

"It doesn't matter. You won't win."

"I should warn you—I don't often lose."

"Me either." I laughed. "Give it up."

He rolled over, tossing the Frisbee aside. He moved as quickly as lightning, grabbing me and tickling.

"No!" I screeched, clawing at the blanket as I tried to scoot from his reach. "Stop, that's not playing fair at all." I gasped for breath at his assault.

"Say it," he ordered.

"Noooo . . . "

He was killing me—I was so incredibly ticklish. He rapidly managed to flip me over, and I flailed, trying to push him away by placing my hands against his rock hard chest. Grabbing me by the wrists he stilled, holding them down against the ground.

He smiled widely, barely winded, knowing he had me effectively imprisoned. "Say the words and I'll let you up."

I shook my head as I huffed, refusing to give in as I lay underneath his muscular frame.

His look changed into something different—something smoldering, and I all of a sudden wondered if he was going to kiss me. His head dipped closer, until his full lips were a mere fraction from mine, and I could feel his breath against my skin. Goose bumps flared over me as he caressed my face with his gaze, and I stopped squirming in anticipation. I wanted him to kiss me.

"Tell me you like me," he whispered. He was so close I could almost imagine the feel of his lips as they moved, but not quite.

I pursed mine together, trying to stop my mischievous smile. "No," I replied.

He shook his head. "That's not an acceptable answer."

"Well, it's the one you're getting." I laughed and he did as well, releasing me and flopping onto his back. The spell was broken.

I placed my hand on my stomach, trying to calm the butterflies that were beating in there more like a bunch of bats gone wild.

"This is not over by any means. I will get you to say it."

"It's on."

He stared at me. "You think I'm kidding, don't you?"

"Not at all. I just think I happen to be a really good person at resisting peer pressure."

He laughed again. "We'll see about that." He propped up on his elbow. "So what else do you want to do today? I'm having too much fun to take you home yet—unless you're sick of me. I don't want to keep you prisoner."

"I'm having a great time, actually. Thank you."

"You're having a great time because you like me, don't you?"

I was silent, and he chuckled again, shaking his head. He climbed to his feet and held his hand out. "What shall we do?"

"I have a place I want to show you if you don't mind driving out of town a little ways."

"Just tell me where to go. I don't mind at all."

"Are you taking me into the woods somewhere to execute me?" he joked as I directed him where to turn.

"No, but on second thought, it might not

have been the best idea to bring your nice car here. I didn't remember the roads being so bumpy."

"That's okay. I'm not in any kind of rush." He cast a glance at me and winked. "I don't mind going slow."

"You're an incredible tease," I replied, unable to help my smile. I was not unaffected by his flirting. He knew exactly what he was doing.

"True . . . , but you *like* it. Don't you?"

I couldn't help the giggle that bubbled up from within me uncontrollably. He was so much fun.

"I'm not going to say." I bit my lip as I smiled, and he shook his head. "You may want to slow down or you will drive your car into the river right around this bend."

He stepped on the brake, and we came to a stop before a sandy stretch of dirt that led down to the edge of the water. It was only about knee deep and around twenty feet wide but had a decent amount of swiftness to it.

"That's what I wanted you to see." I pointed to the far cliff face. The afternoon sun was angled just right, highlighting the ancient Indian ruin, which had been built into a cave in the side.

"This is incredible!" Hunter exclaimed, getting out so he could take a better look.

I followed suit, and we met in the middle, leaning back against the hood.

"There's a visitor center and a hiking trail you can take up into them. It's down the main highway a bit. The last part of the trail is pretty rough, though. I like coming here to sit by the river and enjoy the view instead. It's so peaceful."

Hunter cast a grin in my direction before turning back to the amazing sight. "We should come and hike into it someday. Can you imagine what it must've been like to live in a place like that?"

I shook my head. "Well, I wouldn't have wanted to be the kid constantly being sent after water, that's for sure. I'm thinking they must've been pretty strong to keep on making that climb over and over again."

"I'm sure you're right. I can't fathom the kind of work it would take to make a place like that run properly. I wonder if defense was really that important to survival. Just imagine carrying all that rock up in there to build it. That's some serious dedication." He surprised me when he wrapped his arm around my shoulders, giving me a friendly squeeze. "Thanks for bringing me here. This is awesome."

I felt the heat creeping into my cheeks. I was happy he was pleased with it. It was one of my favorite places to come sit and unwind. "I'm glad you like it. I didn't know if you would. You seemed kind of horrified when I told you about things there are to do."

He chuckled keeping his arm around me loosely. "I guess it's more enjoyable when the person you're with is a great part of the view too."

I snorted and shoved him away. I started walking backward toward the water, keeping him in my sight. "Now you're just laying it on thick."

"And you like it. I can tell by that pretty blush spreading so nicely over your skin. I think it's gonna paint you all the way down to those tiny, cute ankles of yours." His gaze traveled over my entire length and back up. "You really should just admit it."

He was going to do some serious damage to my heart I was afraid. I'd never felt so easily comfortable with someone in my life, not even Clay. There was definitely something about Hunter Wilder that drew me. He made my heart race every time he looked at me. It was exhilarating and scary at the same time.

"I can't admit it. You keep reminding me you don't have room for girls in your life right now."

The smile slid from his face, and he grew serious, his eyes watching me like a hawk from where he leaned. He pushed away and stalked in my direction, catching me by the arms and pulling me against him. My hands slid up his chest of their own accord, and my breath caught in my throat as I tipped my head to look at him towering over me.

"A girl like you tempts me to change my mind."

He literally took my breath away. I wanted him to kiss me, but he held me rigidly, not moving any closer. I wanted to know what his lips would feel like against mine. He made all other guys I'd known pale in comparison. Deciding to take the initiative, I slid my arms farther up, wrapping them around his neck and pulling him down closer.

He resisted at first, but then released a sigh and moved toward me.

I held my breath, waiting for his mouth to touch mine.

The sound of laughter broke us apart and we turned, seeing a man and a woman with a couple of small children walking down the side of the stream.

"Good afternoon!" the woman called to us in friendly fashion. "Beautiful view, isn't it?"

Hunter looked at me. "It sure is." He pulled me into the circle of his arms, and I thought I might swoon on the spot it was so romantic. "Enjoying a day of hiking?"

"Yeah, we went up into the ruins earlier. It's a tough little hike, especially with kids. We promised them they could play in the water when we came back down," the man spoke.

"Sounds like fun. I hope you enjoy it. We're just about to do the same thing," I replied, waving at them as they continued on their way.

"We are?" Hunter asked grinning softly. "Funny, but I thought things were headed in an entirely different direction."

"That's what you get for thinking, I guess." I pushed away and left him, enjoying the sound of his laughter following after me. I sat down in the sand and removed my shoes, leaving them there when I got up and moved toward the water.

I wisely dipped a toe in first and gasped. "Oh my gosh! That is so incredibly cold!" I grimaced and waded in farther.

"Then why are you going in deeper?" Hunter chuckled.

"Because it's fun! Come on! Take your shoes off and join me." I carefully stepped on the slippery rocks, trying to feel each one as I went further in until the water reached my knees and the current splashed up around them. I turned and looked over my shoulder to see if he was coming, but the motion caused me to lose my footing. I wobbled, furiously trying to maintain my balance before splashing down hard.

The cold liquid rushed over me, making me gasp, and my mouth filled with water as the current picked up my body and bumped me roughly against several of the stones on the bottom. I tried putting my hands down so I could push my head out of the water, but I couldn't get enough force underneath me. I flailed, clawing at the slippery rocks as I tried to gain a hold, panicking as my body screamed for air.

Resisting the urge to suck in a breath, I floundered. My vision started going black at the edges and I had the horrifying thought that I was going to drown in two feet of water. My limbs felt heavy, like I couldn't move them properly. I didn't think I could fight it much longer. I opened my mouth, trying to scream, but more water rushed inside.

Strong arms grasped me, picking me up and I coughed, spraying liquid everywhere before dragging a giant breath of air into my lungs. Hunter scooped me up into his arms, and I laid my head against his chest as I clung to him, shaking with both cold and shock.

"Just keep breathing, Cami," he ordered.

I couldn't reply, shivering as he carried me out of the water and up the sand toward his car. He set me down, leaning me against it, pinning my traumatized body there with his hips. He reached down and pealed my shirt off, revealing my lacy bra beneath. He tossed the top on the hood and reached for the button on my shorts.

"What are you doing?" My voice was trembling as I wrapped my arms around myself.

"Trying to keep you from getting hypothermia in this breeze. Can you stand on your own?"

I nodded and he stepped away, pushing my shorts down and instructing me to lift each leg. They joined my shirt on the hood. He reached into his pocket for his keys and popped the trunk, pulling out the thick blanket we'd used for our picnic earlier, wrapping me up in it tightly before hugging me.

"Girl, I swear you just took ten years off my life. Are you okay?" He released a giant sigh as he leaned his head on top of mine, rubbing my back through the blanket.

I started laughing, and then crying. "I couldn't get up. It was so dumb and then I couldn't breathe. I felt like I was just flopping around like a rag doll." I buried my head against his chest. "It was so stupid. The water is so shallow."

"That current was much stronger under the surface than it looked. It felt like it took me a year to reach you."

My knees wobbled, and he grabbed me tighter, holding me up.

"Come on, let's get you seated." He opened the passenger door and lifted my burrito-wrapped body into the car, settling me into the seat before crouching down beside me. "Cami, are you sure you're all right?"

I nodded. "I'll be fine. I'm more embarrassed than anything."

"Don't be embarrassed. Accidents happen. How many fingers am I holding up?"

His question diffused my hysteria, and I started laughing again. "I can still see, Hunter."

"How many?" he demanded.

"Three," I answered dutifully.

"What's your full name?"

I rolled my eyes. "Camilla Noelle Wimberley."

"Who's the president of the United States?"

"Abraham Lincoln," I replied in a snarky tone. "Quit asking me dumb questions."

He sighed but grinned. "I'm just trying to make sure you're okay. You got bumped around pretty good. If you hit your head I should probably take you to the emergency room."

"I don't think I hit my head, just every part of the rest of my body." I slumped back against the seat.

"Let's get you home." He tucked the bottom of the blanket into the car and shut the door.

I watched him as he retrieved my shoes, then took my clothes off the hood and wrung the water out of them before tossing them in the trunk and closing it.

"Somehow I don't think bringing you home mostly naked is going to score me many points with your parents," he said as he slid into the driver's seat.

"Hunter, you just saved me from drowning. I'm thinking they'll probably be pretty grateful." That was when I noticed how wet he was also.

He sighed heavily. "Guess we'll find out." He turned the heater on and slowly made his way over the bumps and ruts in the road. As soon as we reached the highway he gassed the engine and raced the last the forty miles back into Copper City.

HUNTER♥

CHAPTER TEN
Hunter-

What to do? I sat sprawled on the plush black leather sofa in my condo, flipping my phone around in my hand while I tried to decide whether or not I should text Cami and see how she was doing.

Her dad was not at all happy with the nearly naked state I'd returned her in. Her mom was all worry and concern, thanking me profusely for helping her daughter before shuttling her off into the other room. I hadn't waited around long enough to get my blanket back, and it was the actual comforter for my bed.

It had been several hours now. The words, How R U? were typed onto my screen, I hadn't pressed send yet. There were a million things running through my head—things I was having extreme difficulty sorting out.

If I sent this text, it would give the message I was still thinking about her, and I really did care. It made me out as being committed enough to keep an interest in her, which I honestly was, but shouldn't be.

There was a jingle of keys at the door and it swung open. "Hey, Uncle Chris," I said to the tall, thin man as he walked inside carrying his briefcase.

He shook his head. "Would you cool it with the whole uncle thing?" he asked in exasperation. "It's not funny anymore."

I chuckled. "Maybe not for you. I find it quite funny."

"Well, I'm glad I can amuse you, even though I'm way too young for you to call uncle. How are you doing? You look like you could use a little cheering up. You're worried about something, I can tell. What's eating you?"

I sighed, and sat up. He knew me too well. "Can I confess something? I'm really struggling here, and I need a second opinion."

"Sure," he said, tossing the briefcase on the coffee table between us. "What's up?"

I decided to plunge in. "I've met this girl . . ." I held my breath, waiting for the explosion.

"What? You're kidding me. Please tell me you're kidding." He looked astounded.

"I wish I could, but I can't. I'm sorry. I noticed her right from the beginning. I've been trying to fight my attraction for her, but it isn't working so well. Now I find myself jumping from the kettle into the fire. We've had the opportunity to get to know each other a little more, and not only do I like her, she seems to really like me."

Chris groaned and loosened his tie. "This is wrong in so many ways."

I nodded. "I know it is. I'm totally torn. If I walk away from her now, she's going to wonder what happened. She knows there was a real connection there. If I don't walk away from her . . . well, you can see where I'm going with this."

"Hunter," he warned. "This isn't good." He stroked a hand over his face. "What's her name?"

"Cami Wimberley."

Chris rubbed his temples. "How old is she?"

"Seventeen."

He gave me an incredulous look. "She's a freakin' minor, Hunter, and you're not. You can't be involved with someone like that. She's too young, and it's too dangerous."

"I know!" I growled, jumping up and pacing to the window.

"How close are we talking here? Boyfriend/girlfriend status? Have you kissed her?"

"No, I haven't, but I would've today if we hadn't been interrupted. The sad thing is I want to." I leaned against the window and folded my arms. "Being with her is the most natural thing in the world. I swear it's like she's perfect. It doesn't matter that she's all wrong for me. It all melts away when I'm with her. There's just this amazing connection." I pinched the bridge of my nose. "What should I do?"

Chris shook his head. "I don't know, but we

need to maintain a low profile here. We can't afford to draw any undue attention to ourselves right now."

"Well then, I need some advice. I like this girl, and I don't think I can stay away. I want to be with her."

He shook his head. "You're a legal adult. If you cross any lines with her and someone found out, it could land you in jail. We can't have that."

"She'll be eighteen next month. I checked."

"Why'd you ask her out? You know we're trying to lay low."

"She was in a bit of a pickle with another guy who likes her. I decided to help her—thinking it would be just a onetime deal. Things progressed from there."

Chris snorted. "Oh, so now you're saying you're in some sort of a love triangle? You're not supposed to star in your own romance novel! What the heck are you doing when I'm gone?"

I smiled wryly. "Apparently making a big giant mess of things. I'm sorry. I didn't mean for any of this to happen. Do you have any advice?"

"Probably nothing you want to hear. I guess try to be careful and not get involved with kissing her. That's when the lines will get sticky for you and could cause problems."

I nodded. "Okay, so look, don't touch. I got it."

"Be careful. This sounds like it could go south really fast."

"I'm aware. I hate having her in the middle

of this. I don't want her caught in the crossfire if something actually does go down."

He stared at me for a minute. "We're playing a dangerous game here. You need to be careful. How would she handle things if you just up and disappeared? It could happen, you know."

"She'd be terrified. I imagine she'd think I overdosed on something. She's very concerned about my current drug use. She's had a bad experience with that." I ran a hand through my hair.

"So, here's my question. If you've been growing closer since you've been here—why the extreme concern all of a sudden? Surely you've thought of all this before."

I sat down on the couch again. "We went out together today, and she had a near death experience this afternoon."

"What?" Chris sat up straighter.

"It's not as bad as it sounds, but she fell into a river—more like a fast-moving creek really. She got caught in the undercurrent and couldn't get up. I thought she was going to drown before I got there. It was the most terrifying few seconds of my life."

"That sounds horrible. Is she okay?" He seemed genuinely concerned.

"Yeah. She was mostly cold, wet, and exhausted. I wrapped her up in a blanket I had from our picnic and took her home."

"I'm glad you were with her."

"Me too, but something happened out there. Seeing her like that really solidified what I'm feeling. This isn't about trying to help her, like

I've been deluding myself. I really want to pursue . . . whatever this is."

Chris watched me for several moments before he spoke. "I can see this is kind of like walking a tight rope for you. You're going to have to be aware and try balancing things properly. Guess we're finally going to see what you're really made of, aren't we? Be careful. You could end up blowing everything."

He got up and walked into the kitchen.

"That's what I'm afraid of," I said under my breath.

CHAPTER ELEVEN
Hunter-

How R U? U awake? I retyped, pushed send and waited, lounging on my bed while I listened to some music, trying to calm my nervous energy. I couldn't stand not knowing any longer.

My phone buzzed, and I opened the text immediately. Hey. I'm good, thx. I kinda crashed after U brought me home. Sorry.

I breathed a sigh of relief as I read her message and then dialed her number.

"Hello?"

It was good to hear her voice. "I've been worried."

"Don't be. I'm fine, just wiped out. You know you're my hero now, right?"

I snorted. "Hardly, I was scared to death." That was an understatement of epic proportions. I was pretty sure my heart had stopped beating from the moment she slipped under to the second she was finally able to gasp for a breath.

"You didn't show it. You just swooped in and saved the day. You work well under pressure."

"I'm not so sure about that, but I was happy to help." I paused before continuing. "I guess you should go ahead and tell me how your dad is going to ban me from ever seeing you again."

"Actually, he's coming around. After I explained everything he even seemed a little impressed with your quick actions. I think it was my lack of clothes that bugged him the most . . . and knowing you'd seen me that way."

"Well, I couldn't very well leave you standing there dripping wet and freezing."

She laughed. "It's okay, Hunter, really. He gets it. He was nervous about you to begin with. I've never really dated guys like you before."

"Guys like me? Why does that sound like a bad thing?"

"I don't mean it badly at all. It was a compliment. Let's just say the guys I dated in the past were . . . geekier guys, for lack of better terminology. You're definitely *not* one of those, but I think geeky is what he's comfortable with."

"What are you comfortable with?" I wanted to know.

There was silence on the other end for several seconds. "I'm pretty comfortable with you, if that's what you're asking. I didn't think I would be, but I am. It's strange really."

"I'm glad you feel that way. I don't want you to be uneasy around me."

There was a moment of silence. "Would it be bad if I said I miss you?" she asked, and my pulse rate picked up. "I'm sorry I fell. I wanted to watch the sunset out there with you today. My carelessness cut our date short."

"Don't worry about it. There will be other dates." I groaned internally. I was determined to dig myself into a deeper hole it seemed.

"There will be?"

"If that's what you'd like." After today I was pretty much willing to give her whatever she wanted. I just needed her to be safe.

"I'd like that a lot." She gave a short laugh. "Did you know I dreamed about you while I was sleeping? I can smell your aftershave or something on your blanket. Sorry I didn't give it to you before you left. I'll wash and return it."

The image of her body wrapped up tightly in my bedding with her gorgeous red hair splayed about her pleased me to no end. *Seventeen, dude,* I reminded myself. *Rein it in.* "Keep it," I said. "I want you to have it."

"No, I don't want to steal your blanket," she protested.

"You aren't. I just gave it to you. Now you can tell me how much you like me." I grinned.

"Nice try." She laughed, and the sound warmed my heart.

"I will win this," I promised her.

"I don't think so."

"Go back to sleep. You can tell me how much you like me tomorrow at school, and you can fill me in on this dream you had."

She laughed even harder. "Good luck with that, playboy."

"I don't need luck, Goody. It's gonna

happen. Now go back to sleep."

"Yes, sir!" she said in military fashion.

I smiled, wishing I could brush my hand over her beautiful face. "Goodnight, Cami."

"Goodnight, Hunter. Thanks for being there."

The call clicked off, and I missed her already. I sat there for several moments staring at the white ceiling. This was going to be rough. I knew things weren't in a good place right now, and part of me wanted to run far and fast in the other direction. Unfortunately, the part that didn't want to seemed the most in control. I'd been excited for the move here at first, eager to get into the local scene and live the party life. It was easy for me—natural.

I thought back to my stuck-up jock years before this—playing sports, chasing and catching more than my fair share of girls, attending some pretty wild parties. I'd loved being part of all that before things really changed for me, sending my life in a completely different direction.

I chuckled wryly to myself. I was so stupid. This had seemed like it would be an easy playtime for me—lay low, party, chill. I hadn't really planned on knowing people well enough to actually like them, or to have them like me either. I was starting to feel like I was part of them. Now I was falling hard for this girl, and it didn't seem like anything I told my brain made it want to change. If Cami had been a girl in my old high school, I would've grabbed onto her with both hands and never let go. She was different—the kind of girl a guy would want to keep all to himself.

Ugh, I should quit sitting here mooning like a lovesick kid. This was getting ridiculous. I barely knew her.

I rubbed my temples and glanced over to the stack of papers sitting beside my bed. I still needed to go through them and do my homework for school as well. Maybe I could get Chris to do my assignments. I snorted, that request probably wouldn't go over too well. I hated doing all this class work.

I groaned as I pulled myself out of bed and went to my desk chair. It was going to be a long night.

"So I want you to check out your cameras and carry them with you all week. Take pictures of anything in and around the school that catches your eye. Concentrate on building the composition of your images. I want a triangular aspect to your shots, something with three points of interest, which allows the eye to circle through the picture with ease as we discussed in class today."

I was stoked as I listened to Mr. Adams give this assignment. I liked taking pictures and seeing what the camera caught when people weren't looking. Of course, the biggest reason I was excited was because I couldn't wait to get shots of Cami.

"No digital cameras either," Mr. Adams continued. "I want you in the dark room developing this film."

I glanced at Cami who was alphabetically

seated in the desk next to me. "You ready to pose for some pictures, Goody?"

"Pose?" she asked, giving me a confused smile.

"You heard him. We're supposed to take pictures of things around the school that catch our eye. You're what catches mine." I glanced over her and gave my tried and true sexy grin of appreciation.

She blushed right on cue. *Heck yeah*, I thought. *I've still got it.*

"I don't think that's what he meant, Hunter." She laughed sweetly as she closed her notebook.

I shrugged. "I don't care. I don't have any pictures of you, and I want some. You like me enough to do this, right?"

She shook her head in amazement, a wide grin plastered across her face. "You really aren't going to give this up, are you?"

"Nope. Not until I hear you say you like me. It's not that difficult, Cami. Even grade school kids can do it. In fact . . . ," I reached into my binder and pulled out a pad of sticky notes I used to keep track of assignments and started writing on it.

"What're you doing?" she asked, leaning to look.

"No peeking," I teased, shielding it with my other hand while I continued. When I was finished I peeled off the top paper and stuck it on the front of her notebook. "Do you like me? Check a box, yes or no. I can't make it any simpler."

Cami busted up laughing, causing several others in the class to glance at us, but I didn't care. She was gorgeous, mesmerizing even, and I could've stared at her smile all day long.

She shook her head as she stood and walked past me. "Come on, let's go get our cameras."

"You forgot to check your little box thingy on the paper," I said pointing, and she paused, looking over her shoulder. "It's easy. You just take your pen and put in a check. It's a line really, no biggie. No one sweats over a line." I pulled another paper off and demonstrated how to make a check. "See just like that."

She was still grinning as she turned and continued to the front of the room.

"Do you need me to show you again?" I called after her. I couldn't help chuckling under my breath. She was so fun to tease.

I got up and followed after her to where the cameras were lined up on the shelf. They were all identical, so I didn't spend any time choosing, instead just grabbing one and then getting in line behind her to put the serial number and my name on the sign-out sheet.

Her hair was full of its usual natural bounce and curl again today, and I touched it lightly. She looked at me questioningly. I smiled softly. "Just admiring the view. How're you feeling? Not catching a cold or anything are you?"

She shook her head slightly. "I'm feeling pretty okay, actually."

"That's good. I was worried you might get sick afterward."

We both took turns signing the paper before

leaving the classroom together.

"You want to walk around and take pictures with me?" I asked, looking for any excuse to spend more time with her.

"Sure, I enjoy the entertainment your company provides." She bit her lip in an attempt to hide her grin.

"Ah, so I'm just the comic relief, then. I get it." I bumped her with my arm and she laughed.

"Where do you want to wander first?"

"Let's go over by the football field," I suggested. "I bet we could find some good shots over by the field house and stuff. They have the track equipment set up out there for practice."

"Did you ever do track?" she asked as we headed in that direction.

I shook my head. "No, just football and basketball. I did try baseball once with one of my buddies. It was all right, but not really my thing."

"I bet you were really good at basketball. You're so tall. How tall are you?"

"Six foot three, and I was one of the shorter ones on the team."

"Did you play a lot?"

"Yeah, I was a starter—top scorer, actually."

"And were you a starter in football?"

"Yep. I played both ways. Offensive tackle, defensive end."

"Why'd you quit playing?"

I shrugged and gave a little sigh. I wanted to tell her I hadn't quit, that I'd been a first team all star every single year before things changed. I wanted to tell her why things were different now. "Got in with the wrong crowd, after my parents died, I guess." I hated lying to her. Telling her these things was going to kill my conscience.

"I'm sorry about your parents. How'd they die?"

"Car accident into a river," I said casually, repeating the history, which had been drilled into my head.

Her face went white. "Oh my gosh! Yesterday . . . that must've been horrible for you."

My mind scrambled for a second, trying to keep up. "What? Oh! You falling in the water? No, it's okay."

She looked away. "It must've brought so many uncomfortable memories to the surface. I'm so sorry." She seemed distraught.

I slipped the camera strap around my neck and pulled her into an alcove behind the building.

"Listen, Cami," I said as I squeezed both of her shoulders. "Don't feel bad. I honestly never even thought of my parents once yesterday. Any concern I felt was strictly in regards to you and your wellbeing. I won't lie, it was a scary thing to see, but only because I care about you." I pulled her closer, and she slid her arms easily around my waist, laying her head against my chest.

I wrapped mine around her tightly and allowed one hand to drift up the back of her neck, sinking my fingers into her soft curls.

She lifted her face. "I'm glad you were

there."

Our eyes locked, and I felt something strong flare between us. I knew she felt it too because the desire was written in her eyes.

I wanted to kiss her so badly my mouth watered in anticipation. My gaze traveled down to her glossy lips, and the tip of her tongue darted out, licking them slightly. Her breathing increased, and I knew then she wanted me as badly as I wanted her.

It took every ounce of will power I had to lift my chin and place it on the top of her head. I briefly hugged her tighter for one moment longer before I released her.

"Come on. We better go take pictures before someone stumbles on us hiding back here." I walked away without waiting to see if she was following.

CAMI

CHAPTER TWELVE
Cami-

I couldn't help my disappointment as I followed after Hunter. I wasn't going to lie to myself. He was hot, and I desperately wanted him to kiss me with those amazing looking lips of his. For some reason though, he still seemed reluctant, but I couldn't fathom why. If you liked someone you did what you had to do to be with him or her. Right? I wasn't any big expert on relationships, but it seemed easy enough.

I sighed with frustration, and the sound came out a little louder than I intended, causing Hunter to pause and look at me. He waited until I was beside him, and he loosely draped his arm around my shoulders, giving me a gentle squeeze.

He didn't say anything as we continued toward the field, but his actions spoke of attraction. He clearly didn't care who saw him with me, and I wondered if there was a way I could up my game, maybe tempt him into action a little faster.

That scared me, though. Given the tiny bit of information I knew about his past, I imagined he was probably a fire that would light fast—so quick it would consume me whole. Maybe I should be content to stand back and let him work through whatever issues he had. Let nature take its course, so to speak.

Hunter dropped his arm and faced the school, taking a picture of the wide sweeping grounds and buildings, which sprawled behind us. He adjusted his location and took some more of the athletic fields and structures. I wasn't sure what he found so fascinating about the place, but I lifted my camera and started looking through the view finder for things I found interesting, snapping the occasional picture of trees and plant life before casually turning and firing off several of him standing with his camera up to his eye.

He lowered it. "Did you just take a bunch of pictures of me?" he asked, a sly grin spreading across his face as if he were extremely pleased.

"I don't think so . . . ," I replied innocently. " . . . unless I caught you by accident when I was focusing on those buildings over there." I pointed past him, and he looked at the jumble of plain, brick walls across the parking lot.

"Uh huh. Sure." He lifted his camera and pointed it directly at me, clicking several times in succession.

I smiled and he continued to shoot away. "What're you doing?"

"I'm taking your picture." He paused. "Did you hear that? *Your* picture—not the ugly buildings behind you. I just want to show you how it's done."

My goodness he could make me feel so giddy. I couldn't stop smiling as I walked onto the track, shrinking down to take some images of the hurdles lined up on it.

I heard him beside me and looked over as he continued clicking.

I shook my head. "Mr. Adams is going to be mad that you used up all your film on me."

"So, I'll buy him more film." He shrugged it off as if it were no concern. "I like taking pictures of you."

"Well, I hope they don't turn out too scary."

"Not possible," he said assuredly before lowering the camera. We started walking around the track together, making our way to where the giant pole vaulting pad was set up. "You should grab the pole and pretend like you're gonna go for it, and I'll take a shot."

I laughed, running over and jumping on the giant foam mattress, flopping back against it. "This is about as close as you're gonna get! I have no desire to attempt a pole vault."

He looked at me with a smoky stare I could feel all the way to my toes. "This works too." He lifted his camera and took one single shot. "Do you have any idea how beautiful you are with your hair spread out around you like that?"

I shook my head very slowly. "Nope. Guess you'll have to show me."

He swallowed thickly, removing his camera

from around his neck and setting it carefully on the ground. "That could be dangerous."

"I thought you liked danger. Wasn't it you who accused me of not having a real life just a few days ago—making fun of the parties I attend and the friends I have?"

"That was wrong. I shouldn't have said those things." His eyes never left me, and I noticed he was clenching and unclenching his fists as he stood watching. He looked hungry, but hungry more like a predator hiding in the grass, waiting for the perfect time to pounce on his victim. It both thrilled and scared me.

I was no queen of seduction, but suddenly wished I was—wished I knew how to make him close the distance between us. "Hunter," I whispered, not knowing what else to say.

That was the magic word.

He was on the pad in an instant, stretched beside me, leaning over as he slid his hand up my arm and into my hair. "You're so gorgeous." I felt his hand trembling, and he lowered his lips toward my mouth, but at the last second he quickly lifted them to brush against my forehead instead.

I was so confused and frustrated. No one had ever looked at me the way he did—no one had ever made my insides flip the way he could. Yet, he seemed so reluctant to seal the deal. I was tired of beating around the bush.

"Kiss me, Hunter," I demanded, not caring if it was the right thing to say anymore. I slid my hands up his muscle-lined arms, linking them around his neck.

He groaned, releasing a big sigh. "I want to, Goody. You have no idea how much I want to."

His words made my heart sing.

"I can't kiss you, though."

And my heart crashed.

"Why not? What would be so terrible about kissing me?"

He laughed wryly. "Nothing I can think of."

"Then for heaven's sake, what's stopping you?" I felt like a little girl stomping her foot because she wasn't getting what she wanted.

He moved closer, and I could feel his breath on mine as he stared at my lips. I knew the exact moment he decided, and I lifted my mouth to meet his.

"Well, isn't this cozy?" Clay's voice interrupted, and I fell back onto the mat with an exasperated groan as Hunter turned toward him, releasing me as he sat up.

I'd never wanted to punch Clay so badly.

"Can we help you with something, Bradley?" Hunter asked as he looked him over.

I sat up, seeing Clay standing there in another set of designer clothes. His body was tense, face flushed, and his mouth was set in an angry grimace.

"What are you doing out here with him, Cami?" he demanded. "We discussed this."

"Excuse me?" Hunter asked, and I could see things were quickly going from bad to worse.

"I'm here because I want to be. Why are you here, Clay?" I scooted over, sitting at the end of the mattress.

"Why? Because someone needs to protect

you, and it's obviously not going to be him. You are aware half the school can see the two of you canoodling here together, aren't you?" He waved his hand in the direction of the heavily windowed buildings before turning back to Hunter. "You moved in for the kill pretty fast. I told her you were only after one thing."

I thought my eyes were going to bug out of my head, I was so incredible angry.

Hunter folded his arms casually and studied Clay. "You have no idea what you're talking about," he said rather calmly. "But this is my advice—walk away before you make things any worse."

Clay was livid, his face almost purple with rage. "And leave you to pick up where you left off? I don't think so."

"Actually, I was referring to the damage you're doing to your friendship with her right now." He looked at me. "Cami, was I forcing you to do anything?"

I blushed and shook my head. "No. It was probably more the other way around—me forcing you to do something you didn't want."

Hunter placed his hand on my arm. "You weren't forcing me. I'm going to leave you here so you can discuss things with your friend. Are you okay with that? I'll stay if you need me."

I blew out an exasperated sigh. I didn't want him to go, but I knew Clay and I needed to have this out. "I'll be fine."

Hunter stood and grabbed his camera off the ground, glancing between Clay and me. "Text me later, okay?"

I nodded, watching him as he walked away. I waited until he was out of earshot before I spoke up.

"You have the worst timing ever. What possessed you to come barging out here like that?"

He joined me on the mat, hunching over dejectedly. "I didn't like what I was seeing. I was running something to another teacher, and I saw you two walking together, emerging from a hidden corner, him wrapping his arms around you, taking pictures. I knew he was after you. Do you see it now?"

"What you saw, Clay, was me trying to coerce him, not the other way around. I wanted him to kiss me."

"Why?"

I gave a choked laugh. "Because I like him. I thought that was obvious."

"He's a player, Cami."

"No, he's not. You're the one who's placing that label on him."

"The whole school says the same thing." He looked at me incredulously.

"And what does the whole school say about you? Does that mean it's true?"

His face fell as he considered my words.

"Do you know why I've been friends with you all these years?" I asked.

He shook his head.

"Because I like *you*. I don't care what anyone else thinks about you, I think you're fabulous. I don't care what anyone else thinks about *me*, either."

"You care what he thinks about you," he replied, loosely gesturing to where we could still see Hunter's retreating figure walking across campus.

"I do, but only because I like him. I can tell you right now that yes, he has his hang ups. I know he's not perfect, but I like him, and I don't care what anyone else says about him. I'm going to form my own opinions."

He stood up and faced me. "I don't understand. You claim to like me and know me, then why can't you see what's right in front of you?"

"What do you mean?" I knew where this was heading, and I wished there was some way I could correct the course.

"Have you really been that blind? I'm crazy about you, Cami. I have been for years." He stalked away.

"What about Marcy?" I asked grasping at straws.

He snorted. "You want to know about Marcy? Fine, I'll tell you. She isn't real! Just a figment of my imagination made up with the hopes of making you see me in a new light!"

My head was spinning. "What? That's not true. I've seen the texts she sends you. You were talking to a real person!"

"Yeah, my cousin, Shannon, agreed to play the part to help me out. Nothing like getting a little lovin' from a relative, is there?"

I was going to be sick. "Why would you do that? Why not just tell me how you felt?"

"So I could go through the humiliation I'm

experiencing right now? Gee, I don't know . . . let me think!" He shook his head in frustration. "You claim you know me, but you couldn't even see what was most important to me—you! I've done everything I could think of to make you notice. Just when I thought I was finally getting through, then Hunter comes riding up on his white horse and snatches you up and carries you off into the sunset. I waited too long."

He dropped back down mournfully beside me, sliding his hand up my arm, over my shoulder, until he slipped it around behind my neck. "Please, pick me instead, Cami. Let me be the one who holds you in his arms and stares at you like that. I love you. I have for a long, long time."

I was frozen by his declaration, glancing at my clasped hands as I fumbled with what I should say. I looked up just in time to see his lips before they pressed against mine. He slipped his hands to both sides of my face, holding me there until I pushed him away.

"Please, Cami," he pleaded with tears in his eyes. "I've wanted you for so long."

I looked at him, feeling tears of my own and wishing there was something I could say to make him feel better. "I can't, Clay. You've been my very best friend, but I don't feel that way about you. I'd still like you in my life, but I think maybe it would be best if we spent some time apart from each other for a while. There's a girl out there for you somewhere. It's just not me." I stood, my heart twisting in knots. "Sorry. I'll call you if I want to talk."

I walked away, unable to look back and see the devastation I knew was written on his face.

"I don't want another girl, Cami!" he called after me.

I burst into tears and started running.

CHAPTER THIRTEEN
Hunter-

He kissed her! *Kissed her*! That made me want to rearrange his face. Feelings of possessiveness welled up, causing a great amount of anger to roll through me, though I didn't really have time to analyze.

Cool it, man, the sane, rational voice in my head instructed. I tried tapping into that inner place I went when I needed to calm down. I lifted the camera and zoomed in again, snapping a few more pictures of Clay as he stood and kicked the giant mat when Cami ran away. He reached into his pocket, pulled something out, and paused, looking at it. I couldn't tell what it was, but I took another shot hoping I could catch it.

He was certainly exhibiting signs of repressed anger. It scared me a little, wondering if the cracks were starting to show in his carefully maintained demeanor. I didn't want to jump to any conclusions—things really could be exactly as they appeared—but I thought maybe I should keep a better eye on him. I didn't want him hurting Cami in any way.

I struggled with the idea of rushing to check on her as she came barreling by my hiding spot. I started reaching for her but then changed my mind when I heard her sobs. She was obviously upset, and I didn't think she needed me mixing up her feelings even more. She could probably use a few moments to compose herself.

Watching her, I waited until she was safely deposited in the bathroom just inside the back glass doors of the main building before I made my way over to the exterior entrance to the photo lab. The bell was about to ring, and most of the students were back gathering up their belongings. I took my camera and slipped into the dark room, hoping no one would notice. I made sure there were four bins set up with the different developing chemicals, and I locked the door, activating the red light.

Pulling out my film, I set to work, knowing it would take time to develop and enlarge the images I was interested in. I kept a nervous watch on both the timer and the clock on the wall, worried about being interrupted. I maneuvered my way through the process, carefully doing a strip test to see how long to expose my images.

There was a knock on the door. "Is someone in there?" Mr. Adams voice spoke.

I cringed, glancing up through the red haze toward the clock. I'd been locked in here for almost two hours. "Yeah, it's me, Hunter. I used all my film and wanted to see some of my images. I thought the darkroom was open until five."

I had several photos hanging, and from what I could see so far, there were some good captures. The ones of Cami immediately caught my eye. Even in black and white she was beautiful.

"It is. I had a faculty meeting after class and didn't realize anyone was still in here until I saw the Do Not Enter sign was lit. Just be sure to clean up and close everything when you're done."

"Will do," I replied as I continued to hurry about stringing pictures on the dry line. When I was finished I straightened the room, following the instruction sheet on the wall. I was almost done when there was another knock at the door.

"Just a sec," I called as I quickly pulled the pictures down and placed the ones I'd taken of Cami and Clay upside down in a pile on the worktable. I put a few of Cami, along with some of the track, facing up and unlocked the door so Mr. Adams could come in.

"There you are."

I was shocked to see Cami standing there. She stepped inside hugging her binder, and the door closed behind her.

"What are you doing here?" I asked. The red light made her hair look like it was glowing.

"Well, I was waiting for you. Your car was still in the parking lot."

I looked at her, confused.

"I usually catch a ride with Clay, and . . ." she added, shifting uncomfortably.

She'd needed a ride home and I'd ditched her. I felt horrible.

"Oh, man. I'm so sorry. I didn't realize you'd need a ride or I would've been right there. I didn't have anything pressing after school so I stayed to develop my images."

"I kind of figured that when I saw your books were still on your desk. I sat at the tables outside and did homework while I was waiting." She turned toward the stack of pictures. "How'd they turn out?" She sat her binder down on the counter and reached for them.

I felt my pulse kick into overdrive. I didn't want her to see I'd been spying on her private moment with Clay. It would creep her out.

"Some aren't that grand, but I especially like the ones of you. They're gorgeous—like I knew they would be."

She lifted one and studied it with a small smile before reaching for the next one in the pile. "These are really good, Hunter. You're quite the photographer."

I held still, my heart racing, knowing if she continued far enough she'd see what I'd been doing. I would totally come off as the jealous boyfriend—something I didn't want at all. She made her way through until she reached the images that were facing down.

"Those are the bad ones," I said, moving to stop her. "I'm just going to put them in the shredder."

"Don't do that." She placed her hand over

mine, stilling me. "Let me see them first. All the others were so good."

I was desperate, racking my brain for a way to distract her from continuing. "Cami . . . ," I let my voice trail off, and she glanced up at me expectantly.

"Yes?"

I closed my eyes for a second. "Forgive me," I whispered when I looked at her again. I grabbed her cheeks and pressed my lips to hers.

Sparks exploded at the simple contact between us, and I found myself sliding my hands down to her shoulders so I could pull her closer. I wrapped both of my arms around her back and pressed against her, walking slowly forward until she was pinned against the door. Her fingers move upward, locking around behind my neck. She opened her mouth, allowing me access, and I happily invaded, licking and tasting what she offered. It was heaven.

She made a soft moaning sound in the back of her throat—or maybe it was me—I wasn't sure anymore as her hands made their way up into my hair, digging in as she kept me pulled tightly to her. My palms moved lower, cupping her bottom and lifting so she could wrap her legs around me. She did so as if she'd done it a thousand times before, and I moved to trail kisses across her face and down her neck.

She tossed her head back, arching. "Finally," she breathed out as her hands traveled over me.

Seventeen! the warning voice shouted in my head, and I leaned away so quickly I almost dropped her.

"What is it?" she asked, panting, hanging onto my shoulders.

I can't do this, I thought. "We're moving too fast," I said instead, not wanting to make her feel bad.

She looked hurt anyway, staring into my eyes for several seconds before she released her legs from around my waist, and I helped set her upright again. We both stood there—each watching the other—not knowing what to say. She finally broke the awkward silence surrounding us.

"I'm sorry if I'm doing something that's upsetting you, but I liked kissing you. I don't think it's too fast. Well . . . , I mean . . . that was a pretty hot kiss, so yeah, I can see where you might construe that as moving fast. But still . . . I liked it . . . and if that's how we feel then that's how we feel, right?" She blinked. "I mean unless that's not how you really feel. Is it?"

She was rambling, and I couldn't help myself. I started laughing. "I have no idea what you just said." I couldn't stop looking at her mouth. It was a little swollen, and I wanted to kiss her again and again, over and over until she couldn't breathe properly anymore. My libido had kicked into overdrive, and I wasn't having any problem imagining all the things I'd like to do.

"Do you want to kiss me?" she asked plainly.

"Yes," I replied with an exasperated sigh. "Too much, in fact. I don't want to take advantage of you."

"You just keep kissing me like that, and let me decide how much is too much." Her fingers were against my mouth, tracing my lips. "You have no idea how long I've wanted to kiss these."

"While I'm happy to know you dream of kissing me as much as I do of you, I think we should probably try to keep things a little more cool between us."

She rolled her eyes, clearly balking at the idea. "Why?"

I shrugged. "Just trying to keep things a bit safer. If that was our first kiss where do we go from here?"

"Let's find out." She leaned forward, pulling my mouth back down to hers and pressing her lips to mine once more.

I was helpless to resist her—like a fly caught in her seductive web. The more I struggled the more tangled I became. I quit battling and gave in, succumbing to all she wanted. I kissed her hard, aggressively, too aggressively, but I didn't care. I couldn't get enough. She tasted so good, and I loved the way she clung to me with desperation. I knew she felt the same.

There was a knock on the door, and we broke apart, both of us breathing heavily.

"You about done in there, Hunter?" Mr. Adams voice asked.

Cami grabbed up her books. "Meet you at your car."

I nodded and watched her sneak through the exterior door.

"Yeah, I'm done," I answered, taking a deep cleansing breath as I tried to calm my raging, hormonal body. I gathered up my things, and headed into the classroom. "Sorry I took so long." I went to my desk, carefully slipping the images I didn't want anyone to see into my binder, and set the others to the side while I zipped it up.

"Let's see how your pictures turned out," Mr. Adams said, coming over and picking them up. He flipped through them casually, smiling before handing them back. "They look good, though you may want to take less pictures of Cami next time."

I nodded. "Yeah, I got a little carried away."

He smiled and patted me on the shoulder. "She's a pretty girl. I'm sure that's easy to do."

I cleared my throat nervously. "I better get going. My uncle is going to start wondering where I am." I grabbed the items off my desk. "See you later, Mr. Adams."

"Goodnight, Hunter."

HUNTER♥

CHAPTER FOURTEEN
Hunter-

My music was blaring as I sat at my desk with my head buried in my hands. Pictures from today were spread all over in front of me, but I wasn't seeing any of them. All I could see was Cami—her hair, her lips, her skin, her sweet body wrapped around me as I kissed her over and over again in my car, ravishing her until she'd finally pulled away, putting some much needed-distance between us.

I'd driven her home in silence, as my thoughts overwhelmed me. We were explosive together—combustible—and I should've never crossed this line. I had no idea it would be like this. I'd never wanted a girl as much as I wanted her. I shuddered to think what might've happened in that darkroom if we hadn't been interrupted. I'd lost all restraint.

I slammed my fist down against the pictures. What the heck was happening? Where was my carefully maintained restraint? I'd been confident I could withstand anything thrown at me when we'd come here. Now I wasn't so sure. I wasn't in control at all. I was playing around with a chick I was hot for—one that could cause me a serious bundle of trouble. This was completely unacceptable.

My phone buzzed, and I saw it was a text from Cami. R we ok?

I stared at it—almost afraid to touch it—as if acknowledging her would make me combust all over again. I shouldn't reply. I should walk away now and look like the jerk Clay had told her I would be. She'd cry, I was sure, and it would burn her in a big way, but she'd get over it eventually. She could forget about me and move on with her life. She'd be safe.

But would I ever get over it?

I picked up a picture I'd zoomed in on and stared at it. Even if I wanted to, I couldn't walk away from her now. She'd gotten under my skin, and I wanted more . . . a lot more.

Chris was right when he said I'd be walking a tight rope. I hadn't realized at the time how tight it would be. I wasn't sure what was going on yet, but things were starting to unravel in my mind. I ran a hand over my mouth as I tried to figure out what to do.

Sighing, I picked up my phone to text her back. I was going to take the plunge and make an executive decision. From now on the role of boyfriend was going to be played by me. It was definitely crossing a line, and I hoped I wouldn't cook my own goose while I was at it. I wasn't lying to myself anymore. I *wanted* to be with her, so I was going to live my time with her to the fullest and be happy she was part of my life, even if it was for a short while. Man, I felt like a sick bastard.

Hey gorgeous, I replied, laying it on thick. Haven't been able 2 stop thinking of U. That was the absolute truth.

U were really quiet earlier. Thought U were having regrets.

More regrets than you could begin to imagine, I thought. Cami, this afternoon was like, wow, but kinda scary wow, if U know what I mean.

Yeah. I kinda attacked U.

Really? I chuckled. That wasn't how I remembered it at all. I liked it, I replied honestly.

U did?

U couldn't tell? I laughed out loud, even though she couldn't hear me. She was kidding, right? Didn't she realize how close we'd come to sealing the deal right there? Just thinking about it was getting me all worked up again.

Haha. Maybe.

I shook my head. I still didn't have a clue to the way girls thought.

Well, if U can't tell whether or not I liked what went down today then U and I have some serious problems. More like I would be having some serious problems.

Ur a good kisser. She put a little smiley face after it.

I groaned. She had no idea what she was doing to me.

Haha. Thanks. U 2. What ya doing tonight? I was desperate to change the subject.

Homework.

Me 2.

Well, ok. I'll let U go then. Just wanted 2 make sure we were cool.

We R so much more than cool. U have no idea.

Another smiley face. Talk 2 U at school 2morrow.

Do U want a ride? I knew now that Clay had been her transportation.

That wld B nice.

Gr8. Pick U up at 7:30.

Sounds good.

I was smiling when I tossed my phone down. I grabbed my leather jacket, putting it on before I slipped the weapon I occasionally carried for protection into its hiding place. A guy could never be too careful. I grabbed my digital camera and car keys and headed out the door. Time to see if I could score a little celebratory refreshment.

I leaned my head against the leather seats with a sigh before rubbing my eyes. The smoke filled the car around me, but I didn't really care at the moment. Derek sat beside me, taking a drag off his joint.

"I'm glad I finally caught up with you, dude. I've been craving some of this for a while."

He chuckled. "Anytime, man. There's more where this came from. I thought you'd gone all preacher on me now that you're dating Cami."

I frowned a little. "Yeah, she's made it plain

that she doesn't want me to do this stuff."

"I'm guessing you don't care what she thinks?"

"I do. I've decided to try and be clean while I'm hanging around with her. The rest of the time is fair game."

"Gotcha. Glad you got it all worked out."

"I do. Hey, can you get your hands on some meth for me?"

He looked at me pointedly. "It'll cost you, but yeah, I can try to scrounge some up."

"Cool. I appreciate it. Sometimes I just need something with a little more oomph—know what I mean?"

"I do, man, I do."

"So what's the problem with the best friends today?" Russ asked, elbowing me and pointing to where Cami and Clay sat far apart, not talking to each other, in Chemistry lab.

"Me, apparently," I replied with a grin.

"You?" Russ seemed puzzled.

I leaned over so I could whisper in his ear. "Clay's a little angry because he thinks I made out with Cami yesterday."

Russ's eyebrows shot up in surprise. "And did you?"

"I don't kiss and tell, man."

"You did, didn't you?" He gave a silent look of appreciation between Cami and me. "So was it like a onetime thing or are you headed back for seconds soon?"

I shook my head. "I'm headed back for thirds and fourths . . . heck even tenths. I like her. She's super chill."

"You don't have to convince me. I've always thought she was hot. I'm just not as brave as you are." He laughed. "You aren't the first guy to want her, ya know. Outside her geeky little circle of friends, I mean."

I felt a small thread of jealousy shoot through me. "Really? Who else is after her?"

"Well, no one now that I'm aware of, but Jordan Henley was carrying a pretty big torch for her before he died. I heard him making a bet in the locker room with some other guys about how he was gonna smash her." He shook his head. "We all thought he'd strike out. There's no way she would've given him the time of day."

I didn't like hearing about another guy wanting her like that. "I'm sure she would've given him the same lecture I got about how drugs are bad and he shouldn't be doing them." My body was tense as I tried to casually redirect the conversation.

He shrugged. "I don't know. He was never really into the drug scene that heavy. Maybe a joint or two here and there. He drank with us, but he had his heart set on some big athletic scholarship. He tried hard to keep his nose clean, wanting to be in the best physical shape possible for the teams who were looking at him. College football was a really big deal to him. That's why his death was weird. No one could believe he started using so heavily."

"Such a bummer," I said, fingering my notebook as I stared at Cami.

"It's okay, dude. He's not competition

anymore, you can relax." Russ gestured at my clenched hand on my lap, and I realized I was grinding my teeth.

I released everything with a sigh. "I'm okay. Guess I like her more than I thought. Hearing you talk about another guy put me on the defensive a little."

Russ clapped me on the shoulder and squeezed. "You've got it bad, don't you?"

"I do." I knew that simple comment would spread through the school like wildfire, and everyone would know about it before the day was over.

That was exactly how I wanted it too.

CAMI 💜

CHAPTER FIFTEEN
Cami-

"Is it him again?" Hunter asked, leaning to look at my phone resting on the arm of my couch.

"Yes," I replied with a sigh, as I saw Clay's name on the screen.

"Hand it here." He made a motion for me to give it to him, but I hesitated.

"I don't think that's such a good idea. He'd freak out if you answered. Plus, I don't know what you'll say."

"He's stalking you, Cami. Can't you see that?"

"No. He's just jealous of you. Cut him a break, Hunter. He's been a huge part of my life since we were five. He's not used to me ditching him for another guy. He'll catch on eventually."

"So you're just going to let him hound you until that happens?" Hunter's mouth set in a firm line. "This has been going on for, like, two weeks now."

"For the time being. Please don't be angry with me. I want to handle this in my way."

His eyes softened. "I'm not angry with you. I'm just not too thrilled with him."

"I know. Me neither. It'll get better, though. I promise. Clay's had his obsessive moments with me in the past, but he always gets over it."

"Obsessive how?" Hunter's scowl deepened, and I laughed, desperate to diffuse the situation.

"I love that you're so overprotective of me." I brushed my hand over his forehead where it was laying in my lap.

"Well, you are my girlfriend. It would look kind of bad if I didn't care, don't you think?"

"I'm your girlfriend?" I couldn't help the smile that crept over my face.

He chuckled. "I figured that was kind of a given since we can't seem to keep our hands or mouths off each other. Were you not on this couch with me for the last hour, or for the last couple of weeks for that matter?"

"Yeah, I was, but we've never really declared anything official was going on. I thought maybe I was just your new make out buddy. You made it pretty clear you're not into the whole girlfriend thing in the past."

He shook his head and closed his eyes as he lifted his hand, running it into my hair absently. "You're my girlfriend, Cami, unless you don't want it that way." He opened his eyes, looking at me.

I swallowed. "I want it that way."

"Good, because I think we've established I'm never going to get my fill of you." He lifted up, capturing my mouth, and shifted to make room for me to lie next to him on the sofa.

I melted easily into him once again—our homework still lying on the floor forgotten, and neither of us seemed inclined to start it again. Too bad we didn't have a class on physical anatomy together, then maybe we could've passed this off as studying.

My head rested on his shoulder, and I tipped it toward his, allowing him to rain little kisses over my face. He paused, his amazing eyes heavily lidded with desire written plainly in them. Even the way he stared at me made me feel beautiful.

He ran his hand down from my shoulder to lock fingers with mine. "When will your parents be home from work?"

I shrugged. "Probably in thirty minutes or so. Why?"

"No reason. Just wondering when I needed to be ready for your dad to barge in here with a shotgun."

"Why would he need a gun? Unless you're planning on doing something super evil and depraved to me," I teased. I loved being wrapped up with him like this.

"You have no idea how deep the level of my depravity is right now." He chuckled.

"Are you subtly telling me you're the wolf in sheep's clothing?"

"There's no subtle about it. I'm flat out telling you." His eyes roamed over me hungrily, and I knew he was being serious. For whatever reason, I wasn't scared. I felt safe with him.

"I trust you." I brought my lips to his again, and he groaned at the contact.

"You shouldn't," he mumbled into my mouth. He shifted me again so I was lying on top of him. I kissed him heavily while he ran one of his hands into my hair, holding my face to his, the other circling my waist, crushing me against his body.

Our mouths pressed harder together, kissing more and more frantically until he arched suddenly, causing me to roll onto the floor. Instantly he was off the couch and sprawled out on top of me.

I laughed. "What was that for?" I asked, sliding my arms up around his neck and pulling him back down. He sucked on my lower lip, biting it as he reached for first one arm, and then the other, pinning them beside my head.

"We have *got* to cool down. You're driving me crazy."

I bit my lip as I stared up at him mischievously. "I thought that was the whole point."

He shook his head and groaned. "You really want me to get shot, don't you?"

"Not at all. We couldn't do this anymore if you were." I had no idea what made me feel so bold with him. I'd never behaved this way with anyone in my entire life, but I liked it. The things he made me feel were incredible.

"Can I be honest with you? I mean brutally," he asked, keeping me pinned beneath him.

Nervous fear shot through. "Sure."

"There's only so much a guy can handle before things get out of control."

"Okay?" I searched his face wondering where he was going with this.

He laughed wryly. "I'm trying to say I'm there, Cami." He stared at me. "I mean *right* there. I can't take anymore."

I could feel the blush that was rapidly spreading across my face as his meaning sunk in. "Oh."

He grinned, bending to kiss me lightly on the lips before nuzzling softly by my ear. "I love that you're so innocent, but I'm gonna move now. I want you to pick up your books and put them on your lap. We're going to finish our homework . . . from opposite ends of the couch. Understand?"

"Got it," I nodded, secretly thrilled that I could make him feel so unrestrained.

He sighed and dropped to kiss my mouth one more time before quickly moving off me and heading toward the kitchen.

"Where you going?" I called after him as I sat up, reaching for my books and placing them in my lap just like he'd asked.

"I need a cold drink. Do you want something?" I could hear him banging around in the cupboards as he looked for a glass.

"No, I'm okay. Thanks." I didn't want to do anything that would dilute the scent of him on me. I could taste his minty breath from the gum he'd been chewing earlier, and I could smell his aftershave on my now sensitive skin from all the times he'd nuzzled against me. I loved it. I'd had no idea what I was missing out on before this. He made my heart flip out in ways I'd never imagined possible.

I heard the back patio door slide open. "I'll be outside for a second."

"Are you okay?" I laughed nervously.

"No, but I will be. I just need to cool down for a minute."

Wow. I must've really done a number on him. I smiled in secret glee, biting my bottom lip again as opened my English book. I felt so empowered right now. I stared at the assignment in front of me feeling hopelessly distracted. There was no way I was going to be able to concentrate. My skin was still tingling and my heart was racing.

Glancing down, I noticed my disheveled appearance. I got up and went upstairs to my bedroom, pausing in front of the mirror to straighten my clothing before going into my bathroom and quickly brushing through my hair. My lips were swollen and nearly every trace of makeup had disappeared. I looked thoroughly kissed. My dad would freak.

I picked up my face powder and began quickly buffing some over my skin.

"Covering up the evidence?" Hunter drawled, appearing in the doorway and causing me to jump.

"Yes." I continued to apply as he leaned casually against the frame, watching me.

"Good idea, though it kinda just makes me want to mess it all up again."

Tingles shot through my body, and I glanced at him. "You're so bad."

He arched his eyebrow. "You have no idea." He tipped his head slightly to the side, his eyes narrowing.

I paused. "What's wrong?"

Moving behind me, he swept my hair to the side. "You may want to put a little powder here on your neck. It looks like I got a little too aggressive." His thumb brushed over my skin.

"You gave me a hickey?" For some reason a giggle bubbled up out of me.

"Apparently—unless you've been having your neck sucked on by someone else."

I elbowed him in the stomach and he grunted.

"Sorry." He continued to brush his fingers over the mark.

"Don't be. It's close enough to my hairline that no one will notice after I cover it up. Besides . . . I like it."

He smiled, looking surprised. "You do, huh?" He wrapped his arms around me and leaned his chin on my head.

"I do. Maybe you'll give me another one sometime."

He released me and moved away. "I'm leaving before this conversation takes us right back to where we started. See you downstairs."

"Chicken!"

"I'm *so* not chicken," he replied, and I couldn't help my grin. I finished reapplying my lip-gloss and went down to join him.

He was sitting on one end of the couch with

his books propped open beside him and his notebook in his lap. He held a pen carefully poised over the paper, and he glanced up when I entered.

"You look amazing," he said appreciatively. "Now sit over there." He pointed to the other end of the sofa.

"Bossy, aren't you?" I grumbled as I went to where he directed.

"Practical," he supplied, giving me a wink to soften the remark.

I stared at him—something I could do forever and never get tired of—and I suddenly wanted to know every little thing about him. We'd been together a lot during the last couple weeks, but conversation hadn't exactly been high on our list of priorities.

"What's your favorite color?" I asked.

"What?" He looked as if I'd thrown him with my random subject change.

"Your favorite color," I repeated. "It occurs to me that we barely know anything about each other."

He snorted. "I was under the impression we were getting to know each other quite well."

"You know what I mean!" I threw my pencil at him, and he lifted his hands to ward it off, chuckling.

"Red. My favorite color is red." He eyed me. "For obvious reasons."

I grinned. "So, if I didn't have red hair, what would your favorite color be?"

He appeared to consider this. "Probably black. Black looks great with everything . . .

especially red."

"I agree, black rocks. I also like green and gold. They go well with my red hair." I smiled. "What's your favorite food?"

"Anything Italian. I'm a big fan of both pizza and pasta. How about you?"

"I love Italian food, though I probably love Mexican just as much."

"Mexican is good. I can get on board with that."

"How about your favorite movie?"

He scratched his head while he stared off into space. "Pass. I have too many I like to pick a favorite."

"A favorite genre of movie then?"

"Not really. I like lots of action, but there are some great comedies out there too. I don't even mind a good chick flick once in a while . . . as long as it's with the right chick." He glanced over me and gave me a sly grin. "What about you? Do you have a favorite?"

"Lots of them actually—drama, and romantic comedies, but I'm a big fan of musicals as well. I absolutely love Phantom of the Opera, both the play and the movie. Have you seen it?"

He shook his head. "Can't say that I have, but if you like it then I'm willing to give it a try."

I practically squealed in delight. "Really? I love it! It's *so* swoony!"

He chuckled. "And I'm guessing swoony is good?"

I brought my hand up to my heart. "Nothing is better than a good romance, Hunter. Nothing!"

"I'll keep that in mind." He shook his head as he laughed.

"So what kinds of things get you excited?" I asked, loving getting to know him better.

He snorted. "Fast cars and loose women," he answered without missing a beat.

"Oh." I didn't know what to say—he'd caught me totally off guard.

He burst out laughing again. "You're so easy to tease—that gets me excited." His gaze grew more reflective. "Lots of things about you seem to do that."

I really wished he would kiss me again. I thought he wanted to, but he glanced at the clock, and I knew he was thinking about my parents getting home.

"How would you like to go on a for-real date with me this weekend?" he asked.

"I thought we had been on real dates."

"No. We've just been making out, not dating." He grinned. "Not that I'm complaining at all, but I want to take you out on a real date . . . show you some things I enjoy doing, and when we are finished we will go back to my place. We can make dinner together, and we'll watch your favorite movie. If my uncle is home you can meet him."

"That sounds fabulous! I'd love to do that! What day?"

"Let's plan for this Saturday, shall we?"

"That sounds perfect," I replied, unable to stop my huge grin. I was so excited to learn more about him.

"Then it's a date," he said. "Although I wish

we could do something together before then."

"Well, I have a choir concert on Wednesday if you want to come to that. I have a solo, but I don't want to bore you."

"You were gonna sing and not tell me?" He gave me a pointed look.

I shrugged. "I guess. I didn't think it would be your kind of scene."

"Anything with you in it is my kind of scene, Goody. I'd love to come listen to you. What are you singing?"

I couldn't help my excited smile. "I'm actually doing a song from Phantom. It's called *Wishing You Were Somehow Here Again*."

"Sounds like it'll be a perfect precursor to our date on Saturday. Maybe we can go out and get a milkshake or something afterward. I'm sure your parents won't want you out too late on a school night."

Almost as if on cue, I heard the front door open. "Cami, we're home!" my mom's voice called.

"We're in the living room."

My dad rounded the corner, his eyes narrowing as he took in the distance between Hunter and myself on the couch before drifting to our books and over to where the television was still playing quietly.

"Hey kids. What're you both up to?" He came and gave me a kiss on the cheek and Hunter stood to shake his hand.

"English and Government homework," I replied as he set his briefcase down by his chair. "You know—the fun stuff."

He relaxed and chuckled, which eased the underlying tension in the room.

"How's that going?" Mom asked, glancing between us with a smile as she came from the kitchen with a glass of water in each hand, giving one to Dad.

"Honestly, it's tedious. We've been planning future dates, actually. Hunter is going to come to my choir concert on Wednesday."

"Really? You're a music buff then?" Dad directed the comment to Hunter.

"Only in the fact that I like music. I don't know the first thing about it, otherwise."

"Well, music has been Cami's life since she was little. We used to joke that she came out of the womb singing. Has she told you she wants to go away to college? She's hoping to be accepted into the music theater program at the University of Arizona in Tucson."

"She has, and I think that would be an amazing experience for her. Plus, Tucson is wonderful. That's where I'm from. I'm planning on moving back there after high school."

I had to try not to laugh as I watched my dad's plan fail. He was subtly trying to tell Hunter to back off because I was going to college. He looked less than thrilled to find we'd be living in the same town.

"Won't that be fun?" Mom exclaimed, not getting Dad's 'stay-away-from-my-daughter' memo apparently. "If things work out for you two, you can still keep dating." She smiled—her bubbly, incurable romantic self coming straight to the surface.

Dad pasted a fake smile of joy on his face with a slight eye roll before he chased it down with a swallow of water. I was betting he wished he had some liquor in that glass right now.

"Honestly, I'd like nothing better than that," Hunter replied, sending a glance in my direction. "I like Cami a lot."

I wanted to kiss him so badly. I didn't care that my parents were sitting right there. They needed to get used to the idea. I flipped open my notebook to where I'd put his sticky note from weeks ago. I took my red pen and checked the 'yes' box before leaning over to put it on his binder. "You win," I said instead. "I like you."

Hunter grinned widely and grasped my hand, squeezing it, and we all pretended to miss the groan from my dad.

CHAPTER SIXTEEN
Hunter-

I was mesmerized. To be totally honest, listening to her sing made me excited to watch the movie—something I hadn't been sure about before. I couldn't stop staring as she wrapped me up in the sound of her voice and the story she was telling. She was completely in character, and I totally believed she was a young girl pining at the grave of her father.

She isn't good—she's gifted. I was pretty sure it wasn't just me who thought so, either. A passing glance around the theater showed everyone watching intently, some even had tears in their eyes—it was incredible. I stood up and clapped when the performance was over, not caring if it was the right thing to do. She was awesome and getting a standing ovation from me. Thankfully, a few other people did too, so I didn't look like a complete idiot.

Her gorgeous blush stole across her face,

and she gave a quick bow before returning to stand with the rest of the choir for their remaining numbers. I settled back into my chair and watched her every move for the rest of the concert. She was a star in the making; someone who came alive on stage and it was as if I was seeing her for the first time. Suddenly I felt inadequate to be around her.

Who are you to try and lay claim to this girl? I thought. *To sweep in and turn her life upside down—what gives you that right?* My conscience nagged.

She had dreams and goals, things that didn't include me. I'd taken one look and barged right in, without giving a second thought about what was going on with her prior to my arrival. I'd allowed myself to be totally ruled by my attraction for her.

Was it wrong for me to want her so badly? Really? She was almost eighteen, in exactly three weeks to be precise. I actually had the day marked on my calendar because it meant one guilt trip I could finally be free of. I hated all the secrecy I was involved in. I wanted to be open and honest with her, to tell her who I really was. I wanted her to fall for me—the real me, not some fake imposed person she thought she knew. When things were all said and done, I hoped she felt there was enough truth in our relationship to keep seeing me.

I sighed, sinking farther down into my chair. I'd certainly made a mess of things. But there was nothing I could do now, except try and make the best of the situation and hopefully ride it out to the finish.

I glanced around at the people in attendance. There were enough to fill the auditorium about halfway. I'd chosen my customary seat in the back of the crowd, so I could carefully observe everyone, but I'd been too caught up in Cami to notice anything.

They were starting the last number when I noticed Clay sitting across the room. It was obvious he was staring at Cami. I shifted uncomfortably in my seat, not liking him here. Cami still hadn't spoken to him. He'd quit calling, but he continued texting, begging her to talk to him. She wanted to handle it her way, so I stepped back, not offering any more advice. She knew my opinion on the matter.

He turned suddenly, looking straight at me. I didn't look away as he stared me down. I could plainly see he was angry, and I knew he was trying to intimidate me. He had no idea who he was dealing with if he thought he could make me cower. I was totally down for winning a juvenile contest against this hotheaded. We were both legal adults, let him show me how 'man' he thought he was.

Neither of us looked away until the applause after the final number. The choir and instructor bowed, and the students began making their way into the audience to greet friends and family.

I waited while Cami paused to hug her parents, and I saw Clay making his way in their direction. She didn't see him though and turned to hurry up the steps to where I was sitting.

Clay stopped, glaring at me before walking away.

I stood and she threw her arms around me, a giant grin plastered on her face. "Well? What did you think?"

"You were amazing!" I said hugging her back.

"Really? You liked it?"

I leaned away so I could look at her. "Like doesn't begin to encompass what I felt. People told me you were good, but I really had no idea. You were phenomenal. I felt like I should be standing there with a sign that said "that's my girlfriend," or something."

She laughed and slapped my shoulder. "Now you're just messing with me."

I chuckled and pulled her closer. "I'm not. It was fantastic. I could totally see you doing this for a living someday."

She blushed and ran her finger in a lazy circle over my leather jacket. "Really?" Her eyes moistened up.

"Are you okay?" I asked, concerned.

"Yeah. It means a lot to hear you say something like that, though. I know this isn't really your thing."

I nuzzled my face into her hair. "Cami . . . you're my thing. Period."

We sat in the farthest corner booth in Francesca's, where the lighting was softer and we could look out the giant window and watch the traffic go by. I was thoroughly enjoying observing her as she sipped her thick shake from the straw, then licked her lips with tiny repetitive darts of her tongue. It was driving me crazy . . . in a good way.

"Your dad doesn't like me," I stated out of the blue.

She sighed, shaking her head. "I think you're right. You haven't given him a reason to chase you off yet, though."

"Oh, I've given him plenty of reasons, he just hasn't witnessed any of them. I'm pretty sure some of the places I've put my hands on you were not on his list of acceptable locations."

She snorted. "There's no list of approved locations when it comes to where you can touch me. Hand holding is crossing the line in his opinion."

"Then I'm definitely screwed." I grinned and winked, taking a drink of my shake.

"I like it when you touch me."

I choked a little. "Me too," I finally managed, looking over her gorgeous body.

She bit her lip shyly as if she were waiting for me to do something.

"What?" I asked.

"Why are you sitting way over there?"

I chuckled and raised an eyebrow. "Would you like me to sit on your lap? I don't think we can get much closer than we are."

She bumped her shoulder into mine. "No. You're just . . . all to yourself." She gave a frustrated sigh. "You know what I mean."

"Are you saying you'd like me to put my arm around you?" I did it as I spoke, hugging her.

"Yes, that's much better." She snuggle her

head against my shoulder. "I like cuddling with you. It feels nice."

"Can't argue with you there." I placed a quick kiss near her hairline.

"Hey, bro, wassup?" Russ said, sliding into the booth, catching me by surprise. "Hi, Cami." He gave her a little wave.

"Hi, Russ. How are you?"

I loved her leaning against me—comfortable enough to stay where she was.

"I'm good. I was driving by and saw your buddy, Clay, on the corner by Hunter's Camaro, so I figured you all must be meeting here."

Cami stiffened in my arms. "Clay's here?"

I looked through the window and sure enough, there he was, leaning against my car.

"Be right back, okay?" Cami said, sliding from my grasp.

"Cami . . . ," I warned, feeling insecure about her leaving.

"It's okay, Hunter. I need to talk to him. He's not going to drop this until I do."

I didn't want to let her go. "Stay where I can see you—in case you need me." I had to try and play things cool. I couldn't come off as an obsessive boyfriend.

"I will." She gave me an apologetic look and headed out the door.

"Everything all right?" Russ asked, looking concerned.

I shrugged, attempting to play off my worried attitude. "They're still having some issues."

"Were they dating or something?" Russ

seemed confused. "Why's he freaking out so bad?"

"No, they weren't, but apparently he wanted to be. Cami, thinks of him like a brother."

"Hmm. Interesting and a little weird if you ask me," he added.

"My thoughts exactly," I replied, my eyes never leaving the two in the parking lot.

CHAPTER SEVENTEEN
Cami-

"Hey, Clay," I said as I walked up to Hunter's Camaro. I leaned against it, next to him. "What's going on?"

His eyes were downcast, arms folded, and he looked miserable and lonely despite the fresh, new style he was still sporting.

"I miss you, Cami," he finally mumbled. "A lot."

I sighed heavily. "I miss you too. Honestly, I do, but I'm not dealing well with the weirdness between us right now."

"So it's my fault then." He kicked a small rock, sending it shooting across the parking lot.

"Well, kind of, yeah." I didn't know how to make him understand. "I mean, I love the transformation you've done to yourself, but I loved you before. It was always fine with me because you were Clay—my best friend who's always been there since I was a little kid. Do I think you look hot and amazing now? Sure! But just because you've conformed to a new style, it isn't going to change the way I feel about you. I feel the same way I always did. I want my best friend back."

He lifted his head, glancing at the window where Hunter and Russ were both watching us with avid interest.

"This is our place. Why did you start bringing him here? Do you know how much it kills me to come by and see you in there laughing with him?"

"I've had other boyfriends in the past. That never stopped you from walking in and sitting down next to me before. Me being on a date with someone else doesn't make our best friend relationship null and void. You're always welcome to come join us."

"Boyfriend?" he questioned, and I didn't miss the hint of alarm in his eyes. "Is that an official thing or just random terminology you're using?"

I folded my arms and looked at him pointedly. "Yes, he's my boyfriend."

He chewed on his bottom lip and glanced away. "So, I guess that means you've been making out with him."

"That's *none* of your business." I couldn't believe he went there.

"It *is* my business," he replied angrily. "We talked about this—about the kind of guy he is and what he's really after. He only wants you for your perfect rockin' body—like half the other guys in this school who sit in the locker room and talk about all the things they'd like to do to you."

I was shocked. "What're you talking about?"

"You think he's the first?" he spat out. "He's not. Before he died, I sat and listened to Jordan Henley tell a bunch of other guys how he was going get you. They didn't know I was in there. He even made a bet with some of them about how fast he could do it too. Thankfully, fate intervened before he could get his hands on you. This guy is no different. He's only after one thing."

"And you feel you need to protect me?" I was trying to follow his thought process while still reeling from the information he was giving me.

"I'll always protect you, Cami. No matter what."

"Really?" I asked, staring him down.

He nodded.

"Then tell me, what is it *you* want to do with me, Clay?"

He looked at me funny, blinking a few times in confusion. "Wha . . . what do you mean?"

"I mean, what is going on in your head? You claim to have made all these changes for me, so I would notice you, correct?"

He swallowed hard, watching me closely.

"I think you're just as guilty as Jordan. You want to do the same things with me that he did, don't you? You're jealous, and you thought he'd get to me first. Now you're thinking the same thing about Hunter. You don't want me with anybody else because *you* want me. Admit it."

He was silent for several seconds before he

lifted his hand to gently stroke my cheek. "You belong to me, Cami. You've always been mine, even if you don't know it yet. I'm waiting for you to wake up and see I'm the one who's always been there for you. Other guys have come and gone. Hunter will too, you'll see, and when he's finished with you, I'll still be the one standing here wanting you, because I love you."

I was dumbfounded, unable to reply.

He moved closer. "Choose me, Cami. Please." He slipped his hand behind my neck and pressed his lips to mine.

I flattened my hands against his chest— shoving him away roughly—but he struggled to keep hold of me. "Stop it, Clay! Quit doing this! Do you hear me?"

The door to the restaurant banged open, and Hunter ran across the parking lot, followed by Russ. He grabbed Clay by the shirt and slammed him up against the car, hard.

I couldn't help it—I screamed.

"So help me if you ever touch her like that again, I'll have your sorry ass thrown in jail for harassment—after I'm done beating the crap out of you."

"Careful, man," Russ warned, placing a restraining hand on Hunter. "Someone will call the cops if you fight him here."

Clay grinned. "I'll touch her whenever and however I want. You won't be able to do a thing about it. She doesn't belong to you."

A dark flush crossed Hunter's face, and he *looked* dangerous. "No one will ever touch her without her permission—not you, not me, not

the black mascara, which ran down my cheeks in streaks.

"I look like a monster from a horror movie," I complained. I turned the water on and splashed some on me.

"You look beautiful, like always, just a little upset is all." Hunter got some paper towels and handed them to me so I could dry off.

A waitress stepped into the restroom. "Sir, this is the ladies room. I'm going to have to ask you to leave, please."

"Sorry, I wasn't trying to be rude. I was checking on my girlfriend," he apologized.

She held the door open, clearly expecting him to go.

"I'm okay, Hunter. I'll be out in a minute."

He nodded and left the room. The waitress gave me a stern look before she followed after him.

I was so ready for this day to be over.

CAMI ♥

CHAPTER EIGHTEEN
Cami-

Hunter was silent as he drove; the only sounds were the car engine and the low music coming from the CD player. He turned toward the hills outside of town, and I didn't ask him where he was taking me. Regardless of what Clay thought, I trusted Hunter. I didn't know why—there was just something secure about him. He was commanding somehow, authoritative. It seemed an odd way to describe him, but that's how I felt.

I stared at him. He was so incredibly good looking, but there was more. I couldn't quite place my finger on it.

"You seem older than you really are," I spoke.

He gave a chuckle, briefly glancing sideways before returning his attention to the road. "Really? You think so?"

I placed my hand on his thigh. "I don't mean

that badly, or anything. Just sometimes you seem . . . smarter, or more sure, or . . . something. Sorry, I'm not making much sense. I want to know more about you."

A pained look passed over his face, and he slipped his hand down to squeeze mine. "You will. You need to believe me when I say I want to tell you everything, but there are still some issues I'm working through right now. I don't mean to be cryptic, but I'm not ready to talk about those things yet. Please be patient with me. It'll happen eventually."

"Take all the time you need." I certainly wasn't going to press him for whatever skeletons he carried. I was more than happy to wait for him to tell me whatever he needed. I was sure a lot of issues probably stemmed from the death of his parents, which would be very difficult for him to express. I couldn't imagine what my life would be like without mine, nor did I want to.

"I know your uncle's name is Chris, but what's his last name? Is it Wilder?" I asked, wondering about the people in his life.

"Napier."

"Napier. So he's your mom's brother then?" I assumed this was the case, since their names were different.

"Um, yeah."

"Do you get along with him well? I mean are you happy you live with him?"

"Yeah, we've always been close. He's much younger than my mom, only seven years older than me actually. He's more like a brother, and he absolutely *hates* it when I call him Uncle Chris, so I do it often." He grinned widely, and it was infectious, causing me to smile too.

"Will I get to meet him Saturday?" I asked.

"He's going to try to be there, but I can't make any promises. It depends on his schedule."

"What does he do?"

"He's a computer systems analyst. He flies around the country helping companies set up their data to run more efficiently. Then he teaches their employees how to run the new technology. He goes where he's needed so he's gone a lot."

"That must get lonely for you."

He shrugged. "I manage okay."

"Why'd you guys decide to move here then? It's kind of out of the way and not close to any big airports. Doesn't that make it harder for him?"

He laughed. "I'm not sure. He wanted to try it out. He likes new things every now and then. He flies his own Cessna as well, so he can get to the major airports easy enough, wherever he's located."

"He must be making pretty good money then."

"He is."

"I don't know if I could handle being alone that much." I paused, unsure about what I wanted to ask. "Is that how you got involved in drugs and partying?"

"No. I got started while I was looking for girls to hook up with." He cast an appreciative gaze over my form. "But I don't need a party for that anymore."

"I'm not the girl you're looking for if you want a casual hook up, Hunter. That's never been something I was interested in."

"That's not what I want from you," he replied, his hand tightening around mine again.

"What do you want? I've never really been able to figure that out." I bit my lip while I waited for his response.

"I want for us to sit back and let things flow naturally. No expectations, no rush, let's see what happens on its own."

I sighed and stared out the window as we came up on the hill—the lights of the city cast below us in a sweeping view.

"What's wrong?" he asked.

"Nothing." I smiled. "I'm here with you. Life is perfect."

"While I'd love to believe that, Cami, we both know life is far from perfect right now. I need to know what Clay said to you tonight. I don't trust him." He turned the car off and shifted in his seat so he could look at me better.

"He would never hurt me, Hunter, he's just confused right now. I've always understood him better than anyone else, even his parents. He thinks differently and has a different way of doing things. He marches to his own drummer because it's what he understands and makes sense to his analytical mind. Like now, for instance—his whole style change and all these new clothes and stuff—where'd he get the money? Now he's talking about getting a newer car, like a Mustang or something, and he wants me to start dating him. He's been so . . . odd. I gave up on trying to figure him out a long time ago and instead concentrated on being his friend."

Hunter stared at me, appearing to ponder things for a moment. "What did he say?" He wasn't going to let me get around this.

"He told me you weren't the first guy who was after me—Jordan Henley wanted me too. He said thankfully fate intervened to stop it, but now you were here to do the same thing. He told me I belong to him, and he's waiting for me to wake up and see that. And when you've finished having your way with me, he'll be there to pick up the pieces. Then I will understand how much he loves me."

Hunter's face was a mask of cool control. He didn't even flinch. After what had happened at dinner, I'd expected him to become angry again. Instead he stared into the night scene ahead of us.

He slid a hand down his face. "He's wrong about me, just so you know. I've never had any desire to use and abuse you in any way. I honestly care about you, and I've really enjoyed getting to know you." He paused. "It doesn't surprise me that other guys are interested in you. In fact, I already knew it. I'd heard the rumors about Jordan from another source, and I know there are several guys at school who like what they see when it comes to you."

I narrowed my eyes. "I have to say I find that really hard to believe."

"Well, start believing. The truth of the matter is, no one asks you out because they don't like Clay. Forgive the reference, but you're a nerd by association. People don't want to socialize with you because you're always with him, and he makes them uncomfortable. I'm not saying any of this to be condescending. It's just the way things are."

"If I'm so nerdy, then why'd you want to go out with me?"

"I don't care what other people think."

"Neither do I. That's why I've always liked Clay. It's also why I'm dating you . . . someone with a less than stellar reputation."

He smiled. "That's what I love about you, Cami. You're not afraid to lay things out there plainly, no matter how brutal."

I hadn't meant it to sound brutal. His choice of words had me reeling. That's what he *loves* about me? Surely it must've been a slip.

"The way I see it, we have two ways we can play this. We can break up, so it helps to ease the tension between you and Clay. Hopefully this will allow him to straighten things out in his head because he won't see me as a threat anymore. Or we can stay together, and you'll have to promise me you won't interact with him in any way. I'm not saying this to be mean, but he needs a clear message that there never was, nor ever will be, anything between you. You're so kindhearted though, I don't know if you can pull it off. What do you think?"

"I think you're overreacting. I don't think Clay would ever do anything to harm me. We're too close—at least we were."

"I don't want to risk it either way. The decision is yours, though. I'll do my best to trust your judgment."

"Don't break up with me. If you do, he gets exactly what he wants. It'll give him false hope." I sighed, hating how technical and forced everything seemed. "I want what you want . . . to play this by ear and see how it goes. He's got to get used to that sometime in his life."

He leaned across the seat and lightly kissed my lips. "I agree. I'm sorry tonight was so upsetting."

"Don't apologize. It's not your fault."

He opened his door and climbed out, coming around to help me from the car. We walked to the front, and he leaned against it, wrapping me against him in his arms.

"This is a gorgeous view," I said.

"Yes, it is," he replied, bending to kiss the side of my cheek over my shoulder.

I twisted so I could face him, and his lips found mine, kissing me deeply—only to be interrupted by a splat against our faces. We both looked up, blinking as several more raindrops fell.

"Looks like we're about to get wet," I said, stating the obvious.

He laughed. "I don't care." He grabbed me by the waist and turned, slipping me up so I was lying on the hood of the car, pinned there with his body. He ran his hands through my hair, spreading it. "So beautiful," he whispered. He crushed his mouth to mine, devouring it. I felt the thrill of his touch shoot through my entire being, and I met him eagerly, wanting him to continue his delicious assault on my senses as I explored him as well.

The skies opened up, delivering on their warning by pelting us with a cold rain—rain that did nothing to extinguish the intense heat burning between us. If anything, it only heightened the feelings coursing through me. Our clothing quickly became soaked, sticking to us, and the heat of our bodies was much more noticeable as we moved against each other.

Hunter suddenly broke away and started laughing. "We need to go. We're getting drenched. I don't need you catching your death in the rain now. What is it with you and water?"

I smiled, tracing the moist plains of his face. "I have no idea. Just lucky, I guess."

"Then we need to get you some better luck." He lifted me off the car and carried me over the puddles to the passenger seat, quickly depositing me before running around and climbing in the other side. He shook his hair out like a dog, and I squealed, lifting my hands to ward off the spraying drops.

"What? It's not like you can get any wetter!" He laughed and leaned over plastering a damp kiss on my lips before he started the car and headed for home.

I couldn't stop grinning.

HUNTER♥

CHAPTER NINETEEN
Hunter-

"Be careful. You've got to handle it just right. Wrap your hands around it like this and slip your finger right here." I gave a satisfied grunt as she did so, and I wound my arms around her tighter. "You're a natural, I can tell already. Feels good, doesn't it?"

"I guess. It's heavier than I thought it would be, but it's not too bad." She shifted, like she was trying to get a little more comfortable.

"That's good, right there," I whispered in her ear. "Now aim and carefully squeeze the trigger."

She closed her eyes and fired, the shot going wide.

"No, no, no!" I said with a laugh. "You can't close your eyes when you're shooting. It isn't a game of chance—see your target, visualize hitting it. Try again."

I was rewarded with a very exaggerated eye

roll.

"Visualize the target—whatever!"

"What if some poor guy ran in front of you at the last minute? You'd shoot him because your eyes were closed. That would be a bad, bad thing, Goody."

"I don't really think there's any danger since you've dragged me out into the middle of nowhere. Who's around to run in front of me?"

"Me, and I don't particularly relish the idea of getting shot."

"Not even by me?" She grinned. "I'd be gentle, I promise."

I let my eyes drift over her and sighed, shaking my head. "I don't think anything you do to me is gentle."

She laughed, bumping her hip against me before she lifted the gun again and pointed at the soda can several yards in front of us.

"Relax your stance. You're too . . . Charlie's Angels . . . or something."

She snorted. "Quit making me laugh or I'll never hit it."

"But I like making you laugh." I slipped my hands down her waist onto her hips, grabbing them firmly. "Center yourself here, but relax everywhere else, and use your gun sight to focus on the target."

She took a deep breath and held it, squeezing the trigger. The bullet hit the dirt right in front of the can, causing it to fall over.

"It moved! Did you see that?" She cheered, all smiles as she jumped around, and I reached to still her, pointing the gun away from both of us.

"This is still a loaded weapon, honey. Let's try not to kill ourselves with it, shall we?" I couldn't help my smile. She was hilarious. "Do you want to try again?"

She nodded and quickly resumed her earlier stance. Her face was a mask of concentration, and I watched her zero in on her target. She pulled the trigger, and the can jumped as she hit it.

"There you go!" I said, quickly taking the weapon before her next victory dance got one of us shot. "That was much better."

"You do it now," she urged. "I want to see how good you are."

I shrugged. "I'm not too bad, I guess. I just like shooting."

"Show me."

I lifted the gun—my eye zeroing in on the target instantly—and fired the rest of the clip into the can in rapid succession, hitting it every time, even as it bounced around.

Cami's mouth hung open in disbelief. "You're a liar. You're amazing! What are you—some gun-toting drug dealer, and you haven't told me?"

I laughed loudly, enjoying showing off for her. "Yes, that's exactly what I am. You've figured me out." I put the safety on and popped the empty clip out. "I just really like shooting, and I happen to think one can never be too prepared when it comes to safety. You want to try a rifle now?" I hoped she was having a good time. She wanted to know what I liked to do, so

I figured this would be a fun thing. I loved being able to share something real about myself with her, although her comment hit uncomfortably closer to the truth than I'd like.

"Sure, I'll try it."

I smiled—glad she seemed willing to participate. It was a sneaky way to teach her a little self-defense too without her knowing. I went over to the trunk of my car, put the handgun inside, and pulled out the thirty-aught-six and a box of cartridges.

"Now these bullets are a little heavier, so there's going to be some recoil with this one," I warned as I prepared and loaded the gun.

"What does that mean?" she asked confused.

"It means it will kick back into your shoulder a bit when you fire. I'll demonstrate for you first, so you can see what I mean." As soon as the gun was ready, I pointed to the far cans we had set up on a fence railing some distance away when we'd arrived. "Okay, I'm going to shoot at those out there this time." I took a moment to sight the target, firing, watching as the can bounced up wildly.

"You hit it again! That's so awesome!" She squealed, clapping her hands together. "You make it look so easy."

I grinned. "Thanks. Now you try it." I handed her the gun and helped her get into a comfortable stance. "Okay, remember to keep looking at your target and gently squeeze the trigger whenever you're ready."

She blew out a soft breath and fired. The shot went wide again, hitting the next can over from the one she'd been aiming for. "Owww!" she howled, and I couldn't help my chuckle.

"Kicked you good, didn't it?" I rubbed where she'd had the gun nestled against her.

"You could've warned me better. That really hurt!" She looked slightly teary eyed. "I don't want to shoot this one anymore."

I bent to quickly place a kiss against her shoulder. "I'm sorry. I didn't mean for you to get hurt, but I didn't want you to tense up and be scared either. Tell you what. I'll use the rifle and you can use the handgun, and we'll see how many of these cans we can hit together."

She nodded as she continued to massage herself. "Okay. Sorry. I'm not very good at this."

"You're doing amazing," I replied, meaning every word. "I'm happy you wanted to try it."

"I like finding out about the things you do." She smiled and slipped her arms around my waist, hugging me.

I shifted the gun and hugged her back, taking a moment to dip down and kiss her sweet lips. "I like it too."

"I'm glad you were able to get off work," I said as we drove back toward Copper City. "I've enjoyed sharing things with you today."

"Me too. I didn't know if my boss was going to let me since I'd taken Wednesday night off for my concert. I had to beg a little." She laughed.

"Well, I'm happy you did. I'm looking forward to spending the rest of the evening with you."

"We have another spot available at the

theater, you know. If you want a job, you should come apply. We could work together."

"Really?" This did interest me, not because I needed a job, but because it would give me the opportunity to be close to her. I knew Clay worked there, even though she said they didn't get scheduled together much these days. It would give me an opportunity to check into him some more. I'd been forming a few suspicions about him lately and the possible source of his new income. I was beginning to wonder if he might be encroaching on the drug scene. I wouldn't put it past him. He definitely warranted watching. I didn't think he was stable, despite Cami's defense of him. "I'll check it out. Do you think they'd let us work the same nights though, seeing how we're dating?"

"As long as we do our jobs and aren't making out in the supply closets they're pretty good about letting couples have the same shifts together."

"Hmmm. I don't know. The supply closet thing might be a deal breaker. I like pushing you into dark corners and doing wicked things to you." I shook my head and she laughed.

"You're so bad."

I chuckled. "I've tried to warn you. You don't seem willing to listen."

"Maybe I like bad," she challenged.

I placed my hand on her thigh, gripping slightly. "Works for me." She was gonna be the death of me.

She intertwined her fingers with mine— giving me one of her dazzling smiles, and my heart skipped a beat.

"Watch the road, Hunter."

I sighed. "You distract me too much."

"I like distracting you, but I also want to survive." She laughed.

"Good point."

"So what do you want to do for our next date? Or am I monopolizing all your time these days? I know you used to like the party scene."

"I haven't much cared for the party scene lately. I'm finding myself presented with a new drug of choice."

She gave me a disparaging look. "So I'm a drug of choice now? How flattering."

"If you don't like it, I guess I could go back to my old lifestyle. I don't want you to feel like I'm a burden."

She squeezed my hand tighter. "Don't you dare. I like that you've been trying to stay clean. Plus, I'm sure Gabrielle would be there, waiting to sink her clutches into you. She wants you bad."

I groaned, feeling awful I hadn't been totally honest with her on the partying account. True, I hadn't been to many parties, but it didn't mean I wasn't using. Brushing aside my guilt, I focused on the subject of Gabrielle. "Don't remind me. I always feel like I'm part of a petting zoo exhibit when she's around. She's always touching me."

"It's funny, but I would've imagined she'd be exactly your type." She was frowning.

"And why would you think that?"

She lifted her shoulder slightly. "I don't know. I guess because she's been everyone's type before you."

"Which is exactly why she isn't mine." I didn't want Cami thinking Gabrielle was competition.

"You don't think she's gorgeous?"

"She's very good looking, and she knows it and uses it to get what she wants from guys. It's not attractive at all."

"You really don't care for her, do you?"

"Not in the slightest, especially when there are much prettier girls to be noticed." I winked and she blushed.

"How do you know I'm not using *my* looks to get what I want from you?" She grinned slightly as I turned into the parking lot of the grocery store.

I stopped the car and leaned over, pulling her face close to mine. "Cami, *please* use your looks to get whatever you want from me." I pressed my lips to hers. "I like it."

She grinned and kissed me back. "What do you want to make for our dinner?"

"Honestly, skipping dinner and doing this all night is sounding pretty good to me."

Her stomach chose this minute to growl, and we both laughed.

"Okay, message received—food first, kissing later."

"Sounds wonderful." She sighed against my lips, and I had to kiss her one more time. Her stomach growled again.

"Okay, okay. Let's go buy some food." I reluctantly moved away and got out of the car, going around to open her door.

HUNTER♥

CHAPTER TWENTY
Hunter-

Gosh, she's gorgeous, I thought as I sat staring at her from my desk chair in my room. She was asleep, her beautiful red hair spread across my black pillowcase. Her face looked peaceful, flawless in her innocence. She was so trusting. *She's the only girl I ever want in my bed again.* The thought hit me hard, and I closed my eyes. I had fallen for her, and I knew it. I'd never had these kinds of feelings before, but somehow I'd expected it to take longer. I wasn't prepared for it to come racing in this way, capturing me.

I briefly turned my attention to the musical still playing on the television in the corner. We'd been cuddling on my bed while we watched it, but I kept getting distracted kissing her and not paying attention. She hadn't seemed to mind much—fully reciprocating in fact.

She had no idea how many secrets I had

hidden away from her in this room, most of them buried in the bottom drawer to my left. I wondered for the millionth time what she would do when she found out the truth, how badly she'd feel betrayed.

There was a soft knock at the door, and it opened slightly. "You here?" Chris called peeking in. His eyes landed on Cami, and a frown crossed his face. "Hunter . . . ," he whispered emphatically, and I widened my eyes to shush him. "Out here, now," he practically ordered.

I got up and followed him into his bedroom at the end of the hall. He shut the door behind me.

"What the heck is going on?" he asked and I heard the frustration in his voice.

I sat on the edge of the bed. "I'm crazy about her, Chris, that's what's happening. I need your help."

"Hunter, she's seventeen. She's too young."

"I know how old she is!" I snapped, feeling my carefully maintained threads of control unraveling. I sighed trying to calm down. "I don't think you understand. I don't care if she's seventeen or forty. She's the one, Chris. I know she's young, and her life is just starting, but I also know she's the one I want. I feel it burning inside. It's killing me to keep lying to her. I'm gonna blow everything."

"You can't let your feelings for her get in the way, Hunter. If we don't get these deals to go down right, we're screwed. You're putting her in danger too. What if she got caught up in the middle of a drug war? That's bad news, and you know it."

"I'm aware of that, and I'm desperately trying to separate her from that part of our life. I tell myself to walk away, but I can't keep my hands off her."

"So, I'm guessing the no-kissing policy didn't go over so well?" he asked wryly.

"That's the understatement of the year."

"How close are you two?" he asked bluntly.

"Close enough we've talked about how things will work out for us after graduation when we move back to Tucson. I'm not kidding. She's the one I want."

He sank down next to me. "That's not what I meant."

I sighed. "I know."

"Are you going to answer me?"

"No." What Cami and I were doing—or not doing—was no one else's business but ours as far as I was concerned.

He stared at me pointedly. "If you've slept with her, her parents could have you arrested since she's a minor. We'd have cops swarming all over investigating *us*. Most police departments don't take kindly to that sort of behavior, you realize. That's the last thing we need."

I didn't reply to his implied question. "How would you feel if someone was asking you to lie over and over again to Sheridan?" I asked, moving the subject forward by making it personal. "And how would you feel knowing those lies were placing her in a dangerous situation?"

"It would kill me, man."

"Well, I'm there. This is my life, and I hate every second of it."

He sat there in silence, staring at his hands as if they'd somehow provide answers. "Are you sure this isn't just some sort of infatuation? That can happen in high-pressure situations."

I chuckled wryly. "I'm sure. She's not even aware there is a high-pressure situation, and I'm not that desperate. If I didn't think it was real I wouldn't be so concerned. There's been something between us from the very beginning."

"Well, it seems we're caught between a rock and a hard place here."

I nodded. "I'm aware." He looked so disappointed. "I'm sorry I botched this all up. I guess we found out what I was made of and it wasn't any good."

"Don't talk that way. And you're sure this is legit, not just because some other guy is after your girl?"

"I wouldn't do that, Chris. You should know me better than that."

"I do know you well, but you're acting out of character. You've never been one to rule from the heart before."

"That's because my heart never belonged to someone else."

"Does she know how you feel?"

"No. *I* barely know how I feel. It's too fast—too sudden—I don't want to scare her off. I can't tell her when she doesn't really know who I am. If she says it back to me, who is she in love with? Me, or the person she *thinks* I am? It's too screwed up right now."

Chris patted me on the shoulder. "I'm sorry, bro. I really am. Please know that even though things are weird, you're first and foremost my brother—you have been since the first day your sister introduced us. I want you to be happy, and I want things to work in your favor. All I can do is tell you to keep hanging in there. I'll do the best I can to help you, and we'll see if we can work our way through this mess."

I sighed with relief knowing I wasn't in this alone—someone was on my side and understood what I was going through. I was tired of this frantic, worried energy constantly running just under the surface.

"There's a possibility I can get a job at the theater working with her. Should I do it?"

"I'd say go for it as long as your crush doesn't interfere."

I gave a sardonic laugh. "A crush. Thanks for taking me seriously."

"I get it. Just do the best you can. And try not to do anything . . . stupid . . . relationship wise, I mean. That can only lead to more bad for both of us." He glanced at his watch. "When do you need to have her home? It's ten now."

"She has a midnight curfew, but she wanted to meet you."

"Well, go wake her up then, *nephew*, and let's get this awkwardness over with." He shooed me off the bed.

"Yes, *uncle*," I replied with a grin and he groaned.

"I really hate that," he complained.

"I know. That's why I love saying it so much." I left and made my way back to my room.

I hated waking her up. She looked so sweet lying there; I wanted to watch her for a while longer. I ran a hand through her curls, and she stirred slightly.

"Cami, honey," I whispered, leaning closer and brushing my lips softly against hers.

She made a sweet whimpering sound, stretching a little before stilling again.

"Goody, it's time to wake up. My uncle's here and wants to meet you." I kissed her cheek and down her neck, nuzzling my face there.

Her hand drifted up to rest against the back of my head. "Mmm, that feels so good," she mumbled. "I wish you could wake me up this way every day."

I smiled against her skin. "So do I."

"It would be so nice."

Maybe someday, I thought. *If we all get through this unscathed and you decide you can ever trust me again.*

"Did you hear me say my uncle is here? He'd like to meet you."

She stiffened. "Oh no! He came? He must think something terrible is going on with me in your bed this way."

I chuckled. "He was mildly alarmed."

She blushed. "I'm so embarrassed. I didn't mean to fall asleep. I just got so relaxed I drifted off."

"Yeah, I know. It was devastating to my ego. I was right in the middle of kissing you. It made me feel great." I smiled and tweaked her nose.

She made a nervous giggle. "I'm really sorry, Hunter. Honestly, I didn't mean to."

"No worries. We did a lot today. You needed the rest. Besides, I enjoyed watching you sleep. You look very pretty in my bed."

"You're a smooth talker, you know that, right? I can't ever tell when you're being serious, or messing with me. I bet all the other girls eat right from your hand, don't they?"

I shrugged. "I'm not trying to be a smooth talker, there are no other girls, and if I did want someone to eat from my hand I'd want it to be you. How's that?"

She shook her head and grinned. "Yep. I need to watch out for you—definitely a smooth talker." She ran her hand down the side of my face. "Do you have a hairbrush or something I can borrow? I'd like to straighten up to meet your uncle."

"Right through the door there into the bathroom. Help yourself to anything."

I offered her a hand, pulling her to her feet before settling back into my chair as I waited. I wish she didn't have to go home. I liked having her here. It was nice to spend the evening at home with someone for a change.

HUNTER♥

CHAPTER TWENTY-ONE
Hunter-

I tried to remember what day it was. Sunday? Maybe? I sunk deeper into the leather couch at Derek's house. Man, I was messed up—stoned out of my mind, I just wanted to close my eyes and sleep for hours.

Chuckling, I stared at the haze floating in the room. Hell, a person could get mellow just from walking in here. I could barely make out the forms of other people lounging around the room. This was so bad.

My mind casually drifted to Cami, and I closed my eyes as a feeling of panic welled up inside me. If she ever saw me like this she'd probably run screaming in the other direction. That was a sobering thought.

I felt bad. She was working at the theater tonight, so I'd taken the opportunity to hit some people up. I knew she wouldn't approve in the least, and I hadn't intended to get this stoned, but things had gotten a little out of hand. One minute I'd been chillin' with Derek talking about casual stuff, the next he was selling me on the idea of starting to deal with him and how much money we could make if we expanded our reach a bit. He definitely had a head for his business and before I knew it, I was agreeing to it. Afterward Derek and I had gotten a little celebratory, and the party had escalated from there.

Cami couldn't find out. She'd never understand, and I'd never be able to explain why it was so enticing to me. I sighed. She was so beautiful—so good. I tried to keep hold of the picture of her swimming inside my mind, but it was difficult. I wished she was here—so much I could almost imagine her body pressed up against mine right now, the feel of her nuzzling my neck as her hands slid lower down my body, slipping into my waistband.

Whoa! My eyes popped open to find Gabrielle cuddled up against me, her hand traveling in a direction I had no desire for it to go.

"What the heck?" I said, pushing away. "Get off me!" I gave her what I hoped was a good glare, but I could tell she was pretty out of it.

"What's a girl gotta do to get your attention, Hunter?" she whined and poked out her bottom lip in a pout before collapsing against my chest.

Great.

I sighed. "I've noticed you fine, Gabby. You're just not my type." I shoved at her but she didn't budge.

"I'm everyone's type," she mumbled against

my chest, and I felt her kiss me through my shirt. "You need to give me a chance to show you."

"Some other time, then. I'm with Cami now." I lifted my heavy arms in an attempt to push her away again, knowing there would never be a time I wanted this girl.

"I don't see *her* here anywhere. Come on, Hunter. It's not like you have to marry me. Let's just have a little fun together." She moved, straddling me, her hands grabbing the hem of my shirt and pushing it up.

I stared at her incredulously before I grabbed and shoved it back down. "Get off me. Now," I said with what I hoped was deadly calm.

She giggled. "Quit being such a baby. It'll be enjoyable."

"What part of *no* don't you understand?" I asked in exasperation.

She laughed some more. "The 'no' part." She bent and kissed the side of my face.

I shoved her hard enough to send her sliding backward off my knees onto the floor.

"Ow! That hurt!" she screeched, rubbing one of her knees.

Several other people in the room started laughing.

"It's not like he didn't warn you, though." Derek chuckled. "Come here, Gabby, baby. I'll take care of you."

She gave me a glare and moved in his direction.

"Dude, I'm out of here. Sorry." I got up and stumbled across the room over several bodies on the floor. "I'll text you tomorrow."

"Later, man." He was making out with her before I was even through the front door.

I dug my keys from my pocket and got into my car. I hesitated before putting them in the ignition. I was in a pretty bad state. I should definitely not be behind the wheel right now.

Starting it, I carefully drove a mile down the road to the theater. I pulled into the parking lot and sat there for a few minutes. I tried to decide if I was brave enough to go into the theater and face Cami, before making up my mind to sleep it off in the car for a little while. If I could take a nap I'd probably make it home safely.

I closed my eyes and drifted off to sleep.

"Hunter? Hunter?" The voice sounded far away, as did the incessant tapping sound. "Hunter, are you okay?"

Cami. Just the sound of her voice made me smile. I slowly opened my eyes, trying to orient myself.

"Hey." I smiled when I saw her standing outside my window. "What're you doing here?"

She looked at me, puzzled. "I've been at work, remember?" She pointed, and I glanced toward the theater.

Oh, right. Crap.

"How long have you been here?" she asked with a worried frown.

I shrugged. "I don't know. A few hours maybe?"

"Will you please roll down the window or open the door so I can hear you better? Aren't you here to pick me up?"

I was in so much trouble. "Sure," I replied, leaning across the car to open the door on the other side, hoping it would let out any smoke smell clinging to me while she walked around the vehicle. I quickly turned on the car, flipped on the fan and rolled my window down as well.

She climbed inside and turned to look at me in distaste. "What in heaven's name is that odor?"

Damn. I remained silent for a moment.

"How was work?" I asked cordially.

"Oh my gosh! You've been smoking weed haven't you?" She looked horrified.

Among other things, I thought. "It's not like that, Goody," I began to explain.

"Don't call me that. Where have you been tonight?"

"Derek's. He had a party, and I figured since you were working I'd go hang out." I could see the horror and disgust written all over her face.

"Get out of the car!"

Wow, she was really angry. "Why? It's my car!"

"Then you better get out if you want to keep it. There's no way I'm letting you drive in this condition."

"I'm better now that I've slept a little," I complained, but I did as she asked, walking over to her side.

She stormed past me.

"Cami," I said, grabbing her. "Don't be angry with me, please."

She pushed her way from my grasp, going to

the driver's side and getting in. I stood there staring at her for a moment before I got in. As soon as I was buckled up, she put the car in gear and took off.

"Who else was at this party?" She was fuming.

"Lots of people. I don't remember everyone." I leaned my head against the seat. This was going from bad to worse.

"Were you with any girls?" She was clenching her jaw—she didn't want to hear the answer.

"Gabrielle hit on me. I told her no thanks."

"Hit on you how?"

"I woke up and she was cuddled up against me. She tried kissing me."

Her hands were white knuckled on the steering wheel. "Did you kiss her back?"

"What? No! You're kidding, right? I told you how I felt about her."

"I thought you also said you weren't going to do drugs anymore."

I laughed wryly. "I'm pretty sure I never said that."

"You said you hadn't felt the need to continue attending parties."

"Yeah, meaning I was enjoying spending my time with you more, not that I was going to quit using. Don't be putting words in my mouth, Cami."

She gave me an incredulous glance. "Well, pardon me, Mr. Perfect. Excuse me for caring."

I dragged my hand through my hair. This was so not going the way I'd hoped.

"I'm sorry. Things aren't coming out the right way. Please know I would never do anything with the intention of hurting you."

"It doesn't matter whether you intended to or not. The point is you did."

"I'm sorry," I whispered, turning to look out the passenger window. There were so many things I wished I could tell her right now. Things I felt would possibly make it better, or at the very least, help her understand where I was coming from, but I couldn't do it. Not yet.

She was positively rigid as she drove, not speaking at all until she pulled in front of my condo.

"Are you coming in so we can talk about this?"

"No," she answered flatly, tossing me my keys. "I'm going home. I have homework I need to finish before tomorrow."

I dropped the keys back into her lap. "Take my car then. I don't want you walking across town in the dark."

She shook her head. "I don't want anything of yours right now, Hunter."

Her words stabbed me painfully, twisting into my heart. "It's either drive it home, or let me drive you home. I won't take no for an answer."

"I'll call Clay."

Score, Cami: a billion. Hunter: zero. I thought I might actually feel a panic attack coming on thinking of her being with Clay.

"Then call your dad if you need too, but I think you should just take the car. You can come pick me up for school in the morning. I want to work this through with you, Cami. I know what I did was wrong, but I can't fix it unless you talk to me. I know you're angry, so take the car for now, and we'll discuss it later when we've both had a chance to cool down. Okay?"

She sat staring straight ahead for several moments before she finally picked up the keys. "Fine. Now get out."

I did as she asked, and she hardly waited for me to step onto the curb before she was speeding away.

I'd made a mess out of everything.

CAMI

CHAPTER TWENTY-TWO
Cami-

I cried, burying my face in the pillow, not wanting to see the picture, but not being able to look away either.

I told U so, Clay's text read underneath the grainy photo, which showed Gabrielle on Hunter's lap, her hands on his bare chest, his shirt pushed up as he stared at her through heavily lidded eyes. It was amazing how fast a text could spread.

My phone buzzed again. It was Hunter. I'm sure U've seen it by now. It's not what it looks like, Cami. Please believe me.

I didn't answer either of them, instead letting the phone clatter to the floor beside my bed. I couldn't stop the tears from leaking out. Having Hunter tell me about it had been one thing, but seeing it with my own two eyes was something else. He looked like he was enjoying it.

I heard my phone buzzing with more texts,

but I didn't want to check them. Pretty soon it started ringing. I ignored it still, staring at the wall instead.

There was knock on the door.

"Yeah?" I called.

My mom opened in the door. "Are you feeling okay, honey?"

"Yeah, just tired," I replied not wanting to look at her.

"Oh, okay. Well, here's the phone for you. It's Hunter. He told me you were upset with him, but he'd really like to speak with you."

I faced her. "He called the house?"

She nodded with a sympathetic gaze. "I think you should talk to him. He sounds really upset."

I sighed heavily and held my hand out.

"Do you want me to stay?" she asked.

I shook my head. "No. I'll be all right." I waited for her to leave. "Hello?"

"Please, listen for one minute and then if you want to hang up on me you can," he said in a rush. "I swear, I mean I truly promise you, with every fiber of my being nothing happened. Look at the picture. I was sleeping, dozing off and on really. I even dreamed I was with you. I woke up and she was there. Ask anyone who was there. They'll tell you I didn't want anything to do with her. I'm so sorry. I didn't know someone took a picture. Seriously, I feel like she set me up or something to make you mad. I told her I was with you." He paused, and when I didn't say anything he continued. "I swear on my own life, Cami, I'd never betray you this way."

He sounded desperate for me to believe him. I wanted to, but I was still feeling hurt by the whole drug thing.

"Cami?" he questioned again.

"I heard you. I think I'm going to need a little time to sort things out in my head right now. Okay? Give me some space."

"Please don't." The pain was evident in his voice. "You have no idea how much you mean to me."

"I've got to go. My parents will bring your car back to you tonight. I don't need a ride in the morning."

"Cami . . . ," He sounded sick.

"Bye, Hunter." I clicked the phone off, numbly got up and walked out the door. I took it back to its stand and returned to my room, picking up my cell phone. I read through the earlier texts from Hunter before looking at the new one from Clay.

Hope U're ok. Coming over 2 check on U. I need 2 apologize.

I sighed. I wasn't too excited about that, but I supposed it was inevitable. At least he wasn't coming to gloat.

It wasn't long before I heard his familiar footfalls on the stairs, and the door opened.

"Hey," he said, and for some reason I was relieved to have him there—in spite of everything that happened.

"Are you here as my *friend*?" I stressed the word.

"Yes, if you'll have me back."

I stared at him for a moment before I

scooted over and patted the spot on the bed next to me.

"I'm sorry, Cami. I know I've been a pompous jerk, but I've had it in my head for a long time that you and I are a team, inseparable. When we started getting older my feelings for you started changing. I was attracted to you, and I wanted you to feel the same. When that wasn't happening, I thought I could become what you wanted. Then Hunter showed up, and I saw you looking at him the way I wanted you to look at me. It made me crazy. I couldn't stand to see you two together, because you belonged to me."

"I don't belong to anyone, Clay, except myself." I hoped he would understand.

"I get it, Cami. I'm just tired of not being part of your life anymore. It's been horrible." He looked so sad.

"The only reason I asked you to stay away was because of the whole wanting-to-be-my-boyfriend thing. What are we going to do about that? I know you can't automatically turn your feelings off."

He nodded and gave a big sigh. "Will you hear me out on this, and talk to me frankly about it?"

"I'll try." I was super nervous all of the sudden.

"I still want to be your boyfriend, Cami."

I opened my mouth to speak, but he quickly raised his hand and stopped me.

"Let me get this out first, okay?"

I took a deep breath. "All right."

"Knowing you might not ever feel the same way . . . well . . . it kind of kills me a little if I'm being honest." He chuckled wryly. "But being nothing to you is worse. I don't like being without you. I miss my friend."

"I've missed you too." That was the absolute truth.

"So I propose a compromise. Let's go back to being great friends, but I'd like you to not completely shut out the idea of our relationship changing, either. I know I sprung it on you too quickly, but I like the new me, and I want you to like it too."

"Clay." I shook my head. "I don't want to give you any kind of false hope. Even if it were possible to change the way I feel about you, my heart isn't free." I looked at him apologetically. "I have very strong feelings for Hunter."

"Hunter?" He seemed completely confused. "I figured you two were over after that picture."

"No. I'm taking a little break to evaluate some things, but I really want to be with him. He has issues with drugs and stuff. I was mistaken in thinking he'd quit pursuing that lifestyle. It's obviously a big deal for him. I need to sort out what's more important to me and whether or not I can overlook his bad habits. Plus, he's still pretty closed mouthed about things in his life. There's a lot more to know, but he's not willing to share them with me. It's hard to be with someone who keeps secrets."

Clay's face clouded over briefly.

I laughed. "What? Don't tell me you have secrets."

He shifted uncomfortably and smiled. "Who me?" He nudged me with his shoulder.

"Yes, you!" For one moment it seemed like old times.

"My secret is I'm crazy about you, but you know that already."

I closed my eyes and released a big breath. "I'm sorry I don't feel the same. I know you had big hopes."

"Just try, Cami. For me. Please." His expression was so full of sorrow. "I'd do anything for you."

I observed him carefully, taking in his transformation and really looking at him. He was really attractive. I'd always noticed cute things about him but never as something or someone I'd be interested in. I'd placed it over onto other girls, wondering why *they* didn't' like him. I was guilty of the same thing though, counting him off as a nerd, not someone with the emotion and desire to be loved.

I was a hypocrite.

"I won't write you off as a definite no." I gave in, hoping I wasn't leading him on. "That's the best I can give you right now. I really want to see if I can figure things out with Hunter."

"Fair enough." He grinned widely, and I could tell he was happy. "Now tell me what this jerk has been up to and if I need to go rearrange his face."

"Hey, that's mean!" I complained. "I just told you how much I liked him."

"Doesn't mean I have to," he grumbled.

I gave a nervous laugh. Why did life have to

be so complicated?

Hunter looked miserable, and it was killing me. He kept his distance, but it didn't stop him from watching me constantly, hunger always present in his eyes. Our classes together were uncomfortable to say the least. He didn't press me to talk to him, and I didn't try to.

I was doing my best to pretend he wasn't right there, but it wasn't working. I'd look up and catch him staring then glance away quickly. Other times he'd catch me watching with longing, and there was always this giant pregnant pause filling the space between us.

Evaluating my feelings for him was leading me in one firm direction. I was falling head over heels for him but didn't know if he felt the same way, or if he just missed the physical attraction, which was constantly pulsating and throbbing between us with a life all its own.

Trust was also a big issue. I placed a lot of value in it, and there were definitely things I didn't trust about him. The drugs scared me. I couldn't ever forget Jordan's face the night he died. I couldn't bear to lose Hunter that way, and it seemed there was a real risk of it happening.

There was also the fact he was clearly hiding something. He'd never tried to volunteer any information on whatever it was he kept so close to his vest. I knew he seemed to be in some kind of trouble, but I couldn't figure out what it was, and although I wanted to believe in him, it was hard.

That was really all this boiled down to. Could I be with a guy I didn't fully trust? It was a large leap.

"Hey! Cheer up! You look so sad," Clay said, placing his arm around me and squeezing during our Chemistry lab. I heard Hunter's chair shifting from the table behind us.

I could only imagine what his face looked like right now. The tension between him and Clay was almost palpable whenever they were in the same room together. Everyone could feel it, it didn't matter who you were.

"So are we still on for the Masquerade this year? It's always been our thing," Clay spoke in low tones, leaning in close.

"Um, yeah, sure. You did ask me to save all of them for you our freshman year, if I remember correctly." I smiled.

"I did. I wanted a guarantee to get at least one dance with you a year. I knew other guys would be snatching you up."

I snorted. "Yeah, they were really crawling out of the woodwork."

He chuckled. "Not my fault if they're all stupid."

I was a little disappointed. I'd actually hoped Hunter would ask me to the dance. But it was true, Clay had asked a long time ago, so I couldn't back out.

"Come over after school, and we can look for our costumes together."

He smiled widely, squeezing me again as he laughed a little.

There was a quiet cough I couldn't ignore behind me. I looked over my shoulder and found Hunter and Russ staring.

"Can I talk to you after school, Cami?" Hunter asked.

I glanced at Clay who was openly glaring.

"Um, I've actually made plans with Clay. Maybe later? He has to work at five so I'll be free after that." Clay made a snarling sound, and I bit my lip, trying desperately not to roll my eyes.

"Sounds good. I'll be there. Thanks." He didn't smile, but his posture seemed to relax a little.

Actually, I couldn't wait. It was funny how close we'd grown in such a short time. Suddenly imagining my life without him seemed unbearable. I wanted to do whatever we needed to fix things. Hopefully he would feel the same way.

Facing forward again, my eye caught Gabrielle sitting in the middle of the room. She was turned in her seat, looking at me, a secretive grin plastered on her face. She got up and stalked toward me, then slipped a note across the table.

I stared at it, not wanting to touch it and was saved by Clay grabbing it. He opened it and read, his face coloring before he quickly folded it back up.

"What does it say?" I asked, curiosity getting the better of me.

"You don't want to know."

I reached over and took it, unfolding it to

reveal a note written in lipstick.

"Hunter Wilder is the best I've ever had."

My face flushed with anger. I crumpled the note in my hand, grabbed my books and headed for the door, dropping the paper in front of Hunter on my way past.

"Miss Wimberley! Sit down please," the teacher called.

I left and didn't look back.

HUNTER♥

CHAPTER TWENTY-THREE
Hunter-

I quickly scanned the paper, cursing under my breath before crumpling it up myself. I shot Gabrielle a glare before I ran out the door after Cami.

"Mr. Wilder!" the teacher shouted. "You're going to get detention!"

I didn't care. I hurried down the hall and saw Cami rounding the corner ahead of me. I ran to catch up with her.

"Cami, wait up."

"Go away."

"It's not true. I swear to you it's not true. She's screwing around with you, and it's working. Don't let her do this." I was desperate for her to believe me.

She stopped, tears running down her face. I was getting really tired of seeing her so sad all the time.

"Come on." I grabbed her by the hand and

pulled her after me. She didn't ask where we were going. We walked in silence to my car, and she climbed in when I held the passenger door open.

I went around to the other side and joined her.

"We really need to discuss things. I know everything has been messed up, and I know it's my fault, but I can't take seeing you cry anymore. I want you to be happy. Talk to me please, and let's see if we can work this out somehow." I stared while she played with the edge of her notebook.

She finally looked up. "I want to believe you, Hunter, I really do, but you keep so many secrets from me. I know there is stuff going on you don't want to talk about, and I've tried to respect that, but when you combine it with doing drugs and partying I have a hard time trusting you. I was under the impression you were trying to get away from that type of thing. Apparently I was mistaken. Then this very suggestive picture of you surfaces, showing you with someone else. She says she was with you, and the picture seems to support her, but you say nothing happened. It makes me realize—despite how I feel—I don't really know you. Other than making some nice memories of our own, and being extremely attracted to each other physically, you're practically a mystery." She gave a deep sigh as if this let a huge weight off her chest and laid her head against the seat.

I tapped my fingers against the steering wheel nervously, knowing I needed to tread carefully. I wanted to tell her everything, but I couldn't—both for her safety and mine. Things were so royally messed up. I should've never gotten involved with her. I knew this, but I couldn't seem to make myself walk away.

"As far as Gabby goes, I can only tell you nothing happened. Honestly, the play by play went something like this—I was stoned and zoning out. I'd drifted off to sleep and was kind of dreaming or thinking of you subconsciously, and I could even feel you next to me—your hand sliding down my body. I jerked awake, and she was there. I shoved her away and told her I was with you. She said she didn't see you around anywhere, and climbed on top of me, sliding my shirt up. I shoved her off hard enough she fell on the floor. She was mad at me, said I hurt her. Derek called her over, and she started making out with him. That's when I left the party. I worried I was too blitzed to drive so I pulled over at the theater. I considered going in to watch a movie and let things get out of my system a little, but I was really tired—and I was afraid to see the disappointment in your eyes—so I fell asleep in the car. That's it. You know everything. Please tell me you forgive me and we can move past this. I never meant to hurt you."

I waited, every nerve tense, wondering what she would say.

"Are you going to do drugs again?" She wouldn't look at me.

"I'd love to tell you I'll quit right now and walk away, but it's not that easy." I was so frustrated. There was no way I could make her understand why I used, or why they were so important to me.

"It *is* that easy. You just *do* it, Hunter, and let those of us who care for you, help you through it."

I closed my eyes, knowing she couldn't possibly understand what it meant to suffer through an addiction since she'd never been there. But I also didn't miss the hidden message in her words. "Do you care for me, Cami?" I held my breath, turning to look at her. "Is that what you're saying?"

She sighed, holding my gaze. "Yes, and I want to do more, but you won't let me get close enough. All I can say is I care about what I do know, despite our issues."

I slipped my finger under her chin and leaned over, kissing her softly on the lips. Instantly, the burn she created inside me was back. I'd never experienced anything like it before in my life. I didn't care what I had to do to keep her—I had to find a way to have this girl.

"I want you," I whispered against her mouth. "I want everything I know about you now and all the possibilities of what I'll learn about you later. I've never felt this way about anyone. You mean more to me than you could ever understand."

She was crying again, and I continued to kiss her softly, staring into her honey colored eyes, wiping away her tears with my thumbs as I went along.

"This is happening really fast," she said quietly. "It scares me a little."

I kissed her mouth lightly again. "I know. It scares me too, but does happening fast make it any less real?"

"I guess not," she replied in between kisses.

I couldn't stop touching her. "Then the real question is where do you want to go from here?"

My lips traveled over her cheek, continuing my parade of endearments down to her neck.

"Hunter, stop. I can't think rationally when you're all over me like this." She tilted her head, giving me better access.

I smiled against her skin. "That's the whole point, isn't it? Admit it. You're enjoying this as much as I am."

"We aren't done talking, though. This is what always happens. We get distracted by all the physical stuff, and the things we really need to discuss get glossed over. While I love how you make me feel, I kind of hate that this always happens."

I stilled, my face nuzzled in the crook of her neck. I breathed in heavily, letting the light scent of her perfume overwhelm my senses for a moment. I really wished I could lose myself in this girl. I wanted to make her mine in every sense of the word, but I knew it just wasn't possible right now. I slowly pulled away.

"What do you want me to say?"

"Tell me about you. I want you to trust me with whatever your secrets are, and let me help you through them. I want you to let me know *all* of you." A hopeful look shone brightly in her eyes, and it was killing me—ripping me to shreds.

"Cami . . . ," I stroked her beautiful mouth. "I'd love nothing more than to pour out my soul to you and share what you're asking, but I can't right now. I still need some time."

Her expression fell, and it was like a knife straight to my heart. I hated hurting her. I was so tempted to throw caution to the wind and tell her, but even then I was still afraid I would lose her once she heard what I had to say. Anything I did would betray her. I was caught in a web of lies and deceit, and there was no easy way out of it.

She looked down and her lip trembled. "Okay then. When you're willing to trust me, I'll be willing to give things a try. You know where to find me." She picked up her books and reached for the door handle.

"Cami, don't please," I begged her.

"This is your choice, Hunter. You know what you need to do to change things." She got out of the car.

I slumped into my seat as I watched her walk toward the school. My heart felt like it was being sent through a meat grinder. Running my hands through my hair, I sighed heavily. I couldn't blame her, really. It was totally unfair of me to ask her to go blindly into a relationship when she didn't understand what she was getting into. I was being selfish, but I wasn't sure what else to do.

I hoped she didn't think I was just going to walk away from her because of her ultimatum, though. I couldn't tell her things, but there was no way in hell I was going to leave her alone with Clay so he could move in for the kill. I didn't think she realized yet exactly how manipulative her precious bestie actually was, but I'd been watching him closely and it hadn't surprise me at all that he'd managed to worm his way back into her good graces. I knew he still wanted her too—whenever we were around each other, the tension between us was bad.

I dug my cell phone out of my pocket and speed dialed Chris. He answered on the second ring.

"Are you okay?" his voice was full of concern.

"Yeah, I'm fine. Can you call the office and excuse me for the rest of the day? I need a break."

"Sure thing. I'll tell them you aren't feeling well."

"Perfect. Thanks, man."

"No problem."

I ended the call, tossed my phone in the cup holder and headed for the condo.

CAMI ♥

CHAPTER TWENTY-FOUR
Cami-

Clay and I were still huddled together on the couch searching through costumes on my computer for the upcoming Masquerade when the doorbell rang.

"I wonder who that is?" I said, glancing toward the hallway.

"I'll get it," he replied, jumping up and heading from the room. I listened for a second and could hear him talking to someone.

"Who is it?" I called.

"No one," he answered back.

"Apparently I'm no one now," Hunter said with a grumble as he entered the room, coming to sit on the other side of the couch.

Clay stood in the entryway frowning at Hunter. "I didn't invite him in, Cami."

"No, he didn't," Hunter said, glaring. "But it didn't stop me from getting in here anyway, did it?" He glanced at me before picking up the remote and turning on the television.

I had no idea what was going on. "Did you need something, Hunter?"

"No." He waved a noncommittal hand in the direction of Clay. "You two continue with whatever you were doing. I'll just watch something."

"You don't have a T.V. at your own house?" Clay asked, coming to sit between us. He wasn't happy at all.

"I have three actually," Hunter replied.

"And you can't watch them there because . . ." Clay prompted.

"Because Cami isn't there."

Silence. Neither of us knew what to say, but I couldn't help the little thrill that went through me. I was surprised to see him. I figured he would walk the other way after our talk today, but it looked like that wasn't going to be the case.

"Clay, what do you think about this one?" I asked, trying to redirect his attention. He was looking at Hunter like he hoped he would spontaneously combust.

He glanced at the screen. "King Triton and a mermaid?"

"Yeah. It's kind of cool."

"Clay doesn't have the abs to pull that off," Hunter spoke, peering over. "You on the other hand would look fabulous as a mermaid."

I could feel Clay's temperature starting to boil. "I suppose you think you're the perfect one to pull off this costume?" he accused.

Hunter snorted. "I wouldn't be caught dead

dressed up like that, but yeah, my abs would work." He was staring at me with a smoldering look, and suddenly it felt hot. It should be wrong for anyone to carry so much power in one expression.

I swallowed. "Okay, so no mer-people. How about some traditional costumes? The fancy ball gown, tuxedo, and matching masks?"

"Let's look," Clay said successfully redirected again. "I like that idea."

We combed through several images before coming across a beautiful gold dress and mask, with an accompanying black tuxedo, gold vest, tie with accents, and matching black mask.

"I love the mask on this costume, Clay. It reminds me of the Phantom in *Point of No Return*. It's sexy."

Hunter shifted uncomfortably.

"Then that's the one. I know how much you love that musical. I'm more than happy to be your Phantom-come-to-life for the night. Maybe I'll get you to sing for me too."

I laughed nervously. Boy, he was laying it on thick. "Sounds like fun."

"Cami and I watched that movie the other night on my bed," Hunter piped up. "Well, I should say we tried to watch it. We kept getting . . . distracted."

Clay's face colored a shade I'd never seen before.

"Okay, then! Who wants a snack?" I snapped my laptop shut and grabbed Clay's hand, dragging him into the kitchen, hoping to avoid an explosion.

"On his bed?" Clay retorted, frowning.

"Just drop it, okay? It's none of your business."

"Has he tried anything with you?"

I leaned against the counter. "No, Clay. He hasn't done anything I haven't wanted him to do."

"Oh, that makes me feel a whole lot better," he said facetiously, rolling his eyes. "Did you have sex with him?"

"No, and it's none of your business."

"It is my business. You're my best friend, and I need to know if something is going on." His fists were clenched tightly at his side.

"You're misunderstanding the role of best friend, I think. You only need to know what I deem necessary to tell you. This is not one of those things, so quit asking." I was starting to get angry.

"Problems?" Hunter asked, leaning casually in the doorway.

"Yes!" Clay and I both shouted.

"Anything I can do to help?"

"No, I think you've helped enough already. Thanks." I took a glass from the cupboard and got a drink of water, not asking either of them if they wanted one. I didn't care if I was being rude.

Hunter pulled out his phone and glanced at it. "Four-thirty, Bradley. Looks like it's time for you to head off to work if you want to make it by five."

"I'm highly capable of keeping track of the time by myself, thank you."

Hunter shrugged. "Okay. Just trying to help." He walked through the kitchen, outside to the back patio, and stood by the pool with his hands in his pockets.

"What is his deal?" Clay asked incredulously.

I shook my head. "I'm not sure. I'm as surprised to see him here as you are. I kind of gave him an ultimatum today. Maybe he's here to talk about it. I don't know yet."

"I don't want to leave you here with him." He folded his arms over his chest.

"You need to go to work. I'll be fine."

"I can call in sick. I've never done it before. Jon would believe me."

"Clay. Go to work. That's an order. I'll be fine."

"Come with me. You can hangout, maybe catch a movie or something."

I laughed. "I'll be fine. Now go. I need to talk to him. I'll email you a link to the page so you can order your tux later."

He looked so disappointed. "Okay. Don't let him bully you. If you need help, just call me."

"All right," I replied, mostly to get him to leave.

I followed him into the living room and watched as he gathered his things.

"I'll text you later," he said, giving me a hug.

"Sounds good. Bye." I waited until I heard the door close behind him before I turned around, and found Hunter leaning against the wall watching me.

"You should probably know I don't like him."

"Really? Wow. I would've never guessed!

Thanks for telling me." I went over and plopped on the couch.

"I mean it. He gives me the creeps. I don't like it when he's around you. Something about him is off."

"Hunter, he's been my best friend for my whole life. You and I, we've been—whatever we are—for a very short time, even if it doesn't seem that way. You don't get to say who's my friend and who's not."

He came and sat next to me. "I'm not telling you who to be friends with. I'm just saying he legitimately gives me concern. He's very possessive of you."

"And you aren't?"

"I am, but only because I care about you, and I'm concerned."

"Clay loves me and is concerned about me too. He's convinced you're going to hurt me, and he wants to put a stop to it."

"No, he's convinced I'm going to steal you from him, and *that's* what he's trying to put a stop to. He honestly believes he still has a chance with you. I, on the other hand, actually do have a chance. There's a difference."

"Is that so? Have you come to spill your secrets to me so we can move on with this relationship then?" I crossed my arms and bit my lip as I looked at him pointedly.

His face clouded over, and it reminded me of brewing storm clouds. "No, I haven't."

I sighed in exasperation. "Then why are you here? I thought I made myself pretty clear on things."

"Because I like being with you, and regardless of what you said, I still think we are great together—secrets or not. If you don't want me as a boyfriend, that's fine, but I'm not leaving. You can consider *me* your new best friend."

I snorted. "You're kidding, right?"

"Not even a little."

"Why?"

"I need to know you're okay."

He was maddening.

"Why wouldn't I be okay?"

"I thought I just explained all that." He gestured toward the door. "Hello . . . psychotic guy."

"Clay is *not* psychotic. Confused at times, maybe, but not psychotic."

"That's your opinion."

"And it's the right opinion."

"Guess we'll have to agree to disagree."

"I guess so." I was feeling extremely frustrated. I wanted to hit Hunter and then kiss it better. He was driving me insane.

He stared at the television again. When had things become so awkward with us? Wasn't it this time last week we were making out with each other in this very spot?

"Did you get your class work done, or do you have homework you want to do together?" I was grasping for straws to fill the silence.

"No, I'm good. I finished in class."

"So what do you want to do?"

He stared at me pointedly, his gaze wandering slowly over me and back up again.

My breathing increased as if he were actually touching me.

"Do you really have to ask? I thought you already knew exactly what I like to do with you."

I swallowed thickly. "I think I need another drink. I'm so thirsty today."

I went into the kitchen, knowing I was running away, but he was driving my senses crazy. I wanted to forget everything I'd said and make out. I wanted him to share his secrets and be honest with me, yes, but I also just wanted to be with him. This was going to be hard.

Filling my glass, I stood at the sink for a minute, staring out the window into the backyard. I didn't know he'd entered the room until I felt his hands slip along my sides, leaning against the edge of the counter, trapping me there.

"What are you thinking about?" he asked, nuzzling his face against my hair.

My racing pulse and how much I want you to kiss me, I thought with a sigh and closed my eyes for a moment to enjoy him being there. His breath filtered through my hair, sending goose bumps trailing over my skin.

I set my water down and faced him. He was so close, his lips a hairsbreadth away, his eyes, like melted chocolate and caramel, staring with obvious desire. He didn't close the distance though, staying a small fraction away. I held my ground, every nerve in my body screaming in protest, knowing the pleasure that waited if I gave in. I wanted to give in.

He continued to stare, his glance traveling

between my eyes and my mouth, waiting for me to make a move. "Kiss me, Cami." His voice was low and seductive. "You know you want to."

I licked my lips, and his eyes instantly diverted to that spot. "You're right, I do want to," I replied in a quiet voice, wondering if I might melt right here, trapped in the circle of his arms, yet hardly being touched.

"Then do it."

"I can't, Hunter. You know how I feel."

There was hurt in his eyes. "Yes, I do. I wish there was some way you could trust me anyway—some way for you to know I wouldn't ever willingly do anything to hurt you." He didn't move, his gaze continuing to rove over my face as if searching for an answer.

"I want to believe that," I replied honestly. "It's just hard to trust blindly after everything that's happened recently."

"Let me make it up to you." His mouth was so close to mine I could almost feel it brushing against me as he spoke.

"Hunter," I licked my lips again, knowing I was faltering. "I . . . I . . . "

"Cami, we're home," my mom's voice echoed through the house.

"They're early," I whispered in dismay, knowing our moment was interrupted. "We're in the kitchen," I called out louder.

Hunter sighed heavily. "We aren't even close to finished with this discussion." He picked up my glass of water and slipped it into my hand before moving to lean against the counter next to me.

I gulped the water down, trying desperately to calm the fire he'd ignited. How could he stand there so casually, as if nothing had happened? I looked up at him and he winked.

"Later," he promised, and little butterflies of anticipation took flight in my stomach.

HUNTER♥

CHAPTER TWENTY-FIVE
Hunter-

"Morning, Goody. How are you today?" I asked, leaning against the locker next to hers with what I hoped was my sexiest grin.

"Morning," she replied brusquely, slamming her locker and stepping around me. She continued on down the hall.

Crap. Something was wrong.

"Hey, where you off to in such a hurry?" I moved quickly to keep pace with her.

"It's called class, Hunter. I do the same thing every day. Maybe you've noticed."

I searched for a reason she'd be upset with me.

"What's wrong, Cami?"

She shot me a glare. "As if you don't know."

"I wouldn't ask if I knew. Tell me what's wrong."

She stopped dead in her tracks. "Don't play dumb with me. I saw you."

"Saw me?" A little dread crept into my voice. I knew what she was talking about.

"Yes, unless you let someone else borrow your car to sit parked down the street from my house all night. Why are you watching me?"

I scrambled for something to tell her, anything that might make sense.

"Oh. You saw my car." I laughed trying to buy some time. "Um . . . I got a flat after I left yesterday. I called my uncle to come get me, but we had to take the tire in and have it fixed. We just left it there until early this morning when he had to leave." I was lying to her . . . again. I couldn't tell her what I'd really been doing on her street. She'd never believe me anyway.

She visibly relaxed. "Why didn't you come and ask my dad for help?"

"In case you haven't noticed, I'm not very high on the list of people your dad admires right now. Having him stay up to help me get a tire repaired wasn't about to endear me to him any further. Besides, Chris was more than willing to help me." I smiled, trying to soften things. "Can I carry your books?"

"I've got her books," Clay said, sweeping up beside me and taking them before she could respond. "We have band together, remember? Come on, Cami."

He linked arms with her and practically dragged her down the hall. She shot me an apologetic glance, but continued on her way.

I headed toward class, my mood instantly boiling at the sight of Clay. I was tired of having this kid always interfere, and after what I'd seen last night, I *knew* he wasn't good for Cami. I'd been right to call him a psycho, but there was no way I could call him out right now. It would only draw more attention to me—something I couldn't have happen. I'd give anything to go a round or two with him, just to show him what was what. That sparked another thought in my head. If I couldn't beat the crap out of him, maybe it was time to start messing with him instead.

I purposely waited as long as I could so I'd be the last guy into the weight room. Cami had choir class second period, but Clay had this class with me. Casually, I walked in and surveyed the area.

He was against the farthest wall, doing the bench press. I moved to the bench alongside him, pausing and obviously checking out how heavy he'd weighted his bar before adding ten pounds more to my own. He glared at me as I started easily lifting. I pretended not to notice, continuing my workout. He finished one set before getting up to add more weights, so we were equal.

I couldn't help the internal smile. We were *so* going to play this game, and I was going to win. I went through my rotation, got up, added more weight, and started again. Soon after, Clay was readjusting to match me. I had to admit, while I knew he'd been working out, I didn't think he would do so well. Kudos to him, but I was getting tired of this.

I stood and loaded the bar to my max weight, watching his eyes grow bigger and a little desperate looking. There was no way he'd come even close, and he knew it. I finished lifting and moved on to a new station. Clay didn't make any attempt to best me for the rest of the period. Hopefully, he'd get the underlying, subliminal message as well.

I groaned and rolled my eyes, wanting to bang my head aimlessly against the cafeteria table.

"Hey, Hunter," Gabrielle said, sliding into the empty seat beside me.

Could this day get any worse? I glanced at Cami, who was shooting daggers at me. I looked over at Russ. He gave me a confused shrug; there wasn't going to be any help from that corner. Clay on the other hand was looking quite pleased with the whole situation, and I wanted to mash his face in. For once I wished the school had an open campus. Situations precisely like this one would be so much easier to avoid.

"Can I help you?" I asked, trying my best to sound polite through gritted teeth.

"No. I'm fine. I just thought we could hang out together again." She smiled and took a sip of her drink.

"Again?" I was so confused.

"Well, I had fun with you at the party, so I thought we could do something together again."

It took all the control I had not to let my jaw drop. "Are you really this delusional, or actually insane?" I was done being nice to this girl. She had a serious problem with accepting "no" for an answer.

"What do you mean?" She blinked, her eyes wide and innocent.

"I mean that I keep beating you off, and you just don't seem to get it." I was starting to feel a little angry. "Let me make it plain and simple for you. Gabby, I don't want anything to do with you. Give it up already."

She studied the drink in her hand. "There's another party this weekend. I know where you can score some good stuff. You want to go with me?"

I stared at her, my mind going completely blank for a moment. "Did you hear anything I just said?" Everyone at the table had quit eating and was watching the exchange with avid interest.

She nodded. "Yes, but I think if you'll just give me a chance, you'll really like what I have to offer."

I sighed. "And what is that exactly?"

"All the things you aren't getting from her." She gestured toward Cami. "Guys have needs . . ." She let her sentence dwindle off, as Cami rose, her expression mottled.

"Leave now, Gabby," Cami spoke up. "You aren't welcome here. And stay away from Hunter. He's made it plain he's not interested."

Gabrielle shrugged. "You know where to find me if you change your mind." She stood and walked away, trailing her finger across my back as she went.

"What the hell just happened?" I said,

looking at the others.

Russ shook his head and laughed. "She wants you bad, dude."

"Why?" I replied in exasperation, watching Cami sit back down dejectedly. "I've never shown any interest in her whatsoever."

"She's never had a guy tell her no before. I think it's damaging her ego."

"I think you should go for her," Clay piped up, snidely. "You two were made for each other."

Cami elbowed him hard in the ribs, clearly angry. "Stop it."

"No, let him talk, Cami." I looked at Clay. "Since you seem to know Gabby so well, perhaps you can tell me how you arrived at that conclusion. Maybe you've been banging her too?"

Cami choked on her food, and I absently reached over to pat her on the back while staring pointedly at Clay. His face reddened, and he glared at me. I knew he hated me, but I didn't care. I also knew what else he'd been up to—the sick prick.

"Even if I was, it wouldn't be any of your business," he spat out, not denying it. I knew without a doubt he'd done precisely that. Man, he had Cami snowed.

"Exactly," I replied angrily. "So stay the hell out of mine. Quit professing to know what kind of guy I am. You don't know crap."

"I think lunch is over for me," Cami threw her sandwich back into her lunch bag. "I can't stomach anymore of this." She got up from the table and left the room, depositing her bag in the garbage on the way out.

"Quit trying to push the school hooker on me, especially one that's willing to sleep with you." I scowled at Clay. "And quit trying to get Cami to hate me. It doesn't matter what you do or say, I won't leave her, and I especially won't leave her with you."

"She doesn't belong with you," he growled.

"Then that's for *her* to decide." I glanced at Russ. "Come on, man. Let's get out of here."

"You barely even know her," Clay called after me.

"I know her well enough." I was so tired of messing with this dang kid. He had extreme issues. I wished I could make Cami see that.

"She'll always be mine."

He was baiting me.

"I seriously doubt it, but feel free to keep dreaming."

We went through the cafeteria doors into the adjoining hallway.

"Dude, that guy is friggin' nuts," Russ said with a nervous laugh. "Are you sure Cami is worth it?"

"She's worth it."

"You're really into her—like for keeps?" he asked.

"Yes." I scanned the hallway, looking but not seeing her anywhere. I continued around the corner in time to catch her disappearing into the bathroom.

"I'll wait here," Russ said wisely, knowing I would go in after her.

"Thanks, man." I hurried and pushed the door open. She was leaning against the wall with her arms folded. A quick glance at the stalls showed me we were alone.

"One of these days you're gonna walk in on something you'll wish you'd never seen." She glowered. "There's a reason there's a sign that says Girls outside the door. It's meant to keep boys from coming in so we can see to our private needs, you know."

I gave her a lopsided grin and leaned against the wall next to her. "You don't look like you're taking care of anything . . . private. Besides, I need to know you're okay."

"I *am* taking care of something. I'm trying to get away from you and Clay and the testosterone battle going on out there."

I sighed. "I'm sorry. I don't mean for you to feel caught in the middle. The guy just rubs me wrong." I wanted to tell her what I knew, but I didn't know how.

"Yeah? Well, I hate feeling like I'm being forced to choose between the two of you all the time. It's making my life very uncomfortable." She looked angry.

"Oh. I guess I didn't realize there was actually a choice. I wasn't aware you were truly considering him."

She raked a hand through her hair and stood in front of the mirrors, staring at herself. "I don't mean that kind of choice. I'm saying I hate having to choose between my best friend and my boyfriend."

"Your best friend wants to be your boyfriend.

You realize that, don't you?" His little display outside her bedroom window the other night had left no doubt about that. He was beginning to cross the lines of depravity.

She sighed. "Yes, unfortunately."

I moved around behind her, brushing my hands over her shoulders. "Have you stopped to consider that maybe your boyfriend wants to be your best friend too? The jealousy goes both ways, I'm afraid." She needed me to stay close to her, whether she knew it or not.

She stared at me through the reflection in the glass. "Why do things have to be so complicated?"

"Because you're making them that way. The answer is very easy."

"How so?" She looked truly curious.

"Quit thinking about what Clay and I might want or need and search inside yourself. What do you want, Cami? That's all that matters. What will make you happy?"

When she didn't answer, I let my hands drift down, slipping them around her waist. I pulled her back against me and nuzzled my face in her thick hair, placing small kisses there while the two of us stared at the intimate scene in the mirror.

"Tell me what you want," I whispered against her.

She closed her eyes. "I want you to be honest."

I stiffened, pausing as she opened her eyes to lock gazes. "I want that too. I really do."

"Then what are you afraid of?" she asked,

turning to face me.

I shook my head and stepped away. "It's not the right time."

She moved, closing the distance between us again. "What are you afraid of, Hunter?"

I swallowed, watching as she slid her hands up my chest. "I'm afraid I'll lose you."

She stared for a moment before dropping them back to her sides. "I'm afraid of that too." She shifted away.

"Cami, I'd tell you the truth right now if I could." My hands were tied. I felt completely helpless.

"Then what's stopping you? Just do it!" she snapped. She was frustrated and so was I.

"I can't." I knew there was no way to make her understand. "You'll just have to trust me when I say that—for now—it's better this way."

"And why should I trust you?" She pointed her finger. "And don't tell me it's because you'd never do anything to hurt me. You've already proven you can."

I sighed. "You're right, I suck." I meant it. "It's true I've hurt you, but the fact of the matter was I didn't *want* to. There's a big difference."

She made a grunting sound.

"Let's table this discussion, shall we? Go out with me tonight. We'll talk more then."

"I can't, I'm working at the theater."

"Tomorrow then?" I asked, hopefully. Seeing her like this was tearing me up inside. Maybe by then I could come up with something that would appease her.

"I don't know. I'll think about it. Can you please give me some time alone right now?"

I stared at her for several long moments before I nodded and left the restroom.

CAMI ♥

CHAPTER TWENTY-SIX
Cami-

I lifted my punch card and slipped it into the time clock, glancing briefly at the schedule on the wall beside it. I was working with Clay tonight it appeared. I was mildly surprised since we hadn't worked together in a while. There was also the word, "trainee," penciled in by my name. That confused me since I wasn't new.

Jon walked into the breakroom carrying a bunch of cleaning supplies to the closet.

"There's the word trainee written by my name," I said casually. "What's that for?"

"Oh, sorry. I forgot to mention you're helping the new guy tonight." He deposited the items he was holding onto their appropriate shelves.

"So you did hire someone finally. What's his name?"

Jon looked puzzled. "It's your friend you told me about, Hunter Wilder. I figured he would've told you. He came in and interviewed this afternoon with Jen. She seemed quite taken with him."

I turned away so he wouldn't see me roll my eyes as I deposited my purse into my employee locker. I bet she was impressed. Hunter probably laid the charm on so thick she didn't stand a chance.

I leaned my head against the locker and sighed heavily. Hunter and Clay together at my job. This was going to be a long night.

"Are you okay, Cami?" Jon asked, concerned.

Straightening up, I turned, giving him a bright smile. "I am, thanks. Just a long day at school today. I'll be fine. Where do you want me to train Hunter tonight?"

"I'm going to start him off with theater care. I restocked all the cleaning supplies for you two as well. I'll be leaving in a bit, but Jen will be in the office if you need anything."

"Okay. Thanks."

Jon gave me a smile and left.

This was good. Only two people usually worked theater care at a time. That meant Clay would be in the snack bar with Mandy or Shane or in the ticket window. Hopefully, I could keep Hunter and him apart for most of the night.

Of course, this also meant the two of us would be spending a lot of time together without anyone else around. That made my pulse race a little, but I was bound and determined to keep him at a professional distance.

"Hey, Cami," Clay's voice interrupted my

thoughts, and startled, I jumped.

He gazed over me and gave a lazy half smile of appreciation. "Did I catch you by surprise?"

"Yeah. I didn't hear the door open." I fidgeted with the hem of my dark-blue uniform shirt with the red theater logo embroidered in the upper left corner.

Clay looked at my hands curiously, before glancing back to my face. "Are you all right? You seem nervous."

I nodded. "I'm fine. I need to tell you something, though."

His eyes narrowed suspiciously. "What?"

"I'm training a new employee tonight."

He waited for me to give him more information, but I didn't continue. "Who?"

"Apparently Hunter got a job here this afternoon."

Clay didn't say a word, but his jaw clenched. He walked over to his locker, opened it, pulled out his name badge, and began fastening it to his shirt.

"Where's he starting?" he finally asked.

"In theater care. Where are you working?"

"Snack bar," he replied tersely.

"Please try to be civil," I begged him. "This is work. We need to be professional."

He snorted. "Whatever, Cami." He shot me a wounded look. "I can imagine he'll love his new job. He's gonna get paid to follow you around through dark rooms. He's probably thrilled."

"Clay, please."

"He always manages to find ways to infiltrate your life even more, doesn't he?"

I remained silent, and he made his way to the door, flinging it open roughly only to nearly collide with Hunter on his way in.

I groaned audibly.

Clay gave him a stormy glance, but Hunter only looked mildly amused as he slid past him and came over.

"So, I was told to report to you—that you were my trainer." He winked, and I couldn't help staring. I hadn't seen these ugly polo shirts look this good on anyone before. Jon should've started him at the ticket window. He'd have packed the house.

"Why didn't you tell me you got the job?" I asked.

Clay gave a huff and left the room.

Hunter shrugged. "I didn't know until a couple of hours ago. I thought I'd surprise you."

"Well, you did." I glanced at the door Clay had left through.

Hunter followed my line of sight. "Look, Cami. I didn't think he'd be working tonight since you said you didn't get scheduled together much anymore. I swear I'll be on my best behavior. I'm not trying to rock the boat."

"So you're saying you didn't try to get this job because I work here?"

"No, I'm saying I only took this job because you work here. I don't really need the money, but I like being with you, and I hate it when you're at work." He slid a glance over my form before returning to my eyes. "That is when I usually get into trouble you know—when you're not around."

This was something I hadn't thought of. If he was here working, he wasn't out partying with a bunch of losers. Suddenly, things seemed a little brighter.

"Are you trying to make amends?"

"I am." He stepped closer. "I'll do anything I can to prove you can trust me."

There were so many questions I wanted to ask, but now was not the time.

"See that utility cart over there? Grab it. We're going to load it up with our supplies for the night."

He grinned and winked. "Yes, ma'am."

I couldn't help the little flutter in my chest. I wasn't going to lie to myself—I'd never looked forward to a shift as much as this one.

"I don't know if anyone told you, but part of our employee benefits is that we can have all the free fountain soda we want. We can also have one small bag of popcorn per shift. Anything else you want during your break you have to pay for."

"Sounds good."

I opened the closet Jon had just been in. "Most of our cleaning supplies are in here. Occasionally, we may run out of stuff. Our backup supplies are in a storage room in the attic. I'll give you a tour of everything after we are done loading the cart." I lifted a dustpan that was hooked to a long-handled broom. "Most of the time we'll be walking around with these, cleaning up trash and popcorn spills. We'll use them to clean the theaters after each show too. The shows are timed on rotations so we can easily move from one to another. The bathrooms have to be checked every hour and then cleaned again at closing so they are ready for the next day."

"Got it," Hunter said.

I pulled the supplies out one by one and showed him where they went on the cart. "We'll need to move quickly after each movie so the patrons can begin seating for the next showing. The rest of the time will be pretty easy, and if we have a fairly clean crowd, things can even get slow."

"I don't have a time card yet," Hunter interjected. "Jon told me to have you write my hours down for tonight and sign them off, and then he'll get me one made up." He handed me a piece of paper with a time written on it. "This was when I got here."

"Oh, okay." I folded it and slipped it into my pocket. "Let's go to the attic then." I smiled mischievously. "They say it's haunted, you know."

His interest was immediately piqued. "Do they now? And who is they?"

I giggled as I led him out the door and down the back hallway to a wide set of stairs. We slowly walked up them. "All the employees. I think Jon is the only one who isn't afraid of coming up here by himself. This building is old, and there used to be a private theater up here for the family that originally owned the place."

"What happened to it?" he asked curiously.

"Oh, it's still there, but it's locked up. Apparently, the owner back then came in and found his wife dead in one of the seats with a movie still playing. The story goes that he was so distraught, he locked the theater and never let anyone use it again. Many employees have claimed to hear strange noises or smells, and a few have said they've seen the ghostly apparition of the woman herself. They say she's wandering the theater looking for her husband."

"When did this supposedly happen?" Hunter asked, seeming very intrigued with the tale.

"In the nineteen fifties, I'm told. Someone came in later and did the renovations, adding all the extra theaters to it. It used to be one big one downstairs and this smaller one upstairs."

"Hmm. So they use the smaller one for storage now?"

I shook my head. "No. The theater remains untouched. It's kept locked. Even Jon doesn't go in there. He says it's to remain undisturbed out of respect for the dead."

"So there must be some truth to the story."

"Yes. It was an ancestor of his."

"Interesting. You've never seen the inside of the theater then?"

"Only in pictures. I'll show you the album they've kept of the building's history."

Hunter chuckled. "It is kind of spooky. Maybe they should call in the ghost hunters."

"Laugh all you want now," I said, grinning. "It's not so funny when you actually experience something."

"You've seen the ghost?" His eyebrows rose in speculation.

"No, but I've heard the strange noises and

smelled weird things on occasion. Things I couldn't explain away." Goosebumps prickled over my skin as we reached the top of the stairs, and without thinking, I reached over to slip my hand into his.

"Why, Ms. Wimberley, I do believe you are crossing the bounds of appropriate behavior with a coworker. I may need to fill out a sexual harassment report."

"You're right. I should let go."

He gripped my hand tighter. "I don't think so. You should let me hold it . . . for safety reasons of course." His eyes twinkled mischievously, and he winked before glancing down the hallway. "Let's do some exploring later, if we have time, and see if we can stir up the ghost."

I shook my head. "You have absolutely no respect for this story, do you?"

He shrugged as he glanced around. "I'm not trying to discount anything. I'm just being practical. Most things can be explained away if they're researched enough. Has anyone tried to find out what might be making those noises and smells? Do they ever check the theater to make sure it remains undisturbed?"

"I really have no idea. I'm sure there has been some mild investigating by management after the staff complained about it, but I couldn't tell you." I pointed to a set of old, carved, wooden doors depicting cherubs frolicking on them. "Those lead to the theater. The plain door at the far end of the hall is the storeroom."

"It's kind of like stepping back in time up

here," Hunter said as he observed the old red and gold wallpaper and cream moldings lining the walls, along with the art deco wall sconces. "Is this all original?"

"It is. Even the carpet."

He glanced down at the red carpet that was still plush where it ran down the edges in to the very worn center. "I bet it looked really nice back in the day."

"The album is on the shelf just inside the door. They're black and white, but you'll get the idea." I watched him while we walked and started giggling. "Are you sniffing the air?"

He grinned. "Yes, I am. You said people smelled weird things when they were up here. I'm just seeing if I can too."

"And?" I paused, crossing my arms as he moved toward the double doors that lead into the theater.

He turned to face me. "I got nothing." He sighed heavily, looking disappointed.

I laughed. "Most of us run through this hall, not wanting to be here by ourselves very long, and you're standing there *trying* to find something. Aren't you scared?"

He gave me a look of scorn. "Puh-leeze. Why would I be afraid when I have you to protect me?"

I snorted and started laughing hard. "You must be really hard pressed for protection these days."

He smiled widely and walked over, stroking his fingers over my lips. "I've missed hearing your laugh lately."

My smile slowly slid from my face. "Things have been a little stressed."

He nodded. "I know, and I'm sorry. If you really want me to back off, Cami, I will. Tell me now and I'll steer clear, but if that's what you want, you need to know I'll still be watching out for you."

This was my moment. If I really wanted him to leave he would go. He meant it.

"Hunter, I've never wanted you gone. I just wanted the truth."

"And I want to give it to you, really, I do. I'm just asking you to trust me for a little longer, okay?"

I could see the sincerity written in his eyes. I wanted to believe what he was telling me.

"You know what? I owe you an apology. In the very beginning I said I wanted to get to know you better, flaws and secrets aside. Then when things got crazy, I backed out on that. I'm sorry. Take all the time you need. I'll be here if and when you're ready to talk. Until then I'll do my best to trust you."

He relaxed visibly. "Thank you. You have no idea what this means. I'll try not to disappoint you."

HUNTER♥

CHAPTER TWENTY-SEVEN
Hunter-

"Kiss me," Cami said.

"I can't," I replied, trying to hold back a grin.

"Why not?" She looked worried.

"Fraternizing isn't allowed at work." I chuckled as I walked away, heading for the supply room door ahead of her. "I can't get fired—I just started." I twisted the doorknob and entered the darkness, feeling the wall as I searched for the light switch.

I was attacked from behind as Cami barreled into me, launching herself onto my back.

"What are you doing?" I asked, unable to help the chuckle that escaped me. "Now is not the time for piggyback rides. Where's the blasted light switch?"

She slid off me. "It's right here," she said, grabbing my hand and guiding it to the right spot. I flicked the button but nothing happened.

"Hmmm. That's weird." She tried clicking it

several times too with the same result. "Well, I guess we'll prop the door open with this popcorn bucket, and I'll try to show you some things using the light from the hall."

I slid the object she pointed to in front of it. She slipped her fingers in mine and proceeded down the aisle ahead of us, pointing out the general location of all kinds of items, from food to cleaning supplies. When we reached a darker corner behind one shelf, I pulled her into my arms and pressed my lips to her softly. "Sorry, I couldn't wait any longer. I thought you'd fight harder for one." I nudged her nose with mine and released her. "I'll let you get back to whatever you were showing me."

She launched herself at me again, kissing me hard, and I chuckled as I opened my mouth and she slipped her tongue inside. I liked her aggressiveness. I answered by pushing her against one of the shelves, and several boxes clattered to the floor. We both stopped to look.

"Oops," I said, not really caring we'd just made a mess.

She laughed and kissed me again.

My hands slid down to her hips, cupping her to me.

All of a sudden the lights came on, and we broke apart.

"We're back here!" Cami called out as she quickly bent to pick up the boxes that had fallen. "We couldn't get the light to work, and we knocked some stuff off in the dark!"

There was no reply, and I stepped around the corner to see who'd come in.

"There's no one here, Cami." I swallowed thickly and glanced at the fluorescent light fixtures. "Have they ever done this before?"

"Not to me they haven't." She paused, looking up, her eyes wide with hesitation.

I turned and helped her restack everything. When we were done, she grabbed my hand and squeezed it.

"Let's get out of here," she pleaded.

I nodded and she practically dragged me out the door and down the hallway. I couldn't help turning back to see if there was anything there. There wasn't, but the light had turned off again.

"Has anyone ever told you how sexy you are when you're sweeping up popcorn?" I leaned against the dimly lit wall inside the theater watching her as she finished the last row.

She snorted. "It's just the mood lighting in here. It makes everything look that way."

I glanced toward the door to make sure no one was coming in for the next showing. "I highly doubt it, but I can say it's putting me in the mood for something."

She lifted her head, a small smile playing at her lips. "Is that so? What?"

I laughed internally. She'd probably run screaming if she knew exactly what I wanted to do to her. I couldn't help the heated stare the thought caused. She swallowed thickly, and to my surprise returned a smoky stare of her own.

Grabbing her by the arm, I towed her up to the back row of the theater. "See those seats over in the far corner there?"

She nodded.

"If I could, I'd bring you to a movie I thought no one would attend, and we would sit right there—in that corner, in the dark—and make out like two crazy teenagers."

She laughed. "We *are* two crazy teenagers." She stared at me, her eyes sparkling. "Or we could go somewhere we knew no one would be and do the same thing."

The girl was going to set my temperature flaming. I wanted to press her against the wall right now and devour her. "Being alone with you is a dangerous, dangerous game. I think we've discovered that already on a few occasions."

She lifted one shoulder slightly. "Sometimes a girl likes a little danger."

I groaned. "How much of this shift is left?"

She took her phone from her pocket. "Two hours, but we haven't taken our break yet." She grinned.

"Do you have any closets—other than your haunted one—that are good for making out?"

"We could just go to your car. Did you park in back?"

"Yes." I smiled.

"A car with tinted windows in a nice dark alley. I wonder what we could do there?" She bit her lip, an innocent expression plastered on her face.

"Why are we still standing here talking about it?" I asked, my mouth watering in anticipation of kissing her.

"I don't know. Why are we?" She turned and headed down the steps, and I watched her every movement with appreciation as I followed.

We put our supplies in the breakroom and clocked out before exiting through the rear door. She grabbed my hand, pulling me toward my car.

"Hey, Goody?"

She stopped, sighing as she leaned against the wall. "Why do you still insist on calling me that?"

I grinned, looking down, as I pressed my body up against hers. "Because it serves to remind me of the kind of girl you are."

She frowned. "I'm not sure I like that. You really think I'm a goody-two-shoes?"

I shook my head. "No, I *need* you to be a goody-two-shoes."

"Why?" She looked so beautifully confused.

"Because I want to do unspeakable things to you."

Her eyes widened. "Like what?"

I laughed. "I believe I just said they were unspeakable." My gaze traveled over her features. "If you use your imagination, I'm sure you could figure it out."

She pondered this for a moment. "Well, if you can't *tell* me, how about you just *show* me instead?"

I let a strangled chuckle escape. "That would be worse than the telling, I'm afraid." It was all I could do to restrain myself. Thank heavens we were only on a twenty minute break, or I'd be in a lot of hot water.

Cami flattened her palms against my chest before running them over my shoulders and linking them behind my neck. She forcefully pulled me toward her—not that I was really resisting too hard.

"Let's make out like crazy teenagers, as you suggested earlier."

I eyed her carefully and moved in closer. "That might not be a good thing."

"Why not?" She looked perplexed, her tongue darting to lick her lips.

"Because we are now down to eighteen minutes in our twenty minute break. That's not a whole lot of time, you know."

"So quit wasting it." She popped up on her tiptoes and pressed her mouth to mine.

I gave in, slipping my arms around her waist and pulling her the rest of the way against me. The familiar contact exploded between us as we sank into one another, tangling together with our tongues, limbs, fingers, hair, and whatever else would mix together. I didn't want to stop, I just wanted to keep her here pressed against this wall beneath me—she felt so good. We kissed each other as if we were drowning, like it was the only time we were ever going to be allowed to do it—wrapped up in one another until we were both panting.

"Hold on a minute," I said, pulling away. "Let me catch my breath a little." I leaned my forehead against hers, and we both started laughing.

"I think every time I kiss you it's better than the last time. I don't know how that's possible since our first kiss was near perfection." She briefly pecked me again. "It's so intense."

"I agree—it's pretty incredible—but I'm thinking it might be wise not to be alone with you in dark places anymore." I lifted my hand to stroke my thumb over her beautiful cheek.

"Why?" She looked disappointed with my remark.

"Because the rest of my body isn't going to be satisfied with my mouth getting to have all the fun much longer."

She blushed, and I thought it was adorable. "Would that be such a bad thing?" she asked shyly.

Seventeen, that damned warning voice reminded in my head.

"Actually, yeah, seeing that I'm a legal adult and you're not yet." I placed a tender kiss against her lips to soften my words. "Not that I think of you as a child in any way, shape, or form."

She lifted her chin slightly. "I'll be eighteen soon."

I know, I thought. *I've got it marked on my calendar and have been counting down the days.* "True," I said aloud. "But unless you want to visit me in prison after your dad throws me in there, we better work on cooling things down a bit."

She brushed her lips against the side of my face before whispering in my ear. "What my dad doesn't know won't hurt him."

Dear Heaven above, have mercy on my soul. I'm going to end up in Hell.

I smiled, continuing to rub my thumb in little circles on her skin. "While I'd like nothing better,

I'd know, and never forgive myself."

She looked hurt and disappointed, and I thought it would crush me. "Were you so noble with the other girls you've been with?"

I sighed, hating that she felt like I was rejecting her. I tenderly kissed her forehead. "No, I wasn't, but none of them were you, Cami. You're special."

She looked like she doubted my words. I took her face in my hands.

"Listen to me carefully. I mean this. When and if the time is right for us to be together, I want it to be perfect for you. You deserve it all—the candlelight, roses, and romance. There's no need for you to rush. The right guy will always wait for you to truly be ready. He should honor you, worship you, and make it a moment for you to remember forever."

She leaned her head against my chest and sighed heavily. "Stop. You talk about that guy like it's not you. I want it to be you."

I should be so lucky. I pressed a kiss on the top of her head, holding her tightly in my embrace. "I want that too. More than you know." For the millionth time, I silently cursed everything going on in my life right now. I wished I were free to run away with her like she wanted. I knew I still had to tell her the truth, and I knew I might lose her when I did. If she wanted me to let go, then that's what I'd do. I would always put her needs first. Always.

She was strong, though. If that did happen, I was sure she'd survive to find love again. The thought of her wrapped up intimately in another man's embrace made every nerve in my body stand on edge. It made me want to beat something, over and over again until it ceased to exist.

I didn't have the right to claim her, but I wanted to more than I wanted anything in my life. I'd never been so desperate for another person. I just hoped she'd forgive me when the truth finally came to light.

"Please don't ever leave me," I whispered softly against her hair.

She looked up, her eyes wide and innocent. "I won't." She paused, looking hesitant. "I love you."

Her words spun through my head like flashing, colored lights, and I was sure there were fireworks exploding somewhere. *She loves me. Yes! No! Damn it!*

She was staring at me expectantly. I didn't need to search my heart for the answer. I'd known incredibly early on what my feelings were.

"I love you too—so very much." I wished I could bottle this moment so I could enjoy it again later. "I've known it for a while, actually."

She gave me a surprised smile. "You have? Why didn't you tell me?"

I shrugged and grinned. "I don't know. It seemed a little odd to walk up to you and say, "Hi, I'm Hunter, and I'm in love with you," I guess."

She shoved me playfully. "Oh, stop it. You're such a tease. Be serious!"

"I *am* being serious. You stepped out the

254254254254 LACEY WEATHERFORD

door that day and I was . . . I don't know . . .
lost. I've never believed in love at first sight
before, but then it happened. Something about
you called to me. I didn't know what to do about
it, so I tried to ignore it. We can see now how
well that turned out."

"You must have had girls falling at your feet
your whole life with that kind of sweet talk." She
rolled her eyes and crossed her arms, leaning
back against the wall.

"I've never talked like this to a girl in my life.
I've never been in love before." That was the
honest to goodness truth. It had blindsided me
when it happened and had taken me a while to
admit it.

"You haven't?" She seemed kind of
incredulous.

"No. Why . . . have you?" Instantly, jealously
reared it's ugly head inside me, and I was ready
to start beating people again.

"Well . . . there was this one guy," she let
her sentence trail off.

So help me if she said Clay's name I thought
my head might actually explode.

"Really?" I tried to say casually, though it
was difficult since I was grinding my teeth. I
forced my body to relax, mentally demanding
each individual muscle unclench itself. "Who was
he?"

I wished I could pour concrete in my ears. I
didn't want to hear her answer.

"His name was Gullible—or was it Naïve? I
forget." She laughed.

My stress melted away like butter, and I

shook my head, stepping forward to pin her back against the wall. "You've been a bad, bad, girl. You know that, don't you?"

She nodded. "Yes, a very bad girl," she agreed. "I think you may need to punish me . . . a lot."

I groaned as my mouth descended to hers. I was so going to jail.

HUNTER♥

CHAPTER TWENTY-EIGHT
Hunter-

"You out here, Hunter? Oh—hey, yeah, sorry to interrupt! I can catch you later—uh—as you were."

Russ's voice broke slowly into my hormone-driven mind, and it took me a second to pull away from Cami, both of us panting. I glanced in his direction before looking at her. If my hair resembled hers at all then everyone was going to know exactly what we'd been doing. I briefly wondered how many employees lost their job on the first day for fraternizing.

"Hey, man. Hold up!" I called before the back door closed all the way.

His hand came out to catch it, but the rest of him didn't reappear. "Are you sure it's safe?" he asked.

I chuckled at Cami who was frantically running her hands over herself as she tried to straighten her clothes and hair. I couldn't help my widening grin as I ran my fingers through my own, trying to fix it too. I should be shot for attacking her like this in a friggin' alleyway.

"Yeah, it's cool, bro. What's up?"

"Oh, nothing important." He gradually peeked his head around before deeming it safe enough to set out apparently. "I just stopped by to give you crap at work, and Clay told me you and Cami were on your break. He said you'd gone outside."

Good ole Clay. I felt my happy demeanor ice up a bit. "How nice of him to keep tabs on us," I replied. "Whatever would we do without him?" I glanced at Cami, feeling irritated.

She pushed past me. "We still have seven minutes left on our break. Let's go in and get drinks. Russ, we'll get you one on the house."

"Sweet!" Russ grinned and followed after her.

I tagged along behind them, figuring the best thing I could do right now was appear without being attached to her hip. I couldn't help the small smile, which continued to grace my mouth. She was gorgeous, and she was mine. My stubborn inner child wanted to walk right up to Clay and tell him, "Cami loves me." Heck with Clay, I wanted to tell everyone! It wasn't going to happen though, so I would have to content myself with casting secretive glances of admiration in her direction.

She went to Clay, who was working the counter, and ordered her soda. I stopped at Mandy's register. I'd never talked to her before, but she was in some of my classes at school.

She seemed nice enough. When Russ saw I wasn't going to follow Cami, he came over with me.

"What you having?" I asked.

"Dr. Pepper," he replied.

"Mandy, give us two Dr. Peppers, and why don't you let my buddy, Russ, here have my free popcorn. I'm feeling a little generous today."

Mandy smiled, pushing her plastic rimmed glasses farther up her nose. "You seem awfully happy tonight. Are you enjoying your new job?"

"I *am* happy." I grinned and looked over at Cami who was staring at me while she waited for her soda. I winked and she smiled. "As far as the job . . . well, I'm enjoying some of the extracurricular benefits that come with it."

Cami snorted, and Mandy gave us both a funny look.

"Check this out, Russ," I said, pulling him away to stare at some of the Coming Soon movie posters before she could ask me any more questions.

"What?" Russ asked as I glanced to where Clay looked like a volcano ready to explode.

"Nothing. That chick was getting nosy. If people knew Cami and I were kissing outside we both could get fired. While it doesn't hurt my feelings any, I don't want Cami to lose her job."

Russ chuckled quietly. "You better work a little harder at keeping it in your pants then, bro. You two looked like you were ready to go at it right there against the wall."

"Don't remind me." I groaned, trying to

shove the tempting images back down. "I don't know what it is. Whenever we're together things get . . ." I paused.

"Combustible?" Russ offered. "Heated? Enflamed? Frenzied? Intense? Explosive?"

I punched him in the shoulder. "Okay, okay. You get it. I see that. And what's with all the words? Remind me to call you if I'm ever in need of a thesaurus."

He grinned. "Just telling it like I see it. I think even inanimate objects were getting turned on by the intensity rolling off you two. There are cars in the parking lot that are probably pregnant now."

I laughed. "You're such a dork."

"But you love me." He batted his eyelashes, and I punched him again.

"I don't know . . . maybe," I replied.

"Okay, now that was just harsh."

"Can't let peeps think we're having a bromance over here in the corner now, can I? My girlfriend might start getting a little worried."

Russ snorted. "I highly doubt she has any concerns after the performance I witnessed."

"I certainly hope not. That would definitely destroy my reputation."

"Sorry, but it's already destroyed. You took care of that when you made it clear how hard you've fallen for Cami. People are talking about how the good girl caught the bad boy. In fact, the guys are taking bets."

"Bets on what?" I hadn't heard any of this.

"On who will corrupt who first. Will she turn you into a geek, or will you turn her into a smash queen?" He grinned. "I threw a little money into the pot myself. I'm anxious to see how it turns out."

"Really? Did you bet for or against me?" I folded my arms while I studied him. I wasn't sure how I felt about what he was saying.

"I'll never tell." He chuckled, and the two of us turned to look at Cami talking to Clay.

"What if neither happens?" I asked.

"What do you mean?" He arched his eyebrow.

"What if I don't become a geek, *and* I don't smash her."

He looked stupefied for a moment. "Hmmm, never thought of that. I guess I never considered it in the realm of possibilities, given your reputation with the ladies and all."

I grunted. "I'm beginning to think I know which way you bet."

He grinned and shrugged, not offering an answer.

"I like this girl, Russ. Don't tell her about the bet. I don't want it to bother her. Her feelings are important to me."

We both noticed Cami trying to gather our sodas and popcorn together. I hurried over to help, grabbing the popcorn.

"These two are the Dr. Peppers," she said, gesturing to the cups. "Mine's the Sprite."

"Got it." I handed one of the sodas and the bag of popcorn to Russ, and took the other for myself.

"Let's go sit in the breakroom," Cami suggested. "We need to get our carts anyway.

We don't have much time left."

"Is it okay if I go in there with you?" Russ asked, taking a long sip of his drink.

"Ask the boss," I said, gesturing to Cami.

She elbowed me. "I'm not the boss, but sure, you can come with us."

Russ sat at the table when we entered, and I leaned against the wall, giving a quick glance to my phone. Cami and I needed to get back to work, so I punched both of our time cards in.

"You wanna hang out in here?" I asked Russ. "We need to clean a theater."

"Can I tag along?"

"Sure," Cami replied, grabbing her cart. "These are the last shows for the evening, so people won't be coming in behind us. It shouldn't be a problem."

"Well, then, I better come along to chaperone. I wouldn't want your future child to say he or she was conceived in a movie theater."

Cami blushed a bright red and quickly turned back to her cart.

"Russ, you're gonna have to go a little easier on her dude. She's not used to that kind of talk."

She was still blushing when I placed my hands on her shoulders and turned her around to face me.

"You okay?"

"Yeah," she mumbled, not looking at me.

I lifted her chin until she glanced up. "You have nothing to be ashamed of. You better get used to the teasing, though. There's bound to be more if it."

She was biting her lip again. "I'll be all right. Worse things could happen."

I pecked her once on those adorable lips of hers. "Let's go." I put my drink on my cart and gestured for her to go first.

"The next movie should be over any minute," she said. "Let's clean the hallway down here while we wait for everyone to get out."

We grabbed our brooms and dustpans and began quickly sweeping. I tried desperately to ignore Russ's snide comments about watching me become domesticated, and managed to successfully resist the urge to smack him over the head with my broom. The doors opened as we were finishing and the crowd began to pour out. We waited until the last of them were gone before going in. Cami and I had set up a system earlier. I started at the top, and she started at the bottom, and we worked our way toward each other.

"See you in the middle," I teased, slapping her on her cute rear end before I turned and ran up the stairs.

She gave a little squeal and swung her broom at me.

"Ha, ha! You missed!" I laughed.

"Hunter!" Russ's choked voice caught my attention and I turned. He was staring at me with a funny expression.

"What?"

He dropped his drink, spilling the little that was left on the carpet, and he slouched against the wall.

I ran down to his side. "What is it, man? What's wrong?" I grabbed him by the shoulders, noticing he was trembling and sweating profusely.

"I feel funny. My heart is racing."

I slid my hand down his arm, searching for the pulse at his wrist. It was beating wildly.

"When did this start?" I questioned. "Have you felt sick today?"

"No." He looked like he was going to vomit.

I searched his eyes, noticing his pupils were wide and dilated.

"Russ, be honest with me. Did you take something? Drugs?" He seemed to zone out for a bit and I shook him. "Answer me, dammit! Did you take something?"

"No, nothing," he whispered. He slipped further down the wall, and I tried desperately to hold him up. His eyes rolled back into his head, and he started twitching.

"Cami, call an ambulance!" I shouted over to where she seemed frozen in shock. "Get help!" I carefully eased him the rest of the way to the floor.

She quickly dug her phone from her pocket and dialed 911 as she ran out of the room. "Somebody help!" I heard her shout.

"Russ!" I yelled, trying to rouse him again. "Russ, can you hear me?" I briskly rubbed my knuckles against his sternum.

There was nothing. I leaned my ear next to his mouth, listening. A faint breath stirred at my cheek, and I could feel his pulse still racing along. He started foaming at the mouth, and I rolled him to the side to try and keep his airway clear.

"They're on their way!" Cami said as she ran up to my side. "What happened?"

"I don't know, but it acts like a drug overdose. I've seen something similar before. Go wait for the ambulance, and show them where to come."

"Will you be okay?" she asked, concern laced through her voice.

I nodded and she hurried away.

Mandy, Clay, and Shane ran inside the room, all pausing with a horrified look at Russ's body.

"Jen ran to get some things at the store before they closed. I'll go call her and wait in the lobby until she gets here," Shane said.

"What can we do to help?" Mandy asked, and I could see tears in her eyes.

"Bring me some wet paper towels or something. The guy is burning up. Let's try to cool him down."

She grabbed some hand towels from the cleaning cart and ran out of the theater, leaving Clay and me alone with Russ.

"I hope you're getting a good look at this," Clay said, advancing closer. "This is what happens to stupid kids like you who won't lay off the dope."

"So help me, Clay, if you say another word I'm gonna get up and rearrange your face. Now's not the time." I continued to hold Russ on his side. "Besides, he said he didn't take anything."

Clay snorted. "You would believe him. You're

as stupid as he is."

I lifted my head, anger suffusing through me. "That's a little like the pot calling the kettle black, don't you think?"

His eyes narrowed. "I have no idea what you're talking about."

"Well, then let me refresh your memory before you continue on with your high and mighty rant. I've had my eye on you, Clay. I know what you've been up to, and if anyone in this room qualifies as stupid, it's you."

Russ made a loud, gurgling sound, and I quickly checked him, turning his head some more as a bit of fluid rushed from his mouth.

Clay cleared his throat uncomfortably. "I'm going to go keep the hallway clear. There are still shows letting out."

"Fine, you do that," I replied. "But before you go, you might want to know that I saw you that night—under Cami's window."

Clay's eyes widened, and I saw a touch of fear pulse through them.

"That's right. Who's the sicko now?"

"Did you tell her?" he choked out, not denying anything.

"Hell no. The last thing she needs to hear is that her beloved BFF is sexually fanaticizing about her while he watches outside her window. You're a pervert." Fury surged through me as I remembered following him that night.

"What're you going to do?"

"I haven't decided yet, but you can bet your ass I won't ever be leaving you alone with Cami. She's *my* girlfriend, Clay. Back off. So help me if you ever try to touch her, you're dead meat—but now isn't the time for this conversation. You and I can chat later."

Clay swallowed hard, his eyes darting around quickly before he turned to leave without a word.

My heart was racing, and I tried to calm my adrenaline, refocusing on the situation at hand.

I was alone with Russ now. "I don't know if you can hear me, Russ, but keep hanging in there okay? Help is on the way. Just a little longer—you can do it."

Mandy came running back into the room. "Where do you want these?"

"On his head and neck, and maybe in his armpits too, if you've got enough. Just be careful to keep things away from his mouth so he can breathe."

She quickly did as I asked, and I was grateful when the soft wail of sirens filled the air.

Soon, Cami returned followed by a policeman and two firemen.

"What happened?" the policeman asked as the firemen quickly opened a bag and began hooking Russ up to some equipment.

"He was fine, and then he suddenly complained of being sick. He just slumped over."

"Do you know if he took something," he asked.

"He said he hadn't."

"Does he have a history of drug use?"

I shrugged. "I only know of him smoking some pot before."

The officer gestured for me to follow him. "Let's step to the side and let these guys do their job. The ambulance will be here shortly."

"His name is Russ Weston," I said to the fireman next to me. "He turned eighteen on the seventh of this month."

"Thanks," he said, never pausing. "Don't worry, we'll give him the best care possible."

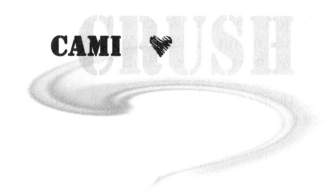

CAMI ♥

CHAPTER TWENTY-NINE
Cami-

I laid my head against the table in the break room. I was so tired I truly believed I could fall asleep right here. I didn't know how many more questions Hunter and I could answer.

We'd been questioned by the police and theater management, explaining every detail of our night and what we were doing with Russ. We'd even had lights shined in our eyes as our pupils were checked to see if it appeared we were on anything. I felt like a filthy criminal, and I was completely innocent of any wrongdoing.

Hunter had been brutally honest too, telling everyone exactly what we'd been doing out back. I wasn't sure if either of us had a job anymore.

Clay, Mandy, and Shane had been released to go home after the cops questioned them. Hunter and I were the lucky ones to stay behind, since we were the people "involved."

The only plus side was the others had finished doing our jobs for us, so we didn't have to stay and clean.

"Can we go now?" Hunter asked, his irritation at being detained evident. "I'd like to get over to the hospital to check on my friend."

"Yes, you may leave. We'll let you know if we need anything else. Thanks for your help." The officer closed his notebook.

"Can I call you later about our jobs?" He glanced between Jon and Jen.

"You still have your jobs. You were technically off the clock when you were outside," Jen said. "Go home and get some rest. We can discuss it later if needed."

Jon didn't say anything, but there was a worried frown on his face and his brow was wrinkled together.

"Thank you," Hunter replied before turning to me. "Come on, Cami. Let's go." He grabbed my hand and pulled me to my feet. I followed after him without speaking as he made his way down the hall toward the back exit. My nerves were shot. I didn't know how much longer I'd be able to hold it together.

When we reached the car, Hunter opened the passenger side door, and I slipped inside without a word of thanks. He didn't seem to notice, closing the door and going to his side and getting in.

"You okay?" he asked gently, placing his hand on my knee.

I saw the concern in his eyes. That was the last straw. I started bawling, unable to keep the sobs back as I buried my face in my hands.

"He looked exactly like Jordan did."

Hunter leaned over, holding me against his shoulder. "I'm so sorry, honey . . . so sorry you had to see that again."

"Do you think it was drugs?" I asked, slightly hiccupping with my tears.

"I hope not, but it looks like it." He kissed the top of my head.

"You have to stop, Hunter! You can't ever use again. I know I said I'd try to understand, but I can't. Don't you see? It could've been you lying there! That would've killed me! Killed me! Please, *please*, stop before you get hurt." I knew I was hysterical, but I had to make him realize somehow.

"I will, Cami. I'll do anything to make you feel better—anything to stop you from crying. You're breaking my heart." He squeezed me tighter.

"Don't say it to appease me, Hunter. I mean it. No more drugs or . . . or . . . we are through. I can't handle knowing you're treating your life so carelessly. That could be you . . . it could be you." I couldn't stop the tears; they were flowing faster than I could wipe them away. I'd never been so scared for someone before. I loved him—but I was angry—with him, with Russ, with Jordan, all of them. Couldn't they understand how they were hurting the people who loved them?

He lifted my chin, and I looked him straight in the eye, *wanting* him to see all the hurt there.

"I'm serious," he said, never breaking his

gaze away. "You have my word. I won't use again. You win."

"Why? Why now? Why not when I asked you earlier?" I knew I was pushing, but I didn't care. I wanted some answers. He'd always been so stubborn before.

"That was . . . a . . . scary thing," he replied slowly, carefully, as if he were deliberately choosing his words. "But I also don't like seeing you this way, either. I know it brings up painful memories for you."

I pulled away and glanced through the window, trying to calm myself down. "I still have nightmares about that night, you know . . . with Jordan. Sometimes I'm afraid to fall asleep."

"I didn't know. I'm so sorry, Cami—for everything."

I wiped my eyes as silence hung in the car between us. "Let's go check on Russ," I said.

"Are you sure you're up for it? I'm more than happy to drop you by your house on the way there." He ran his hand down my arm, and squeezed my hand.

"No. He's your friend. I want to be with you when you go."

He stared as if he were measuring my capability of handling it.

"Really. I want to go—if you want me there."

"I always want you with me. You should know that by now." He smiled and lifted his hand to wipe one of my tears away.

I gave a choked laugh. "I love you."

He smiled softly, his eyes roaming over my face. "I love hearing you say that. I love you too."

The emergency room waiting area was blessedly empty. We were told Russ's parents had arrived shortly after he did and were with him while he was being worked on. A nurse had come and said only one of us could go back. I told Hunter to go, I'd wait here for him. He'd been gone for a while now, giving my mind plenty of time to wander freely, covering many topics from drugs, to Clay, back to Hunter, our relationship, and even death.

Death. It was one thing I'd never deluded myself over. I wasn't like those teens who thought they were invincible. I'd had enough close friends and relatives die to know life was both fleeting and precious—not to be wasted. I was determined to live mine the best I knew how, and I'd made the personal choice to avoid certain things—one was drugs and drinking alcohol, the other was sex.

A friend of mine was killed in a drunk driving accident with her father a few years ago, and an uncle of mine—who had been very sexually active in his youth—was diagnosed with AIDS. I knew my decisions were a little fear based, but my opinion was better safe than sorry. I didn't want those things to happen to me.

I'd done well holding up to my moral values until recently. I met Hunter and suddenly realized why kids sometimes did the things they did. He put off this natural charismatic energy, which drew me to him like a moth to a flame. I couldn't quite describe it . . . he had all this swagger and confidence, but it was more than that. I simply looked at him and knew he was my weakness, my temptation. I'd heard the term, 'like sex-on-a-stick', and thought it described him perfectly—he was carnal, delicious, something I craved. I'd never felt that way about anybody before. It was both thrilling and terrifying because I knew, under the right circumstances, I'd be willing to cross the line I'd so carefully drawn around myself.

This brought up all my old fears. I knew enough about Hunter's past to know he'd been with other girls . . . but what did that mean to me? Was it safe for me to be with him? Was I really ready for it or only being driven by hormones?

I pushed a breath out the side of my mouth, blowing some of my wayward curls from my eyes. None of this really mattered, because—for whatever reason—he didn't seem to be ready to cross that line with me. I couldn't for the life of me figure out why. He *acted* like he wanted to, but he always put the brakes on, and his weird little speech earlier made it sound like he didn't think he'd be the one I would do it with. Why not?

I was so confused.

The doors to the emergency room swung open and Hunter came out. I stood to greet him, noting the solemn expression on his face. He embraced me, burying his face in my hair.

"How is he?" I asked as I slid my arms around him.

He didn't answer for a moment. "He's bad.

They're flying him to a larger facility in Albuquerque. He's in a coma, and things don't look good."

"Did they figure out what happened?"

"They did a drug screen. It showed he had amphetamines in his system."

"So it was a meth overdose?" I felt sick.

"That's what it's looking like." He squeezed me tighter.

"Why would he lie to you about it? Wouldn't he want you to know so you could help him?"

Hunter released me and walked away, running a hand through his hair. "That's the weird part. He was with us the whole time. I never saw him take anything. Did you?"

I shook my head. "What are you saying?"

"I don't know. I guess . . . things don't seem to add up. Did you call your parents?"

"Yeah. I told them I'd be home as soon as we were done."

"Well, I better get you there. Come on, let's go." He held out his hand, and I slipped mine into it.

"I'm really sorry about Russ."

"Me too, Cami." He sighed heavily. "Me too."

HUNTER♥

CHAPTER THIRTY
Hunter-

Everything had taken on a melancholy air since Russ's accident. Cami had been like a ghost beside me this last week, following me everywhere as if she were afraid to let me out of her sight. She didn't talk much; she was just there, and I found her presence comforting, though it made it difficult for me to find time to catch up with Derek and talk to him about our deal. We'd both agreed to back off the drug scene for a bit until things cooled down again.

Unfortunately, her constant attendance also meant Clay was around a lot. He'd wisely kept his mouth shut—at least when it came to talking to me—and didn't attempt to revisit the crass remarks he'd spoken in the theater. We'd never had a chance to talk about my accusations either. I was sure he was constantly staying with us in hopes it would prevent me from relaying the information to Cami. We were at a stalemate—he and I—neither would allow the other to be alone with her.

I hated having him around because I felt like it hindered Cami and me from talking about things that were going on between us. At the same time, it was kind of a relief, because I knew she had questions I couldn't answer. I longed to tell her everything and get it out into the open so we could deal with it, one way or another. The tension in the air seemed to thicken around us daily, and I was certain things would come to a head soon. It was almost time for me to step up my game.

Today was the day I'd been dreading. Tonight was the Masquerade dance and knowing Cami was going to spend the whole evening wrapped in Clay's arms did little to calm my nerves. I felt a restless energy coursing through me whenever I thought about it. I didn't like Clay, and I definitely didn't trust him. Out of respect for Cami and her feelings towards him, I was doing my best to stay out of the way and let them do their thing together.

I was especially missing Russ at the moment. We were all seated in the cafeteria, and I had to listen to Clay and Cami go on about their costumes and last minute preparations. Russ would've distracted me with conversation of his own so I didn't have to hear all this. I suppose I could've played the possessive boyfriend card and insisted Cami go to the dance with me, but I wasn't the sort of person who would force her to do anything. I knew Cami was stressing, so I thought attending the dance would be good—but there was no way I'd leave Clay alone with her. I could barely stomach seeing the two of them together.

As far as I was concerned, they wouldn't be best friends much longer. I was planning on telling Cami about him when it was right, and hopefully that opportunity would present itself soon. This was her tradition with her friend, and I didn't want to intrude—intrude meaning I wouldn't do anything to stop them from going together. I sure as heck would be at the dance, so I could keep an eye on her.

My cell phone started vibrating in my pocket. I pulled it out and glance at the number, wondering who was calling me when I didn't recognize it.

"Hello?" I answered.

"Hi. Is this Hunter?" a female voice spoke on the other end.

"Yes it is."

"Hi. This is Cheryl Weston, Russ's mom."

"How are you? Are things okay?" I asked, feeling nervous. I'd given her my number so she could call me if there was any change in Russ's condition.

"I'm doing fine, and yes. I called to tell you Russ finally woke up. He didn't talk much, but he recognized us, and he asked about you."

Relief washed through me, and I felt tears begin to well up in my eyes. I blinked them away rapidly.

"I'm so glad to hear that."

"He went right back to sleep again, but doctors anticipate a full recovery. Now maybe we can get some answers from him."

"I hope you will. Thanks for letting me know."

"Thank you for helping him, Hunter." Her voice choked up. "The doctors said if it hadn't been for your quick response, we probably would've lost him."

"Please don't cry, Mrs. Weston. I was happy to help. Keep in touch, and let me know how it goes. I'll see if I can get over there to see him soon." She thanked me again and we hung up. I looked up to see Cami and Clay waiting expectantly.

"Russ woke up," I said with a relieved sigh. "He knew who his parents were and asked about me. They think he'll make a full recovery. He's sleeping again now, but they're going to question him when he wakes up again to see if they can figure out what happened."

"Hunter, that's wonderful news," Cami said, throwing her arms around me in a giant bear hug.

I slipped my arms about her waist and placed a kiss against the side of her head, basking in the moment of relief in her embrace. Clay stared at us with a distasteful expression. He didn't appear the least bit happy.

"Maybe you and I can drive to Albuquerque this weekend to see him, if it's all right with your parents," I said.

"I'd love to. I'm sure they'd let me go. We have the dance tonight, but we could go tomorrow. My aunt lives there too. I bet she'd let us spend the night at her place, and we could come back on Sunday since it's such a long trip."

I released her. "I think that would be great. I'd enjoy spending the extra time with you."

Clay didn't speak a word, but he looked positively enraged. I was sure he'd do everything he could to dissuade Cami from going the minute my back was turned.

"Let me call my mom and tell her what's going on," Cami said, pulling out her phone.

I nodded and continued eating my lunch, pretending not to notice Clay staring at me as if he'd like to strangle me right there.

"She says I can go, and she'll call my aunt to set things up for us." Cami was beaming as she hung up, seeming happier than I'd seen her in days.

"Sounds good," I replied. "Thank you."

"I can't wait. It'll be great to see Russ again, and it will be fun traveling with you." She leaned over and pecked me on the cheek. "I love being with you."

I couldn't help my grin and chuckle. "I feel the same. It'll be nice to be alone together. We haven't had much of that lately."

"No, we haven't."

I wondered if Clay realized she'd practically forgotten he was still sitting with us. Cami had made no secret over how she felt about me, but he continued to hang around and act like he had a chance with her. It made me feel uncomfortable. He didn't seem able to get the message.

Tomorrow . . . maybe tomorrow I could

finally tell her about Clay.

The bell rang, signaling it was time to get back to class, and the three of us gathered our things. I listened to Cami chatter happily about her aunt as we walked down the hallway to class, and it was great hearing her sound like her old self again.

The music was pulsating loudly in the transformed gymnasium, complete with a false fabric ceiling and giant, glittering, decorated masks strategically placed around the room. A huge silver disco ball hung in the center, casting its fractured light about the space. It made all the shiny surfaces reflect and glow as if tiny jewels were implanted in their surface.

Masked teenagers danced about the room in rhythm with the pounding beat, dressed in various styles of costumes—from the crazy to the elegant variety.

I hadn't dressed up, only wearing a black t-shirt, jeans, and shoes. I had worn a black half mask, simply to blend into the crowd a little easier. I wasn't here to participate. I was here to observe.

I managed to easily spot Cami and Clay from where I hid—leaning against the corner wall in the shadows. Cami was simply the most beautiful girl in the room, her gold dress set off her red hair perfectly and made her skin look like peaches and cream. Her mask was attached to a long, slender stick, so she could lift it to her face or pull it away while she was talking to people. I was glad she didn't hold it up a lot. I liked seeing her eyes flash and shine in the light as she danced and laughed. She was clearly having a good time . . . with Clay.

It was plain to see she only thought of him platonically. There was never anything romantic in her gestures, purely those of a girl enjoying some fun with her good friend.

Clay on the other hand looked like the cat who'd swallowed the canary. His eyes never left her, and anyone who looked at him for more than two seconds could clearly see he was head over heels crazy about her. It was all I could do to stay here instead of marching over to whisk her away from him. He was constantly caressing her in some manner—whether he was softly running his hands down her bare shoulders and arms, or lowering his head to speak closely into her ear—his body was always touching hers.

I peered at my watch. Two hours down. If I could hang in there for another hour, the dance would be over, and I could make sure he took her safely home. Then tomorrow she'd be mine again for the weekend.

"I knew you'd be lurking around here somewhere," Gabrielle's voice interrupted my thoughts as she approached. "There was no way you'd let your precious Cami out of your sight for so long, especially when she's with another guy."

I didn't bother to answer her.

She stroked her fingers over my bare arm as she walked up beside me. "They make a gorgeous couple, don't you think? Especially since Clay decided to ditch the nerd look. They belong together—can't you see it? It's the way it's always been."

"And what make you such an expert on their relationship?" I asked glancing at her. She was dressed up like a cat burglar in a form-fitting spandex suit, which tightly hugged every one of her generous curves. Her heavily made up eyes glistened as she stared at me through her sleek, black mask.

"Clay and I are . . . close."

I snorted. "If you mean to say you're banging him, I already figured that out."

She looked surprised.

"The only thing I don't know is how long it's been going on," I added. "Or why."

She gave a sly smile and brushed closer against me. "I could tell you the answers . . . if you really want to know."

"By all means, go ahead." She had my full attention.

"It'll cost you." She walked her fingers up my arm toward my shoulder.

"Really? What?" I asked, ready to play her game.

"You know what I want." Her gaze flitted over me.

I paused, mulling over what she was insinuating. "All I can promise is to give you the ride of your life . . . once . . . that's it. You won't get anything else from me."

She smiled victoriously. "Once will be enough. Then you'll be hooked like every other guy in this school."

"You can't be *that* good. Now spill your

secrets or no deal."

She sighed, brushing her hand down past my shoulder, pausing to squeeze my bicep. "Clay has wanted Cami for a long time, and what he wants, he gets. You shouldn't mess with him. He's dangerous. Jordan Henley found that out the hard way."

My eyes narrowed, and I grabbed her by the arm. "What do you mean?"

"Ouch!" she said, pulling back. "You don't want to bruise the merchandise, sweetie."

I relaxed my hold. "My mistake. I thought you'd like it rough for some reason." She smiled, rubbing her hand over mine, and I let her. "What were you saying about Jordan?"

She frowned a little, and I could see her hesitation. "I shouldn't have said anything."

I tightened my grip and dragged her behind one of the decorative walls. "Tell me what you know or the deal is off." I forced myself to reach out and stroke the side of her face, trying to pretend I was into her. She leaned into it and closed her eyes.

"That feels nice."

"Tell me what you know," I pressured her again.

She rested against the wall and beckoned me seductively with her long nailed finger. "Come here first."

I moved, pinning her body with mine.

"Kiss me," she said, licking her lips.

I lowered my head. "Not until you tell me what you know, Gabby. That's the deal." I was so close to her it almost made me nauseated.

"Clay poisoned Jordan. He's a chemical genius, you realize. He knows how to cook his own stuff. Jordan said he was going to get Cami one way or another the night of the Winter Formal. Clay slipped some meth into Jordan's drink, hoping to incapacitate him, but he accidentally gave him too much, and it killed him instead. He didn't know I'd seen him do it until I threatened to expose him. He told me he'd give me the drugs to sell, and I could keep half the profit if I wouldn't tell anyone. So that good party you've been looking for? I'm the one who's able to give it to you. You should've been hooking up with me this whole time."

I was going to be sick. The pieces of the puzzle were suddenly falling into place. In the theater, Clay must've spiked the drink he thought was mine, but when Cami moved them they got mixed up.

"Russ's drink . . . it was meant for me." I'd been the target. Russ's illness was my fault. He had come after me. And now my girlfriend was dancing in the arms of a killer. I had to get her out of here.

Gabby laughed. "I told you not to mess with him. He's sadistic."

"Kind of like you, huh?" I replied, feeling nothing but complete scorn for this stupid, stupid, girl.

"I can be, but the important thing is I kept my end of the bargain. Now it's time for you to keep yours."

"Oh, trust me, Gabrielle. I always keep my word. You will most definitely get the ride of your life," I leaned in closer so my lips were nearly brushing her ear, "in the back of a police car."

She looked confused and then a little scared. "Wha . . . what do you mean?"

"I mean, dear Gabby, my real name is Dylan Wilcock, and I'm a twenty-one year old undercover police officer who was sent here to investigate the suspicious activity surrounding Jordan Henley's death." I couldn't help a sly grin as I cocked an eyebrow at her. "You just propositioned a cop, admitted you were selling illegal drugs, covered up a homicide, and had knowledge of an attempted homicide. I think you've—how do they say it—cooked your own goose? You're under arrest."

She shoved me and attempted to run, but I grabbed her and quickly pinned her to the wall.

"Let me go!" she shouted, struggling.

"Not a chance. You're gonna go out there with me right now and confront Clay, and I'm going to call for a squad car to take us all down to the station."

She looked at me, horrified. "I can't. It's too late."

"What's too late?"

"I was the diversion. He knew he could never leave here with her while you were watching so closely. He has other plans for her tonight. They left as soon as you quit watching."

"What?" I bellowed, my rage boiling straight to the surface. "Why? Why would you put her in the hands of someone who could hurt her? Do you really hate her that badly?"

"I'm tired of competing," she whined like a spoiled child. "All the guys want her, and she doesn't even know it! I'm the one who's always there for them, and all they can talk about is how gorgeous she is and how they'd totally do her. I thought if I helped Clay, it would take care of my problem. He loves her. He wouldn't hurt her."

"The guy is psychotic! How can you know what he'll do? Tell me where they're going!" I pulled her after me, heading toward the door.

"I don't know. He didn't tell me." She was crying in earnest as we entered the hallway together.

I ripped my mask off and started running toward the exit, practically dragging her along. I stepped outside in time to see Clay's ugly little car leave the parking lot. I hurried over to my Camaro and stopped. The tires had been slashed.

I turned to Gabby. "Give me the keys to your car."

"I don't have them. They're in my purse in the gym."

"Listen to me carefully. I'm letting you go, and you're going to get them for me. If anyone asks you what's wrong you'll tell them you don't feel well, and you're heading home. If you help me out now, I'll put it in my report and testify to it. Hopefully that will shine a good light on you. But so help me, if you run, I'll catch you and make sure they throw the book at you. So what's it going to be?"

"I'll help you," she replied without hesitation.

"I promise."

"Okay, let's go back in. Don't forget, I'm watching."

She nodded, and I released her.

I pulled out my phone and dialed Chris's number. He answered on the second ring.

"I've got the evidence we need, and I found a witness. It's the Bradley kid. I knew something was off about him, I just never imagined *this*. He's got Cami, Chris. I need to find her."

"Hang on. I'll be right there, and I'll send the squad car over for your witness."

"I can't wait. I've got to go after them. He slashed my tires, so I'm taking the witness's vehicle. Put out an APB for his, please. The info on it is in the file I gave you for review."

"Already on it," he replied.

Hanging up, I dialed Cami.

"Cami's phone," Clay answered.

"Put Cami on the phone, now," I demanded.

"No problem. It happens," he replied, making no sense, and instantly the line went dead.

Damn.

I watched from the hallway as Gabby went to retrieve her purse and came back. She dropped her keys into my hand and followed me outside as I went over to my car.

"What are you doing?" she asked when I popped the trunk.

"I need to grab a few things." I got my underarm holster out and slid it on before slipping my gun into it. I put my leather jacket on over the top to conceal the weapon. I didn't want to freak Clay out if he saw it when I found him. I slid my badge into my pocket and grabbed a pair of handcuffs.

"I can't believe you're a cop," Gabby whispered. "You don't seem that old."

"That's how I got picked for the job." I grabbed her wrist. "I'm sorry to do this, but you're my key witness, and I can't have you running." I handcuffed her to the trunk latch and placed her purse in my car so she couldn't call anyone from her phone. "Someone will be here to get you soon."

She nodded as the tears continued to roll down her face.

"Are you sure you don't know where he took Cami? It would be somewhere he felt safe."

"He never said."

I stared hard at her.

"Honest. I'd tell you if I knew. I need all the breaks I can get."

"Where does he cook his meth?" I asked, an idea suddenly forming.

She looked worried.

"Tell me, Gabby."

"At the theater."

"The theater?"

"There's an abandoned theater on the second floor that's all locked up. Everyone thinks it's haunted. He found another entrance into it from a set of service stairs no one ever uses. He has a key."

The strange noises and smells coming from the theater . . . it all made sense now. It was

Clay all along.

"Where are the service stairs?" Cami hadn't shown me those.

"There's a locked door by the back entrance. There's a narrow staircase behind it. You'll need keys to get in. He stole his boss's and made his own set so he could get in any time."

I was already running toward her car.

"You really love her, don't you? It's not an act," she called after me.

"I do," I replied over my shoulder. I only hoped I wasn't too late.

CAMI

CHAPTER THIRTY-ONE
Cami-

"I have a surprise for you," Clay said with a smile as he pulled me into the hall.

"A surprise? For what?" He was quite handsome in his tuxedo and mask tonight. I'd noticed several of the girls staring at him. It made me hopeful he'd soon have a girlfriend all his own.

"Well, if I told you it wouldn't be a surprise now, would it? Turn around."

"Turn around?"

"Yes. I'm going to blindfold you so you won't see where we're going until we get there."

"I don't know. This seems awfully suspicious," I teased, but I did as he asked.

He fastened a soft, silky cloth over my eyes. "You can trust me, Cami," he whispered in my ear, then took my elbow and guided me along.

"So what brought on this surprise?"

"A couple of things actually. The end of our

senior year is coming up, and you'll be turning eighteen soon. We're moving on into different chapters of our life, so I thought we should celebrate all the time we've been friends with something special."

"You're always so sweet and thoughtful. Thank you, Clay. I can't wait to see what you have planned."

I heard a car door open. "Watch your head. I'm going to help you get inside."

I grabbed his arms to steady myself as I sat down. "Make sure you get all of my dress into the car."

"Got it," he answered, closing it.

I touched the cloth over my eyes.

"Hey! No peeking!" he ordered as he slid in beside me. "Keep your hands in your lap or I'll have to tie them too. We can't have you ruining the surprise."

"Yes sir!" I laughed as I dropped them.

The car started and we were moving.

"This is weird. Why don't you tell me where we're going? People are going to think you're kidnapping me or something."

He chuckled. "Nice try. You're going to have to be patient."

I felt my cell start to vibrate in the tiny clutch I had strapped to my wrist. "Oh. My phone is ringing."

"I'll get it for you," Clay said, and the strap slipped off my wrist.

"Hello, Cami's phone." He paused. "No problem. It happens." I heard a beep. "Somebody calling for Julie."

"Ah, wrong number then."

"Yep."

"Are we going far?"

"No. We'll be there in a couple of minutes."

"So it's a close surprise." I tried, but couldn't figure out where he might be taking me. "I had a lot of fun with you at the dance tonight."

"Me too. It was just like old times, wasn't it?"

"Yes, it was. I couldn't help but notice all the girls staring at you. I think your new style has garnered quite the fan club."

"Nah. I don't care about any of those girls anyway. If they didn't like me before, why should I care what they think now?"

"Well, it's their loss then."

He reached over and squeezed my hand. "You're the best, Cami. You know that, right?"

"Just happy to call you my friend."

His hand slipped from mine, but he didn't reply. We sat together in silence until he stopped the car.

"Stay here. I'll come around to help you."

In an instant he was at my side, helping me out.

"Can I take my blindfold off now?"

"Soon, but not yet. Come on lets go."

We walked for a little way before he paused and guided me up a step. I heard some keys jangling and the sound of a door opening followed by more keys and another door.

"Okay, we are going to walk up some stairs, so be careful."

He wrapped his arm around my waist and

escorted me inside. I heard both doors close behind us, and the air suddenly smelled stale and musty.

"Where are we?" I asked again, starting to feel uncomfortable with this.

"You'll see in a second. You're gonna love it, I promise."

We carefully made our way up the steps, pausing when we reached the top. I heard him fiddling with yet another lock before he guided me inside, the sound of the latch clicking behind us. I could hear music playing and realized it was a song from Phantom of the Opera. He knew me so well.

"What are you up to?" I asked, a grin sweeping over my face.

"Making your dreams come true." He laughed. "Before you take your blindfold off here's a toast to the future. Then you can see where you are." He thrust a thin stemmed glass into my hand. "Drink up!"

I lifted it to my lips and took a tiny sip before starting to giggle. "Is this fruit punch in a champagne flute?"

"I know it's your favorite, so come on, bottoms up. I have a glass of my own." He clanked his against mine.

I smiled and quickly downed the rest of the contents. "Okay, show me what you've got going on."

"All right. Let me put these glasses over here real quick, and then I'll help you with the blindfold."

He was back in a few seconds, working at

the knot behind my head. "Here you go!"

I opened my eyes, but they blurred and it took a moment to adjust to the light. I gasped. "Are we in the old theater?"

"Yeah, amazing isn't it?" He smiled and slipped his arm around my waist.

"Where did you find so many white Christmas lights this time of year?" It was like we'd stepped back in time—the old wallpaper had yellowed but was still beautiful, surrounded by thick sculpted moldings. The red covered seats were still in pristine condition, and so was the carpet. Every surface had small white lights strung across it. They were on the walls, over the backs of the chairs, and down the red velvet drapes that hung in front.

"How'd you ever get Jon's permission to use this place? I've never even seen *him* come in here. It's so beautiful."

He ignored my question and pointed to the ceiling above the curtains. "The theater screen actually rolls down in front of the curtain there. Behind them is an actual stage. I guess they used to have a few family performances here as well. When I saw this, I knew I'd chosen the perfect place to bring you. It reminded me of Phantom of the Opera. I know how you love that play."

"It's perfect!" I turned and gave him a big hug.

He held me tightly for a few seconds, before suddenly releasing me. "Wait! There's more!" He hurried over to the stage and disappeared behind the curtain.

"What are you doing?" I asked unable to suppress my grin.

"Just a second!"

I heard a squeaking sound, and the drapes spread apart, revealing a large candelabrum with candles aflame on it. Fog began creeping out across the stage, and I laughed, clapping my hands together in delight.

Clay stepped onto the stage with a grin and beckoned me. "I told you I'd be your Phantom come to life. Come sing for me, Camilla!"

I shook my head as I walked up the aisle toward him, laughing. "Not on your life."

"Really?" He looked genuinely disappointed. "I brought karaoke and everything! I wanted this to be your big moment."

He took my hand and helped me up the steps.

I hugged him again. "I can't believe you went to all this work just for me. This is incredible!"

His hand slid up to my neck, and he leaned back so he could look into my eyes tenderly. "I'm so glad you like it. I'd do anything for you. Anything." He paused for a moment, glancing over my face before his mouth descended toward mine.

He caught me completely off guard, and I shoved him away, causing him to stumble backward. "Stop it, Clay. Don't ruin this . . . not now when things are finally starting to feel normal again between us."

"But I thought . . . I thought you liked it . . . I thought you could finally see." He seemed utterly astonished.

"See what? Why can't *you* see? Why can't you hear what I'm constantly telling you? I'm in love with Hunter." My skin flushed as my temper rose.

"No you aren't! You don't even know him. You and me," he gestured between us, "we've been together for years! It's meant to be. Why do you keep resisting it?"

Tears started rolling down his panicked face.

"I'm sorry to hurt you. But I don't feel the same. You're my best friend, Clay. That's all there is."

"You have no idea the things I've done to have you, Cami. I wasn't lying when I said I'd do anything. I'm tired of waiting for you. I won't take no for an answer anymore." His expression turned to something hard and determined, and suddenly I was scared.

"What have you done?" I was honestly afraid to hear the answer.

"I removed the competition."

I stepped away nervously as he stalked forward. "What did you do to Hunter?" I asked, dread shooting through me.

"Hunter?" He seemed confused for a moment. "Nothing to *him*. He should be happily wrapped up in Gabby's arms by now doing what the two of them do best—screwing people."

"Gabby's involved in this?" I was grasping at straws, trying to keep him talking while I made my way backward across the stage. Hunter had been right all along. Clay was off—he . . . was crazy. I didn't know how I'd missed it.

"She saw me slipping something into Jordan's drink the night he died. She's been blackmailing me for a while now. I told her I'd help her get Hunter if she'd help me get you. We compromised."

A cry bubbled up from inside me as I realized what he was saying. He'd *killed* Jordan.

"Do you see now how important you are?" He reached for me again.

"Stay away!" I shouted, shoving him roughly and sending him sprawling. I turned with a sob and fled off the stage toward the main door of the private theater, clutching the knob. I had to get out of here, but it was locked tightly, and wouldn't budge.

"Someone help me!" I screamed, pounding against the thick, old, wooden panels so hard I thought I might break my hand. "Please! Help!" A sudden wave of light-headedness overcame me.

"Not so fast, Cami," Clay growled, seizing me, and we both fell onto the plush carpet with him sprawled on top of me.

I pushed at him frantically, trying to squirm my way out of his hold, but he grabbed my hands and pinned them to the side. "Well, this is convenient, isn't it?"

"What do you mean?" I couldn't help the tremble in my voice, nausea suddenly overwhelming.

A wicked gleam appeared in his eyes. "I mean you should stop fighting me. I made sure I had a little insurance policy in place. There's no way you're escaping me tonight."

My vision suddenly tipped and swam, and I had to blink several times to see him clearly. "You slipped something into my drink, didn't you?" Hysteria welled up inside, and my mouth went dry. "Are you going to kill me too?"

He looked appalled. "What? No! I'd never do anything to hurt you."

"But you *are* hurting me." I struggled to break free of his hold, but felt myself growing weaker. "Don't you understand that?"

"No, I'm helping you. I'm going to show you how good we can be together. I finally realized if you could just see . . . if you could understand the depth of my feelings for you . . . then you'd want me as badly as I want you." He almost sounded sweet, like he truly believed everything he was doing was for the best.

The room tipped again, my strength seeping farther from me. Tears leaked from my eyes as I tried to keep focused. "And you're gonna do that how, Clay? By forcing me? That isn't going to endear you to me at all."

"Relax, Cami." He lowered his mouth to my neck, brushing a kiss near my ear. "I'll be gentle," he crooned. "I promise. It'll be so good."

"Get off me!" In a burst of last-ditch energy, I swiftly lifted my knee, hitting him with all the force I could muster—hard. He groaned in agony and rolled off me to his side, clutching his privates.

I climbed to my feet, leaning against the wall for support. Strings of hanging lights swung wildly about, some falling as I grabbed at them in a desperate attempt to stay upright. I stumbled toward the door before remembering he had the keys on him, so I weaved my way back and began digging in his pockets. Everything was swimming, and I could barely focus, but I felt the cold metal touch my skin and I clasped it, dragging them from him as he lunged for me again. I managed to escape his grasp, and I staggered back to the door, trying desperately to stop my hands from shaking long enough to slide the keys into the lock.

The first two didn't work, but the third one did. I felt like I was going to vomit as I turned the knob, but before I could exit, Clay tackled me again and I went flying, hitting my head hard on the floor. It was over. I knew I'd lost. I was too drugged to attempt another escape now.

"Please don't, Clay." I was crying uncontrollably, desperate to reach him somehow. "If you ever loved me at all, please don't do this. I'll make sure you get some help." My lips trembled violently as I tried to form the words.

"I don't need help. I need you," he said brusquely. His mouth descended to mine, and I turned my head sideways trying to avoid him, but there was nowhere to go. I was pinned beneath the length of his body. He grabbed my chin roughly and turned it back, pressing his mouth violently against my lips. His other hand slid down my thigh, bunching my dress as he pulled it up between us.

"Stop!" I begged, tasting my own tears as I

tried again to push him away. "Stop!"

He squeezed my leg before propping up to undo the buckle on his belt.

I tried to take advantage of the situation, attempting to roll over and crawl away from him.

"Oh no you don't!" he snarled, flipping me back and repositioning himself over me. I heard my clothing rip, and I started flailing against his chest with my fists.

The heaviness in my limbs was sapping my strength, but I couldn't stop fighting. I couldn't let him do this. I screamed loudly, the terrified sound of my voice echoing off the walls of the room.

Clay flinched, but didn't stop.

I gave into sobs. "*Please*," I begged him. "*Please* don't do this. Don't do this, don't do this, don't do this . . ." I repeated over and over again trying to block out the sensation as his hand slid up my leg.

There was a loud clicking sound, and Clay suddenly froze. I looked up to see the barrel of a gun pointed at his head . . . a gun held by Hunter.

"Get up, Bradley," Hunter said in a menacing voice, and a strangled cry escaped my lips at the sight of him. Relief poured through every part of my being. Hunter was here. Hunter was here. I couldn't stop my hysterical tears.

Clay slowly got up, lifting his hands into the air, his pants hanging loosely at his waist. "Don't shoot. I'll do whatever you say. You can put the gun down. You and I are totally cool."

"We're not anywhere close to cool right now," Hunter said, his features dark and mottled with rage. "Cami, are you okay?" he asked without taking his eyes off Clay.

"I will be," I tried to say between sobs.

His jaw clenched, flexing hard. "Did he . . . was he . . ."

I knew what he was trying to ask. "No. He didn't . . . thanks to you." I swallowed thickly, my tongue feeling dry and swollen. "He drugged me with something, though. I feel really sick."

"Did you give her meth?" Hunter demanded, glancing at me for one second with terrified concern.

Clay dove toward the gun, knocking it free from Hunter's grasp as they both fell. It slid down the sloping aisle toward me. Both of them scrambled for it as I sat helplessly watching, but Clay was closer and grabbed it first. Everything suddenly seemed to move at incredibly slow speed as he swung around toward Hunter, lifted the gun, pointed, and fired.

"Nooooo!" I screamed as Hunter grunted loudly, falling beside me, blood immediately spreading across his shirt in a dark, wet, stain.

Clay laughed, a wild look in his eyes as he approached closer, still directing the gun at Hunter. "How quick do you want to die? I'll let you decide where I put the next bullet."

"Don't, Clay! Please don't kill him!" I sobbed. Rolling over, I tried to protect his body with my own—my hands trying to cover the place where he was hemorrhaging.

"Get out of the way, Cami," Hunter said,

trying to push me, but I clutched onto him.

"No," I whispered, hoarsely, collapsing against his chest.

All of a sudden the world was exploding around me, and I flinched as several shots of gunfire rang through the air. I couldn't make sense of what was happening as hands grabbed me around the waist, dragging me off of Hunter.

"No!" I screamed, fighting until a familiar voice echoed through my hysteria.

"Cami, it's okay. It's me, Chris. Are you shot?"

I shook my head. "Help Hunter," I begged, trembling as he laid me back on the floor. That was when I saw Clay, obviously dead in a pool of spreading blood—Hunter's gun lying several feet away. I turned, unable to stand looking at him.

"Code 999, code 999!" Chris yelled into his radio as he grabbed Hunter's gun before turning to shout out the door. "The scene is clear, and I need a medic! I have an officer down!"

An officer? What officer? I glanced around the room, looking for another victim before turning to Hunter, who was still bleeding heavily beside me. I tried to lift my hand to put pressure back on the wound, but I could barely move.

"Cami," he choked out as Chris knelt beside us and quickly tore off a part of my dress, holding it over the bullet hole in Hunter's chest.

"Hang in there, Dylan," Chris said, his face a mask of worry. "Don't you even think of dying or your sister will kill me. I promised her I wouldn't let you get hurt."

"Dylan?" I questioned, their faces both blurring as I glanced between them.

"My real name," Hunter wheezed. "I couldn't tell you. I wanted to, but it would've blown the investigation." Little bits of blood came out of his mouth.

"You're a cop?" I whispered, trying to fight the blackness swimming at the edges of my consciousness.

He nodded slightly, grimacing.

"So, it was all a lie . . ." I couldn't hang on any longer. I let the darkness envelope me.

CAMI

CHAPTER THIRTY-TWO
Cami-

He was buried a week later. Sadly, there were not many people in attendance besides his family, my parents, and me. I didn't cry—I couldn't. I was still in shock over everything. I couldn't seem to make the pieces fit together in my mind. I kept trying to figure out the moment when my best friend had turned into a monster.

His parents felt horrible—said they had no idea he'd become so deluded. They thought we were dating from the things he'd told and shown them—everything from fake letters and emails, to pictures he'd photo shopped of the two of us together. He'd been living a totally phony relationship with me in his own head. The police profiler told me Clay was delusional—he really believed us to be a couple—and none of this was my fault. But he was dead now. That felt like my fault.

I'd woken up in the hospital attached to

I.V.'s, which had been used to help flush the strong date rape drug Clay had given me from my system. Hunter was the first person I asked for. They said he'd been flown by helicopter to a larger facility, but no one would tell me how he was doing. I tried calling his cell phone, but it said the number had been disconnected.

Chris came to the hospital when he heard I'd awakened. He asked me a lot of questions about what had happened with Clay that night. I kept waiting for him to tell me something about Hunter, but he never did. I finally asked him.

"I can't discuss Hunter with you, Cami, since this is part of an ongoing investigation." He looked really sad. "But I promise you'll get answers as soon as possible. You're going to have to trust me, okay?"

I snorted. Trust. Who knew what that word meant anymore?

"Can you tell me if he's alive, at least? He did get shot trying to protect me after all."

"He's alive."

Relief washed through me.

"Is he going to be okay?" I had to know.

He stood and went toward the door. "He was listed in critical condition the last I heard. I'm on my way to see him now. Is there anything you want me to tell him?"

A million things raced through my mind, I love you being first and foremost. "Tell him I . . ." Confusion raced through my heart, making me second-guess everything. What if he didn't really feel the same? What if it was just an act? He'd pulled away from me so many times. He had to be several years older than me. Could he really be in love with a teenager? "Tell him thanks."

"Is that all?" Chris asked, his eyes full of concern.

"Are you really his uncle?" I wanted to hear the truth about something from someone for a change.

He shook his head. "No. I'm actually his brother-in-law. At least I am until his sister gets ahold of me. She's gonna have my head for allowing him to get hurt." He sighed, rubbing a hand over his face. "The whole family is in quite an uproar over everything."

"I'm sorry he got put in danger because of me." The tears began leaking from my eyes without my permission, and I tried to rapidly blink them away. I felt like I was barely clinging on to my sanity by a thread.

Chris came over and grabbed my hand, squeezing it. "None of this is your fault, Cami. Hang in there, okay? I'll see to it you have the answers as soon as I'm able."

He walked out the door, and that was the last I heard from anyone. The next Monday at school a dozen kids were arrested in a giant drug sting. I knew Hunter had to be alive then. Someone had given them names.

Yet, still I heard nothing from him.

I walked into my room when I got home and threw myself on the bed, desperate to escape all the stares and whispers that followed me the whole day.

"Can I get you anything, Cami?" my mom

asked, coming to check on me. She'd hardly left my side, coming home from work early so I was never home alone.

"No thanks, Mom. I just want to take a nap." I was doing a lot of sleeping lately. It was sometimes the only relief I had—when the nightmares didn't get me.

"All right." She gave me a concerned look. "I'm here if you need me."

"Thanks," I said as she closed the door behind her, and I rolled over to face the wall, finally allowing myself to shed tears—over everything. I couldn't wrap my head around it all. I was hurt—sad—angry with Clay. He'd been my best friend my whole life! How could he betray me in the worst way possible? He'd destroyed everything good I could remember about him in just a few moments . . . a lifetime worth of happy memories forever tainted with the stain of his final acts. But despite the trauma he'd put me through, he wasn't the reason I woke up gasping for breath in the middle of the night.

I missed Hunter—craved him—longed to be wrapped again in his embrace. I missed his kisses, the way he stared at me, eyes smoldering as his hands trailed hot caresses over my skin. I missed the tender words he often whispered in my ear and how beautiful they made me feel. Hunter—the one I'd imagined my future with—only to find out he wasn't even real, nothing but a character contrived to deceive others. Ironically, that seemed the worst betrayal of the two, constantly spinning one question over and over in my head.

Is it possible to love someone who never really existed?

It was my birthday. I didn't feel much like celebrating, though. My parents must've understood this, because they didn't pull out the extravagant hoopla they usually did. There were the traditional birthday pancakes, complete with bacon smiley faces—despite the fact I was turning eighteen—and a small wrapped package at my plate.

"What's this?" I asked, tucking some of my wild, wayward hair behind my ear. I hadn't bothered changing out of my pajamas—what was the point when all I did was spend my time in bed these days.

Mom shrugged. "Who knows? It was delivered here this morning."

I reached for the small box and shook it. "It feels empty."

"Why don't you open it and find out?" Dad suggested, and he looked like he was trying to hold back a sly smile.

I undid the ribbon and lifted the lid. "It's a piece of paper." I glanced between them, confused.

"Well, read it," my mom said.

Picking up the paper, I opened it to find two words scrawled on it:

Forgive me.

I recognized the scrawling loops of his

handwriting immediately and my stomach dropped. "Where is he?" I asked, my breath catching as tears sprung to my eyes.

Dad smiled. "He's in the living room waiting for you. We'll be outside on the patio if you need us."

I turned and ran through the doorway, coming to an abrupt halt just inside the room. My heart raced when I saw him standing at the fireplace with his back to me while he ran a finger over a framed photo of me resting on the mantle. I closed my eyes and opened them again to make sure he was still there and I wasn't dreaming.

He chose that moment to turn around, and for a few seconds I couldn't look away from his sorrowful eyes. I didn't notice the sling until I glanced over the rest of him. "What's that for?" I asked, concerned. "No one told me your arm was injured too."

He looked down. "It's not. I just have to keep it still. The bullet nicked my lung and lodged into the shoulder blade. It's going to take a little time to heal correctly."

All of a sudden I was angry, my worry over the last few weeks boiling to the surface. "Where have you been, Hunter? The last I heard from anyone, you were in critical condition. Not one word since! I didn't know if you were dead or alive. I didn't even know who to ask to try and find out about you. Nothing! From anyone all this time!"

He sighed and gestured toward the couch. "Do you care if we sit? I'm sure this will take a while, and I get tired easily."

Trying to calm myself, I exhaled a deep breath and sat down. He joined me, giving me plenty of space by sitting on the opposite end of the sofa. It was strange to see him purposely keep his distance. After all the times I'd fantasized about being back in his arms—it hurt.

"Tell me everything," I demanded, unable to take my eyes off him. He appeared tired, stressed—maybe a bit thinner too, but he was still capable of making my insides flip-out just by looking at him.

"Okay." He seemed so stiff and formal. "First things first, I guess. My name is Dylan Hunter Wilcock, and I'm twenty-one years old. I'm a newly graduated police officer from the Tucson Police Department in Arizona. I haven't been on the force very long. When the Copper City police contacted us for help on this case I was recruited as part of an interstate team."

"What case?" I asked, curiosity taking the place of my annoyance.

"Jordan Henley's family felt there were suspicious circumstances surrounding his death, and according to other witnesses, he wasn't one to use heavy drugs like methamphetamines. Not only did he die from an overdose, but he died with an obscene amount of the drug in his system. There were enough questions brought up by the autopsy that it warranted further investigation. I was sent here to gather information and profiles on the students in this school and to see if I could infiltrate the drug scene and find who was making or selling the meth. When I got here, I was trying to get in friendly with Derek Johnson to see if I could discover who he was supplying and buying from. It was important I appear involved in every aspect of the lifestyle to keep from raising any suspicions."

"That's why you were using? You were trying to keep up your cover?"

"Yes. I couldn't make you understand why without blowing it. I wanted to tell you, but I couldn't."

That stung. "I would've kept your secret. Or didn't you trust me either?"

"I trusted you, but it was safer for you not to know. Besides, *had* you known, it could've changed the way you acted around Clay, and he was on my list of potential dealers after you told me about how he'd suddenly come into money. I didn't want you to tip him off."

"So everything you told me was a lie, a way to get closer to Clay so you could find out what he was up to?"

"No. I wasn't sure about Clay until the very end, but I'd had my suspicious. I'd caught him sneaking around your house one night after you'd gone to bed. That was the day you accused me of spying on you from my car. I knew there was something off, and he needed to be watched. He honestly was stalking you, but you didn't know it. I had no solid proof to pull him in for questioning, so I had to sit back and wait. I was trying to figure out a way to clue you in on things without exposing my identity, but you were so certain he was innocent. I didn't know what else to do at the moment, except stay close and hope I'd be able to properly protect you."

There was an awkward pause, and I played with the hem on my pajama shirt. "Well, I guess I was wrong about him, wasn't I?"

"I'm sorry about everything involving him. I know this all must be very difficult for you. He was your friend for a long time." He actually did look sorry, which made me feel he genuinely was. I knew how he'd felt about Clay.

I shrugged, not wanting to relive the recent horror Clay had put me through. "He shouldn't have shot you. He'd be fine if he hadn't started messing around with stuff he had no business being involved in."

"He was sick, Cami. I honestly believe he'd never have tried to hurt you if he'd been in his right mind. Something made him snap. It's unfortunate, but it's the truth."

I narrowed my eyes. "Why do you sound like you care all of a sudden? You never liked him."

"No, I didn't, but that was because I saw him as a threat to you."

I snorted, trying to distance myself from the ache and emotion coursing through me. "I was just part of your lie though—your excuse to get close to all those kids. Why did it matter if he wanted me too?"

"You're kidding, right?" He looked exasperated. "Do you honestly have no idea how much I care about you?"

"I haven't heard from you for weeks, Hunter . . . err . . . Dylan—whoever you are! I had no idea where you were or if you were alive! I think you proved exactly how much you care about me!" I lashed out. "Do you know what that was like . . . constantly worrying and wondering if you were okay? Waiting day after day to hear from you—anyone—and given the courtesy of knowing how you were doing? You left me all alone, without a word to your whereabouts!"

"I couldn't call you, Cami! I wasn't allowed."

"Why not?" I yelled, wondering if my parents could hear me outside.

"Because I've been suspended by the department pending an investigation."

"What does that have to do with contacting me?" I asked, my mind spinning in a thousand fragmented directions.

He gritted his teeth. "The investigation is to make sure I wasn't involved in any sexual misconduct with a minor."

"What?" I was completely astounded. And suddenly everything made sense with perfect clarity. "This is why you kept pushing me away, isn't it?"

He rubbed a hand over his face before dropping it into his lap. "I'm twenty-one, and a cop. You were seventeen. I crossed the bounds of propriety. I asked to be pulled from the case several times because of it, but the department felt I was right where I needed to be to discover the truth, so I was directed to proceed with caution. I was told not to get involved in anything like kissing or the lines would get sticky.

"I couldn't help myself. I tried to stay away, but I couldn't. Once the investigation was brought up, I was ordered by a judge to have no contact with you until you turned eighteen. You have no idea how many times I wanted to call you or send Chris to tell you what was going on, but that's all considered contact. I wasn't free to speak to you until today, and I've been here since daybreak, waiting for you to get up. I've already explained this to your parents."

"What are you saying?" I asked. I was so confused, yet I couldn't help the bud of hope that was beginning to bloom in my chest.

"I'm saying I love you, Cami. All of that was as real for me as it was for you. I'm asking if you'll stick this out beside me. I'm willing to lose my badge and even be dishonorably discharged if that's the case. I just don't want to lose you."

I wanted to throw my arms around him and kiss him at his declaration, but something held me back. "I don't know what's true about you and what isn't. I thought I knew a lot, but it turns out it was actually very little."

He sighed and rubbed his face again. "I've made a mess of everything, haven't I? Let me just say I wanted you to fall in love with me . . . the real me . . . so I tried to tell you the truth as often as possible. I was the hotheaded jock in high school. I partied with the best of them and hooked up with lots of girls. All of that was true, but I never loved any of them. I excelled at sports, and hoped to continue on with them in college. Then my sister got married to this amazing guy who was a cop, and we became best friends. I adored him, followed him around like a puppy, and one day I decided to go into the police academy instead. My parents are alive and very happy, and the only time I've used drugs during this investigation was when it was necessary to keep my cover. The first time I kissed you, I was trying to keep you from discovering the pictures I'd taken of Clay so you wouldn't be suspicious. You were so determined, I couldn't think of another way to stop you, so I just did it. It was a line I should've never crossed, but once I did, I couldn't go back."

I didn't know what to say. I sat there trying to absorb everything he was telling me, watching him while he sat stiffly on the couch. He looked so uncomfortable. "I don't know what to call you," I finally said.

"Call me Dylan, or Hunter if you want." He relaxed a little for the first time since he sat down. "Honestly, I don't care what you call me as long as you're calling me *something*. I want you by my side." He slid off the couch onto his knees in front of me, not touching me at all, but more like an act of submission. "Please tell me it's not too late to fix this. Tell me you still love me. I've never wanted anything as much as I want you. I'll risk everything that's important to me, just to hear you say you want me in your life."

My gaze trailed over his gorgeous face, and I longed to touch him. "I don't want you to risk everything for me. I'm not worth it." I brushed back the lock of hair that hung over his forehead.

"You are worth it. I've had a near miss with death and it showed me there's only one thing worth living for and that's love. I love you. Please give me another chance."

I shook my head as tears fell down my face. "My dad didn't like you before. I wonder how he feels about you now?"

"Is that a yes?" He looked at me hopefully.

I nodded, smiling. "Yes, but only if you're completely honest with me about everything from now on."

"Oh, Cami. I never wanted to be dishonest with you in the first place."

He leaned forward, wrapping his free arm around me and kissed me, giving me the contact I so desperately craved. The familiar spark ignited hard and fast between us, causing us to clutch each other tighter as our mouths eagerly explored one another. I didn't ever want him to stop kissing me.

"Wait," I said, pulling away, my breathing slightly ragged. "Is there a chance you can go to jail because of our involvement?"

"I don't think so. Chris said since I asked to be removed so many times, the department is at fault also. Because I didn't do anything illegal, and I had your parent's permission to be with you—and they aren't pressing charges—everything should be okay."

I let out a big sigh of relief. "That's good, because I don't want to lose you ever again."

"You won't, I promise." He smiled.

I traced my fingers over his lips. "People are going to say I'm too young for you."

"I can live with that. Can you handle the ones who'll say I'm way too old?" His thumb drifted in a lazy circle over my cheek.

I grinned. "Don't you know me yet? Since when have I ever cared what people are saying?"

"There's my girl." His eyes drifted down over me with the same old heated stare before returning to my face. "Chris thought I simply had a crush on you."

"Really?" I laughed. "Is that what you thought?"

He shook his head. "I knew the first moment I saw you I was in trouble. I wanted to kiss and do all sorts of unspeakable things to you."

"There's those darn, unspeakable things again. What am I gonna do about those?" I smiled as I lightly kissed his lips.

He grinned, his caramel flecked eyes twinkling with mischief. "I guess I'll just have to show you."

About the Author:

Lacey Weatherford is the bestselling author of the popular young adult paranormal romance series, Of Witches and Warlocks, and contemporary series, Chasing Nikki. She has always had a love of books and wanted to become a writer ever since reading her first Nancy Drew novel at the age of eight.

Lacey resides in the beautiful White Mountains of Arizona. She lives with her wonderful husband and children along with their dog, Sophie, and cat, Minx. When she's not out supporting one of her kids at their sporting/music events, she spends her time reading, writing, blogging, and visiting with her readers on her social media accounts.

Visit Lacey's Official Website:
http://www.laceyweatherfordbooks.com
Follow on Twitter:
LMWeatherford
Or Facebook:
Lacey Jackson Weatherford

Coming Soon
From
Moonstruck Media:

BESTSELLING AUTHOR

FINDING
Chase

LACEY WEATHERFORD

The much anticipated sequel to the #1 best seller *Chasing Nikki*! Finding Chase, by Lacey Weatherford!

Things haven't been easy for Chase Walker. He's experienced tragedy, and at times he's not sure he wants to continue living. But he made a vow to go on with his life, and he intends to keep it.

After getting a college scholarship to play football, Chase heads off to school, hoping his time on the field will help to bury the intense emotions that still linger in his heart. Fate doesn't work that way though, and he soon finds himself having to face all the things he's carrying inside, or he may miss the one shot he has to learn how to love again.

Available December 2012

TESTING FATE

Belinda Boring

Mystic Wolves Series Book Three

The next installment in the bestselling Mystic Wolves series, Testing Fate, by Belinda Boring.

Nothing beats the heat of the refiner's fire.
Continue the journey as Darcy faces her greatest challenge to date and fights for her right to mate Mason, the alpha of the Mystic Wolves.

Whisked away by the Fates, separated from Mason and Pack, and relying on her friendship with Devlin, this is make or break for Darcy.

Everything is on the line . . . will she crumble under the pressure or emerge stronger for testing fate?

"She thought she was all alone...he proved her wrong."

Saving Me

KELSIE BLANTON

Saving Me, a young adult contemporary novel from new author, Kelsie Blanton!

16 year old Peyton Jones had it all: straight A's in school, the perfect boyfriend, and nothing to worry about but keeping her GPA up. Then one night it's suddenly ripped away from her. Everything she has ever known changes and she goes from having a perfect plan to watching her world crumble around her.

Steve Gibbons was the quarterback of his high school football team...until the new guy showed up and stole his spot, causing him to lose his chance at a scholarship.
Football was his life and now he feels like he has nothing.

Drawn together after losing hope for their futures, Peyton and Steve become best friends, but as they grow closer something happens that changes everything. Will Peyton be left to face things alone, or can she trust enough to let someone else in?

The God Chronicles

Zeus

Kamery Solomon

Book one in The God Chronicles: Zeus, from bestselling author, Kamery Solomon!

Vegas is not where Karly had imagined herself to be at this point in her life. She was supposed to be living in California, soaking up the sun and enjoying the life of an artist. Instead, she's just moving out of her parents and going to a school that could loosely be called her second choice.

When she meets Zeus Drakos, owner of the new hit casino and resort in town, he seems just like every other jerk guy out there. How was she supposed to know he was the exiled god of Mt. Olympus?

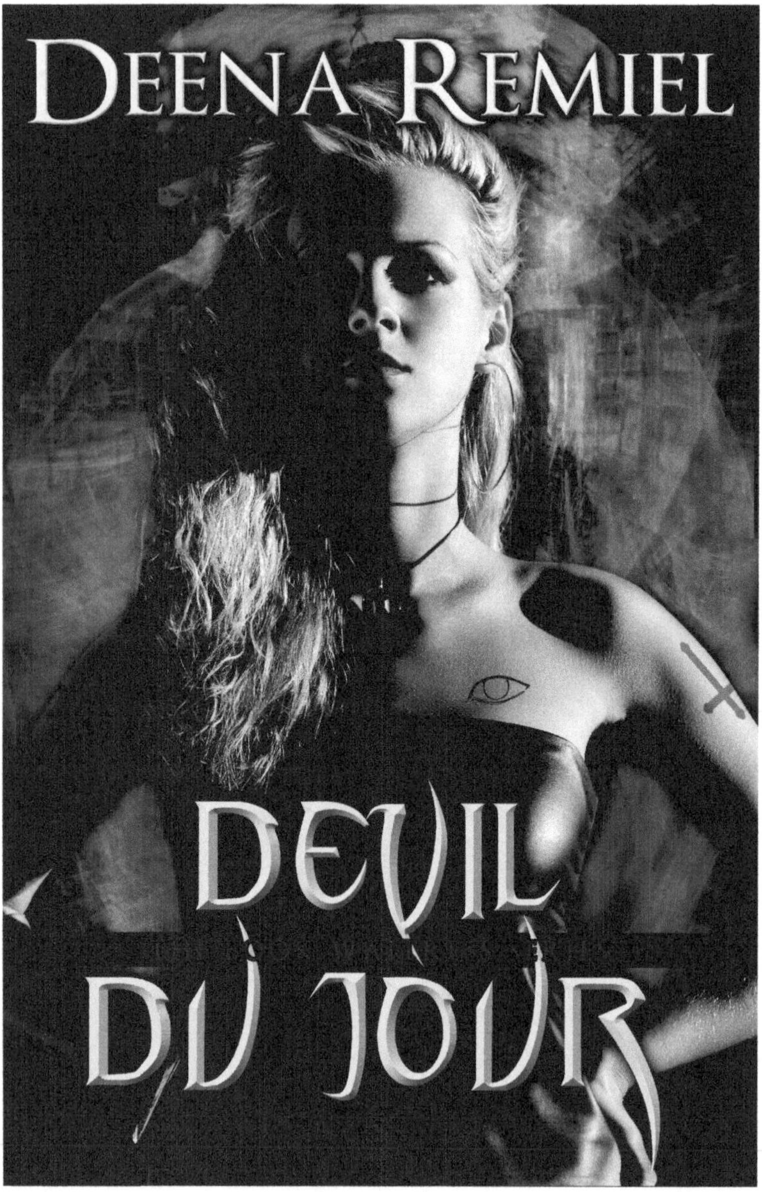
DEENA REMIEL
DEVIL
DU JOUR

Book two in the highly acclaimed Book Waitress series from bestselling author, Deena Remiel!

The Book Waitress, Camille Dutton, has luck on her side. Good and bad. On the upside, she narrowly escaped death and Satan claiming her soul. On the downside, a portal has been opened, and she can feel every time a creature from Hell crosses over to our world.

Derek Galloway is one tenacious man. His curious nature won't let him rest until he closes Hell's portal and finds a cure for Camille's affliction. Satan will have one helluva fight on his hands if he tries to claim her again.

Camille and Derek, an unlikely couple, have found each other in the darkest of times. Will they find the answers they need to free her and the world from Satan's grip? Or are they in for the longest, darkest battle of their lives?